Purchased with funds from a bequest
by Lucille J. Owens
to benefit Outreach Services

JACKSON COUNTY
Library Services

Watchdog

**Center Point
Large Print**

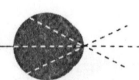

**This Large Print Book carries the
Seal of Approval of N.A.V.H.**

Watchdog

Laurien Berenson

CENTER POINT PUBLISHING
THORNDIKE, MAINE

This Center Point Large Print edition
is published in the year 2006 by arrangement with
Kensington Publishing Corp.

The text of this Large Print edition is unabridged. In other
aspects, this book may vary from the original edition.
Printed in the United States of America.
Set in 16-point Times New Roman type.

ISBN 1-58547-733-8

Library of Congress Cataloging-in-Publication Data

Berenson, Laurien.
   Watchdog / Laurien Berenson.--Center Point large print ed.
      p. cm.
   ISBN 1-58547-733-8 (lib. bdg. : alk. paper)
   1. Travis, Melanie (Fictitious character)--Fiction. 2. Women dog owners--Fiction.
3. Dogs--Fiction. 4. Connecticut--Fiction. 5. Large type books. I. Title.

PS3552.E6963W38 2006
813'.54--dc22

                                                        2005028593

Acquiring a dog may be the only opportunity a human has to choose a relative.
—Mordecai Siegal

One

Never lend money to relatives. It isn't one of the Ten Commandments, but it ought to be.

So when my brother, Frank, came to me with his hand out, I didn't have to think twice about what to say. I turned him down flat. Unfortunately, with Frank it's never that easy.

"Trust me, Mel," he said. "It's the opportunity of a lifetime."

The opportunity of *his* lifetime, maybe. Mine? I doubted it.

For more than a quarter century, ever since he was old enough to walk and talk, I'd watched my little brother maneuver himself into and out of tight spots. He was bright, charming, and impetuous. What he'd never been was practical.

That was my job apparently. I was the diligent big sister who, more often than not, had to stay behind and pick up the pieces when Frank dropped whatever he was doing and went barreling on to his next grand scheme.

"At least let me tell you what it's about," he said. "You can't turn me down without giving me a fair shot."

"Sure I can. Watch me. N-O."

"I'm not listening." Frank raised his hands and put them over his ears. "I can't hear you." With a maturity level like that, you can see why he would come to me rather than going to a bank.

I glared at him for a moment, but the effort was half-hearted. It was 8:30 on a weekday morning. In the normal way of things, I wouldn't have expected my brother to be out of bed yet, much less across town and standing in my kitchen. He must have really thought this was important.

"You've got ten minutes," I told him. "No more. Davey's bus already picked him up and I was just on my way out the door. You're not making me late for school."

Davey was my son, six years old and filled with all the joy and wonder and mischief of his age. In short he was a great kid, at least in his mother's eyes. He'd started first grade a month earlier and was delighted to be riding to school on the bus.

The year before, we'd commuted to Hunting Ridge Elementary together. I'd been employed there for the last six years as a special education teacher. Over the summer, however, I'd taken a new job at Howard Academy, a private school near downtown Greenwich. Four weeks into the school year, I was still trying to make a good impression.

"Relax." Frank glanced at the clock over the sink. "You've got plenty of time."

My brother is an expert at relaxing, probably because he gets so much practice. I was tempted to drum my fingers on the countertop.

People meeting us for the first time often comment that we look alike. Though we have many of the same features—straight brown hair, hazel eyes, and the strong jawline often associated with stubbornness—I've never been able to see the similarity. Maybe I don't want to see it.

While I waited for Frank to get to the point, I walked to the back door and looked out. The small yard behind the house was enclosed, and Faith, Davey's and my Standard Poodle, was having a last bit of exercise before I left for the day. When I opened the door, she raced across the short distance between us and bounded up the steps.

"That is one strange looking animal," Frank said as Faith came sliding into the kitchen, did a quick turn on the linoleum floor, then jumped up and waved her front paws in the air waiting for the biscuit she knew I'd be holding.

I flipped the peanut butter tidbit into the air and watched Faith catch it on the fly. "Nine minutes. You know, most people hoping to borrow money from me wouldn't start by insulting my dog."

"With that hairdo? The comment wasn't an insult, it was a statement of fact."

All right, so Faith's appearance was a little odd. It wasn't my fault. At least, not entirely. She'd been a present from my Aunt Peg, a devoted Standard Poodle breeder whose Cedar Crest Kennel has produced a number of top winning Poodles over the years. Like her ancestors before her, Faith was a show dog.

Accordingly, her hair was being maintained in the continental clip, a modern descendant of an old

German hunting trim, and one of only two dips adult Poodles were allowed to wear in the ring. Faith's dense black coat was long and scissored into a rounded shape on the front half of her body. At the same time, most of her hindquarter had been clipped down to the skin. There were pompons over each of her hip bones and just above her feet on all four legs. A bigger pompon wagged at the end of her tail.

Because the topknot on her head was nearly a foot long and needed to be kept out of the way when she wasn't in the ring, I'd sectioned the hair into a series of ponytails, which were held in place by brightly colored rubber bands. The long, thick fringe on her ears was protected by matching plastic wraps, which were doubled under and banded in place.

Standards are the biggest of the three varieties of Poodles. Faith is twenty-four inches at the shoulder, which means that she and Davey stand nearly eye to eye. Maybe that explains why they get along so well; or maybe it was just that kids and Standard Poodles are a great combination.

Faith also has wonderfully expressive dark brown eyes. Sometimes I could swear she knows exactly what I'm thinking. Like now, as she gazed at Frank with her head tipped to one side. No doubt she was wondering what he was doing there and why I hadn't left for school yet. I reached down and gave her chin a scratch.

"Fine by me," I said to Frank. "You want to discuss the dog's trim, it's your eight minutes."

"Nine," he said, probably hoping to impress me with his counting skills. "I've still got nine."

I waved a hand. It wasn't worth arguing.

Frank waited until I was still, then made his grand announcement. "I'm starting up my own business, Mel. This is your chance to get in on the ground floor."

Probably just where I'd remain, too.

"What kind of business are you going into?"

It wasn't an idle question. In the half decade since college, my brother has held a variety of jobs—everything from bartender to sales clerk to general handyman. If he had chosen a career path, I had yet to see the signs.

"I'm opening up a coffee bar. You know how popular they are. Everyone's looking for a neighborhood hangout, and I've managed to secure a great location."

From the sound of things, Frank was going to need every minute of the time I allotted him. I went back to the table and sat down. Faith hopped up and draped her front legs across my lap, then angled her head upward so her muzzle rested just below my shoulder.

As she settled in, I could feel the creases being pressed across the front of my skirt. Luckily I buy most of my clothes at Eddie Bauer and L.L. Bean, so they can take a few knocks. I burrowed my fingers through the Poodle's thick coat and rubbed behind her ear.

"Where is it?"

"Right here in north Stamford. Remember Haney's

General Store out on Old Long Ridge Road?"

I nodded, picturing a small clapboard building with a wide porch and room for four or five cars to park out front. In the early fifties when the farms and open acreage of north Stamford were being developed into affordable housing to accommodate the post-war family boom, Mr. Haney had opened his small general store. It served as a convenience for harried mothers who hadn't wanted to run all the way into town for a carton of eggs or a bottle of milk. In those days, he'd done a thriving business.

But as the city of Stamford continued to grow by leaps and bounds, supermarkets and strip malls had sprung up within easy reach of almost every shopper. Mr. Haney grew older and the wares that he stocked weren't replenished nearly as often. It had been at least two years since I'd been to his store, and even then the building had begun to look run-down.

Signs covering the front windows advertising the weekly specials couldn't disguise the fact that the glass needed a good cleaning. The red paint on the front door had faded to a musty pink. To top it off, the gallon of milk I'd purchased had been sour. I hadn't been back since.

"Is he still in business?" I asked.

"Not anymore. That's what I'm trying to tell you. As of last month, Mr. Haney retired and moved to Florida. I'm the new owner.

"Owner?" That got my attention. "Frank, how could you afford to buy a building?"

"Maybe partial proprietor is a better term. I don't exactly own the place."

No surprise there.

"I have a long-term lease, and I'm doing renovations. Haney's General Store is going to become Grounds For Appeal. By Christmas we'll be ready for the grand opening."

"Grounds For Appeal?" I frowned. "It sounds like a cut rate law office."

"That's not set in stone yet," Frank said quickly. "I'm still working out some of the details. You could help. Like I said, things are just beginning to get moving. Now would be the perfect time for you to invest."

"Why?"

"Why?" The question seemed to puzzle him. "Well, to be perfectly honest, because I could use some cash." As if I couldn't have guessed. "Actually, Frank, I was wondering why you think this would be a good idea for me."

"Because once the coffee bar gets up and running, I'm going to be making a ton of money. What kind of a brother would I be if I didn't offer my only sister to have the chance to get in on it?"

"Solvent?" I ventured. I checked my watch. If I wasn't out the door in five minutes max, I was going to miss the first bell. "Look, I don't really have time to discuss this right now. And as you know perfectly well, I don't have any extra money. At least not the kind you're looking for."

"You've got Bob."

Bob was my ex-husband and Davey's father. After a four-year absence from our lives, he'd shown up unexpectedly in the spring looking to get reacquainted with his son. At the same time, he'd reinstated the child support payments he was supposed to have been making all along.

Thanks to his contributions, Davey and I were a good deal better off than we had been. We'd been able to have the house painted and take a modest vacation over the summer. We were not, however, in any position to be looking for investments.

"Bob went home to Texas, Frank. He has a new wife there."

"He also has an oil well."

"That's his money, not mine."

"You could ask him for some."

"I could," I said, nudging Faith off my lap so I could stand. "But I'm not going to. Whatever you've gotten yourself into this time, you're just going to have to take care of it without my help."

"Okay, if that's the way you want to be. Most people would jump at the chance to get into a deal with Marcus Rattigan, but if you're not interested, I guess that's your business."

I was halfway to the door but I stopped and turned. "Marcus Rattigan? What do you have to do with him?"

"He's the guy who bought the building. Didn't I mention that?"

He knew perfectly well he hadn't.

Marcus Rattigan was a local entrepreneur whose influence in the construction and development business was well documented in Fairfield County. Over the last decade more than a dozen apartment complexes had sprung up in surrounding towns, their signs sporting the familiar blue and gold logo of his Anaconda Properties.

Rattigan was known for buying up tracts of land, then bending local zoning laws to the breaking point in order to accommodate the greatest possible housing density. He supplied my newspaper with a steady stream of front page stories, and town officials in most municipalities kept a wary eye on the proceedings while fervently wishing him elsewhere.

"Marcus Rattigan bought Haney's General Store? Why would he be interested in a little place like that?"

"Dunno," said Frank. "But he snapped the place up when Haney sold out. The way things have grown up in north Stamford, the store is surrounded by houses now. It's a nonconforming property in a two-acre zone. He can't build on the lot or enlarge the building that's there. I guess that's why he was happy to let me have the lease."

"He knows you're planning to turn the place into a coffee bar?"

"Sure he knows. I certainly couldn't do it without his approval. He and I are partners on the deal."

"Partners. You and Marcus Rattigan?" It was all a little much to take in.

"Sure. Fifty-fifty. He supplied the building. I supply the know-how."

Interesting. As far as I knew, my brother didn't have any know-how.

"He even co-signed my loan at the bank."

"He did?"

"Yup. Happy to do it, he said. Seeing as we were going to be partners and all."

I stared at Frank suspiciously. "If you have a bank loan, what do you need me for?"

"As it happens, I'm running a little low on funds. You know how it is with construction. Estimates never seem to cover the final cost. In the beginning—"

"The beginning? How long ago did you get involved in this project?"

"It's been about six weeks."

"And I'm just hearing about it now?"

Frank shot me a look. As siblings went, we weren't close. Though he only lived one town away, we'd never spent much time together. Our temperaments were just too dissimilar for us to really enjoy each other's company. In fact, now that I thought about it, bad news was much more apt to bring us together than good.

"It seemed like the right time," said Frank. "You know, with the opportunity for you and all. It's not like I need the moon. I figure five thousand should do it."

"Five thousand *dollars?*" I'd always suspected he was daft. Now I knew. There was no way I had that kind of money lying around, and if I did, I certainly wouldn't have trusted Frank with it. "Where on earth would you think I'd get five thousand dollars?"

"All right, so you don't ask Bob. You've been living in this house for what, eight, nine years? You must have some equity—"

"No." I cut him off swiftly. "This is Davey's and my home. I'm not going to risk losing it when you decide to go off and tilt at another windmill. You said Rattigan's your partner. Why don't you go to him?"

"I can't. No way. Marcus put me in charge and I told him I could handle it. How would it look if the first time there was a problem I went running back to him?"

Not great. Even I had to admit that. "Look, Frank, I'm sorry. I just don't have the kind of money you need."

My brother took one last meaningful look around the room, but didn't argue. Instead he pushed back his chair and stood. "Okay, I figured I'd ask. It was worth a shot."

I picked up my jacket and pulled it on. "What will you do now?"

"I don't know. I'll have to think about it." After a moment his expression brightened. "You're not the only family I have, you know. Maybe I'll talk to Aunt Peg."

That would go over well, I thought, but didn't voice the opinion aloud. As things turned out, I should have given him the money. It would have been easier than his next request.

Two

Howard Academy was founded in 1928 by Joshua A. Howard, an enterprising gentleman of the early twentieth century who made a fortune in shipping, munitions and, it was rumored, bootlegging. Joshua, however, discovered rather too late in life that he might have been happier had he devoted half as much time to his wife and his children as he had to making money. Neither of his two sons had the brains to manage the empire he'd built; and his four daughters, all of whom had received the traditional education afforded to young females of the time, were vastly disinterested. Having accrued more money than he could ever hope to spend, and arriving at the unfortunate realization that his descendants could not be counted on to manage the fortune wisely, Joshua turned to philanthropy.

Aided by his spinster sister, Honoria Howard, he had founded Howard Academy, whose lofty aim was "to form the ideals and educate the minds of the young ladies and gentlemen who will shape America's future." Joshua chose as his setting what was then twenty acres of prime farmland, and was now a multimillion dollar enclave just north of downtown Greenwich. Howard Academy had taught the sons and daughters of senators, ambassadors, titans of industry, and at least two presidential candidates. Its alumnae and alumni had marched forth bravely into a world of power and privilege that was waiting to receive them.

With the passage of time, however, Howard Academy, which had once blithely assumed it would have its pick of Fairfield County's best and brightest students, began to feel the heat of competition. The academy was now one of several private schools in Greenwich, all offering a superior education and all vying for the same children and the same limited endowment dollars. Not only that, but the administration had slowly come to realize that the rarefied atmosphere of white, upper class entitlement they'd prided themselves on was neither as desirable nor as politically correct as it once had been. Accordingly, some changes were in order.

Seeking a more culturally and economically diverse student body, Howard Academy hadn't needed to look far to find a pool of qualified candidates. What they *had* needed to do for the first time in the school's history, was hold a scholarship drive. As the twentieth century drew to a close, minority enrollment at Howard was nearly twenty percent.' Student aid was also at an all-time high.

The school's administration would have denied it, of course, but with an eye firmly fixed on the bottom line, Howard Academy now found itself with a strong incentive to admit students who might not reach the school's high academic standards but whose parents were capable of paying full tuition. And if those parents were the generous sort, the kind likely to have checkbooks open and pens at the ready when the annual fund raising drive came around, it was said that admission could be virtually guaranteed.

Course material too rigorous for Junior? Curriculum too varied? That's where I came in.

For the last half dozen years, I'd been happily employed as a special education teacher for the Stamford public school system. I liked the job and I loved the kids. Still, it was hard to be a working mother and a single parent. I needed more time to spend with my son, and more money wouldn't have been all bad, either.

When I'd heard over the summer that Howard Academy was interviewing for the position of on-campus tutor, I spruced up my resume and sent it in. The idea was a lark, and nothing more. Aware of the school's hallowed reputation and penchant for maintaining its ideals, I hadn't thought I'd stand a chance. And then, with nothing to lose, I'd walked in and aced the interview.

Now, as of early September when the fall semester began, I was Howard Academy's newest teacher. Ms. Travis. My first minor skirmish with the authorities had taken place over that quasi-feminist form of address. Apparently, I was the first woman teacher in the history of the school who wasn't comfortable being pigeonholed as either a traditional Miss or Mrs.

I'd had to point out that miss was hardly appropriate since I was the mother of a six-year-old son, and what sort of example would that set for Howard Academy's impressionable youth? As for Mrs., that was out, too.

I wasn't married and had no intention of maintaining a charade that implied otherwise.

Russell Hanover II, the school's headmaster, had given in gracefully once I'd explained my position. Flexibility didn't seem to be a strong suit of his, but as leader of one of Greenwich's toniest private schools, he had beautiful manners. No doubt his mother had taught him at an early age that ladies were to be humored when it came to their preferred mode of address. How else to explain that the office staff, none of whom was younger than fifty, was collectively referred to as "the girls"?

Fortunately, at almost nine o'clock on a weekday morning, the traffic was moving briskly on North Street when I got off the Merritt Parkway and headed south toward downtown Greenwich. My new Volvo station wagon, a gift from ex-husband Bob to make up for four years of missing child support payments, clung to the bumps and curves in the road like a burr in a Collie's tail.

Usually I like to go slowly and enjoy the view. With its landscaped lawns, imposing manor houses, and two-hundred-year-old stone walls, Greenwich is beautiful in any season of the year, and especially so in the fall when the weather is crisp and the leaves are shot through with vivid streaks of color. Today, there wasn't time to look at anything but the clock.

Like many of the homes in the area, Howard Academy is set back from the road. The driveway is flanked by a pair of stone pillars. A small, discreet sign, gold lettering on a hunter-green background, announces that you've reached your destination.

The school itself sits on a wooded hilltop, one of the highest sites around. On a clear day it's possible to see the Long Island Sound if you know just where to look. And if not, as any visitor quickly finds out, Russell Hanover will be delighted to show you.

Honoria Howard had envisioned her students doing their lessons in a milieu that was much like home, and on first approach, the building she'd commissioned for her school looked much like a grand turn-of-the-century stone mansion. It wasn't until the driveway dipped and turned that the newer wing to the rear became visible. Added in the sixties, it was a soaring spectacle of glass and concrete complete with its own astronomy tower.

Kindergarten through fourth grade were housed in the original building, fifth through eighth in the new wing. There were large classrooms, plenty of amenities, and a low student-to-teacher ratio. I had to give Honoria credit. Seventy years later, her vision of what could be was still an educator's dream.

I drove around the building to the teachers' parking lot in the back. A spot was open near the cafeteria door. From there, it was just a short walk down the main hallway to my classroom in the new wing.

Classrooms in the original building were a model of old world charm. There were ten-foot ceilings, intricate molding, and working fireplaces. By contrast, those in the new wing featured recessed lighting, cable hookup, and central air. I've been a teacher for long enough to choose function over beauty any day.

Most mornings I stop at the teachers' lounge on my way in and pick up a cup of coffee. Today I just ran. Even so, I wasn't the first to arrive in my classroom. Spencer Holbrook, my nine o'clock student, was sitting atop one of the two round tables in the room. His eyes were closed, his legs swinging back and forth, his butt bouncing rhythmically in time to a song only he could hear.

As I closed the door behind me, he opened his eyes. In his uniform of navy-blue pleated pants, white button-down oxford cloth shirt, and rep tie, Spencer was a typical Howard Academy sixth grader. Eleven going on forty, with attitude to spare.

He lifted his left arm lazily and checked the diving watch on his wrist. "You're late."

"I know, I'm sorry." I pulled off my blazer and threw it over the back of my chair. My purse went into a desk drawer.

"Big night last night?" His gaze roamed over me, searching eagerly for telltale signs of debauchery.

"I wish. Pesky brother this morning. Why didn't you start working while you were waiting?"

Spencer shrugged. "Why should I?"

"Because you want better grades?" I suggested. A firm hand on his shoulder encouraged him to hop down from the tabletop.

"You want me to get better grades. I think I'm doing okay."

"On the contrary, your grades are immaterial to me. I don't have to take your report card home and show it to my parents."

"I don't have to, either." Spencer smirked. "It comes in the mail. Goes straight to Big J's office. His secretary's the one who has to deal with it."

Big J was Spencer's father, James Holbrook. That was the only way I'd ever heard Spencer refer to him. I'd been tempted to inquire whether he called his mother Big Mama, but in keeping with the school's tradition of genteel behavior, I hadn't quite dared.

I pulled out two chairs and we both sat down. In my folder was a math test Spencer had taken earlier in the week. His math teacher, Leanne Honeywell, had given it to me the day before. I pulled it out.

"Have you seen this?"

Spencer glanced down, then nodded. His dark brown hair, which looked as though it had been neither combed nor cut in recent memory, fell down over his eyes. I resisted a maternal urge to brush it back.

"What'd you think of your grade?" The D slashed in red above his name was damning evidence of his feeble grasp of fractions.

"I guess it's not too good."

"You *guess?*"

I lifted the test and flipped through the pages. There were more red *x*'s and blank spots than there were correct answers. From what I could see, a grade of D had been generous.

Spencer shrugged again. He took a pencil out of his

pocket and began to twirl it between his fingers like a baton. "You care to tell me what happened?"

"Nothing happened. I just blew the test, that's all."

"I can see that. What I'm wondering is why. Miss Honeywell says you got off to a great start in math this year. Your homework's been neat and on time. It shows a real understanding of the concepts. This test should have been a breeze for you."

"Well, it wasn't, okay?" Spencer's voice rose. Quickly he lowered it to a more moderate tone. "I guess I got confused about a few things."

I took out some fresh paper. "Why don't we go over the test together? You show me where you got confused, and I'll explain what you should have done."

I sent him on his way at ten o'clock, a little wiser in the ways of fractions, and hopefully a little closer to realizing that good grades wouldn't automatically come his way because his father was a powerhouse in the telecommunications business. Like many of the kids on my roster, Spencer was of average or better intelligence, with perhaps a slight tendency toward learning problems. Though the students I tutored were having trouble keeping up with their regular course load, they weren't, by and large, learning disabled.

What they lacked was motivation, or self-esteem, or sometimes basic organizational skills. With children who'd been given so much, it was often difficult to make them understand that knowledge was something they would have to work to attain.

I arranged; I explained; I pushed; I prodded. When

all else failed, I played the role of cheerleader. I wouldn't have traded my job for anything.

Two weeks passed without another word from Frank. To tell the truth, I'd pretty much forgotten about his latest venture. My brother's not above bailing out when times get tough. For all I knew, he might have gone back to reading the want ads.

Between the new job, taking care of Davey, and a dog show for Faith coming up on the weekend, there was plenty to keep me busy. I had twenty students from a variety of grades in the tutoring program, so my schedule was full. Just to keep things interesting, it also varied from day to day.

On Wednesdays I got out of school around the same time Davey did, so I swung by Hunting Ridge on my way home and picked him up. When I reached the elementary school, the buses were loading. Davey was waiting for me at the curb near the front door. His best friend, Joey Brickman, was with him.

The two of them were swinging their backpacks and shoving each other playfully. Any minute they were bound to fall off the curb and into traffic. I'm a mother, so that's the way my mind works.

I slid the Volvo into an empty spot and tooted the horn lightly. Davey looked up and waved when he saw me. Both boys shouldered their packs and scrambled in my direction. Joey was pug nosed, freckle faced, and built like a linebacker-to-be. When he threw himself into the backseat, the car shuddered from the impact.

Davey was smaller and more slightly built, but what he lacked in heft, he made up for in speed. He moved with his father's grace, and also had the same heavily lashed, chocolate brown eyes. Today they wore a serious expression as he climbed into the car and shut the door.

"Seat belts," I said, although the boys hardly needed a reminder. They were already reaching around to get the straps in place before I'd even put the car in gear. "Everything okay? You two have a good day at school?"

"It was awesome!" cried Joey. "I lost a tooth. Wanna see?"

I looked in the rearview mirror, thinking he'd show me the tooth. Instead Joey was angling his head upward, mouth agape, pudgy finger pointing at an empty space.

"Pretty impressive. Aren't you a little young to be losing teeth?"

"That's what the teacher said," Joey said proudly. "I'm the first in the whole class."

I glanced back at Davey, who had yet to say a word. "How about you, champ? How was your day?"

"Fine."

"Just fine? That's all?"

"It isn't fair." Davey pushed out his lower lip in a pout. "I wiggled all my teeth and none of them are even loose. I want the tooth fairy to come to our house, too."

"It's so cool!" said Joey. "She's going to take my

tooth and leave me money instead."

Davey crossed his arms over his chest and stared out the car window.

"Don't worry," I said. "Your turn will come."

"But I want my turn now."

That's my boy. He has many wonderful attributes, but patience isn't one of them.

I switched on my blinker and turned up our road. Our house is a small, snug Cape; one of many that all look pretty much the same in a neighborhood that was built in the fifties. The homes have small yards, mature plantings, and streets that are quiet enough for children to ride their bikes. Considering the price of real estate in Fairfield County, I could have done a lot worse.

Joey's family lives at the end of the street. His father's a lawyer in Greenwich and his mother stays home with his two-year-old sister, Carly. Alice Brickman and I have been friends since the boys were small.

I pulled into the driveway, and Davey and Joey spilled out of the car. Faith, whose internal clock is more accurate than my Timex, was waiting just inside the front door. I could hear her excited yips as I fit the key to the lock.

When the door swung open, she was dancing on her hind legs to greet us.

Problems forgotten, Davey gathered Faith into his arms and gave her a hug. His face disappeared into the thick ruff of her mane coat. Standing upright, the

Poodle was taller than he was. Hopping together, they managed an awkward dance of greeting around the front hall.

"Sheesh," said Joey. "She's only a dog."

"She is not." Davey shook his head, and Faith's ear wraps flapped around him. "She's the best dog in the whole world."

Joey was not impressed. "Big deal. What have you got to eat?"

The three of them headed for the kitchen. Davey knew how to unlock the back door and let Faith out into the fenced yard. The milk, glasses, and shortbread cookies were on shelves low enough for them to reach. Confident that they could fend for themselves, at least for a few minutes, I headed upstairs to change my clothes.

A few weeks earlier, at Aunt Peg's suggestion, I'd started roadworking Faith. It's not easy being beautiful, even if you're a dog, and especially if you're a Standard Poodle whose grandfather won the group at Westminster and whose breeder has plans for you to finish your championship. Sixty years old and more autocratic than ever, Aunt Peg has a way of always getting what she wants. Certainly I've never figured out how to turn her down.

Which was why Faith and I were now running two miles around the neighborhood several times a week.

The steady, rhythmic jog was developing Faith's muscle and building up her hindquarter. As a nice bonus, it had also knocked a couple of pounds off of me. So far, my biggest problem had been finding the time to fit jogging into my schedule.

Luckily, Alice seems to think that having two six-year-old boys entertain each other is easier than having one at home by himself, and she'd volunteered to watch Davey while I ran. As soon as I was suited up in sweatpants, T-shirt, and trusty sneakers, I walked both boys down to her house and dropped them off.

Though I've heard of something called a runner's high, I had yet to experience it. For me, jogging was hard work. Not so Faith, who completed the entire distance with head up and tail wagging. I guess that's the difference between four legs and two. We stopped and picked up Davey on the way back, then walked the length of the street to cool down.

Davey was chattering on about a new board game Joey had just gotten, and I was thinking of a nice hot shower, when we let ourselves in the door. My answering machine is on the kitchen counter, and its message light was blinking. I pressed the button, then picked up Faith's bowl and refilled it with fresh water while I waited for the tape to rewind.

"Mel!" Frank's voice sounded tinny, but I could hear the urgency in his tone. "I'm at the coffee bar. You know, Haney's old place? Where the hell are you? I need you to get over here right away."

Three

I threw a heavy sweater on over my T-shirt and we headed out.

The drive was a quick one. Frank's building was only a couple of miles away on back roads that twisted and curved through the Connecticut countryside. The area wasn't as densely populated as the neighborhood Davey and I lived in, but it was clearly residential.

Surrounded by houses on large wooded lots, the small store sat wedged next to the road. There was a bit of space for parking in front and more on one side, but most of it was currently taken up by a dumpster the size of a semitrailer. Frank's black sportscar was parked near the door and I slid the Volvo in beside it.

"Wow!" Davey gazed at the dumpster in awe.

Knowing my son, I figured he was wondering how to climb inside. Quickly I moved to forestall that idea. "How about if you take charge of Faith and make sure she doesn't get into any trouble?"

"Okay," he agreed happily. At his age, it's a thrill to be put in charge of anything.

I ran my fingers around the Poodle's neck, making sure that her collar was lying close to the skin. She doesn't usually wear a collar since it causes the hair to mat, but I hadn't had a chance to take it off after our jog. I handed the end of the leash to Davey and we got out.

The exterior of the building had clearly been worked

on since the last time I'd seen it. The formerly sagging porch had a new floor; rotted boards in the walls had been replaced; and the old-fashioned multipaned windows had been removed, a single large picture window taking their place. All the place needed now, at least on the outside, was a new coat of paint to tie the job together.

The front door was standing open. Davey and Faith scooted up the steps and ran inside. I was about to follow, when something caught my eye. Off to one side, a small piece of white cardboard, torn jaggedly along the bottom edge, was nailed to one of the new boards.

I looked down and saw the rest of the poster on the porch floor below. Its surface was covered with footprints, heavy boot prints actually, probably from the construction crew. Squatting down, I turned the paper over. Large block letters had been printed in a vivid shade of red: GO AWAY. WE DON'T WANT YOU HERE.

I felt a chill wash over me. A noise on the porch made me jump to my feet and spin around.

"A message from the local welcoming committee," said Frank. He took the poster out of my hands, bent it stiffly in half, then strode out and tossed it in the dumpster.

I followed him, looking around curiously. There was a buffer of woods in three directions. With the leaves still on the trees, only one house was visible and it was on the other side of the road. "The neighbors don't like what you're doing?"

"Apparently not. Some of them have even organized themselves into a protest group."

"I don't get it. The last time I saw this place, it was really run down. I would think they'd be glad to have you come in and fix it up."

"I would, too, but it hasn't turned out that way. Haney'd been here for decades. I guess they'd gotten used to the idea that there was nothing they could do about him. But now that he's gone, they're protesting any sort of commercial usage."

We walked back up the steps together. "How much trouble can they cause for you?"

"Legally none. Luckily for us, Haney'd been serving coffee in the back of his store for years. As far as the zoning board's concerned, we're just enlarging on his business. You'd never get a variance today, but it doesn't matter. Nonconformity runs with the land, not the ownership. The right to have a coffee bar here is grandfathered."

"Only because of a technicality," I said, frowning. "Have you been down to the town hall to check that everything's in order?"

"I didn't have to. Marcus deals with details like that all the time and he told me it's all set."

"Hey, Mom, it's cool in here! Come in and see!"

Davey burst through the doorway, with Faith a step behind. His sneakers were soaked and his jeans were wet nearly up to the knees. Faith was dripping water, too. The bracelets of hair on each of her legs hung in sodden clumps.

"What happened to you two?"

Frank grimaced slightly before Davey could answer. "That's why I called. I need your help."

"With the neighbors?"

"No, with the water."

"What water?"

"Come on in. You'll see."

Inside, the building was still very much a work in progress. The deep shelves and high dividers I remembered from Mr. Haney's occupancy were gone. So were the refrigerated bins.

In their place stood two sawhorses, with a wide plank of wood balanced across them and a sheaf of plans scattered on top. A granite-topped counter had been built along the back of the room, and behind the counter a kitchen was partially installed.

The general store had always seemed dingy and crowded, but now the room had a light, airy feel. I let my gaze slide upward. The low ceiling had been opened up and a pair of skylights installed on either side of the peaked roof. The transformation was nothing short of amazing.

"It looks . . ." Wonderful, I'd started to say. Then I realized that my toes felt squishy inside my shoes. I was standing in two inches of water. "Frank, what happened?"

"That's what I've been trying to tell you. I think a pipe burst."

"A pipe burst!" Davey cried happily. He jumped up in the air and landed solidly on both feet. I leapt back as water sprayed in all directions.

"You think? Don't you know?"

My brother scowled. "Do I look like a plumber to you? All I know is that when I checked in at noon everything was fine. When I got back at three-thirty, the place looked like this."

I sloshed across the room, looking for the source of the leak.

"The problem was back there behind the counter," said Frank. "One of the pipes that will be under the sink when it's installed. The thing was spouting water like crazy when I got here, but I think I got it under control. There's a spigot around the corner, and when I turned it off, the water stopped."

His grasp of technical jargon was enough to make my head spin. I leaned down and looked at the pipe he indicated. Beads of water bubbled around the joint where the two ends met. "Did you call a plumber?"

"No. I'm sure someone on the crew will know how to fix the damn thing in the morning. But in the meantime I've got to get this mess cleaned up, pronto."

"That's why you called and told me to get over here? Because you wanted me to help you *mop?*"

"Well, yes," said Frank, looking somewhat aggrieved. "You've got to understand. It's Wednesday."

"I've understood that all day, Frank."

My brother wasn't pleased by my response. "On Wednesday afternoons, Marcus usually stops by to see how things are progressing. He'll probably be here in half an hour or so. I can't let him see the place looking like this."

So instead of going to work on the mess, he'd picked up the phone and called me. For Frank, that probably made perfect sense.

"You'll help, won't you?" he asked.

"I guess so," said the spineless sucker who'd taken over my body. "What have we got to work with?"

"There's some stuff in the cellar that Mr. Haney must have left behind. I've been using an old bucket to bail water out the back door."

The cellar was at the bottom of a flight of cramped, rickety wooden steps. A lightbulb dangled from a wire in the ceiling and I pulled a string to turn it on. The stuff Frank had seen consisted of a ratty looking broom, an ancient mop, and an old carpet sweeper that was probably made before I was born.

The mop and the broom were both stiff with accumulated dirt. A pile of musty rags sat on the floor beside them. My next find was an old snow shovel, bent at both corners, and propped against a wooden post beneath the steps. I added that to the haul and took everything but the carpet sweeper upstairs.

When I rejoined the others, Frank had gone back to bailing. Davey had fashioned a boat out of a Styrofoam cup he'd found on the counter, and was playing captain of the seas. I handed the shovel to Frank.

"I think you'll be able to move more water if you try pushing it out the back door. Be careful you don't scratch the floor, though."

"Don't worry, it hasn't been redone yet. Just get the water out of here any way you can."

The mop was the old-fashioned kind, with long fingers of white hemp gathered together at the handle. I shook it out and watched the dust fly. "Tell me something. If you got here at three-thirty, how come nobody from the construction crew was still here?"

Propelled by Frank's shovel, a wave of water rippled across the floor. "I guess they'd already knocked off for the day."

"Isn't that kind of early?"

"You know how these guys are."

"No, I don't." I mopped along in Frank's wake. "How are they?"

"They, uh . . . , kind of set their own schedules. It depends on things like availability of parts, and doing each job in the right order. Sometimes they don't exactly work a full day."

"What about the guy that's in charge? The general contractor."

"Actually, that would be me."

I stopped and stared. "You? What do you know about being a general contractor?"

Frank pushed a stream of water out the back door. "It's not that big a deal. The hard part was figuring out who to hire for each job. Now all I have to do is keep on top of everybody and make sure that all the work they're doing is coordinated."

"And this is what you call staying on top of things?"

Frank's shoulders stiffened. "Cut me some slack,

would you? What happened today was a fluke, an accident. Look around. You have to admit, other than a little water, things are coming along pretty well, aren't they?"

An objective observer probably would have conceded his point. But I was his sister, so instead I said, "How's the money situation coming?"

"I've got everything under control."

Right. Custer had thought the same thing, and look how that turned out.

Leash dragging behind her, Faith bounded across the floor and pounced on the mop with both front feet. I waited while she pinned it in place and lowered her muzzle for a delicate sniff. Abruptly her head flew up, lips curled in disgust.

"You should have asked me," I said. "I'd have told you not to do that."

"Not to do what?" Frank looked up.

"Sorry, I was talking to Faith."

"Sure," my brother said sarcastically. "Like that's normal."

"I want to help," said Davey. We'd lowered the water level enough so that his boat would no longer float. "Good. Go get a couple of those rags and start pushing them around the floor, okay?"

Crawling in mud—judging by the look on my son's face, it was a job tailor made for a six year old. Hopefully, he wouldn't feel the need to relive this experience at show-and-tell tomorrow.

By the time we heard a car pull up outside, the place

was in pretty good shape. The floor was still damp in spots, but considering it was already pitted and scarred, the new damage was scarcely noticeable. Frank dashed around the room, gathering up the mop, the bucket, and the sodden rags. He threw them out the back door, then slammed it shut and slipped Davey a wink.

I ran for Faith. She takes her duties as a watchdog very seriously, and when Marcus Rattigan's silver jaguar sedan pulled up in front of the store, she ran to the window and began to bark like the ferocious beast she thinks she is. Considering that her protective instincts had saved my life over the summer, I take her abilities seriously, too.

More to the point, I was afraid she'd jump up and plant her muddy paws on the front of Marcus Rattigan's expensive suit.

Through the window I watched him climb out of the long sedan. I'd seen Rattigan's picture in the paper, but that flat rendering didn't do justice to his presence or his bearing. His movements—closing the car door behind him, shading his eyes against the low sun as he looked up at the front of the building—were controlled and precise. He didn't look like a man who'd be easy to ignore, or to turn your back on.

Rattigan's features were regular, but they added up to a face that was more ordinary than handsome. I judged him to be in his early fifties. When the slanting afternoon sun washed over him, I decided not to rule out the possibility of a face-lift.

Davey and I hung back, but Frank strode out onto the porch to greet him. They shook hands; my brother expansive and voluble, Marcus Rattigan, quieter, as though reserving judgment until he saw things for himself.

"Everything's coming along great," Frank said. "We're still on target to open before Christmas. I'm sure you'll be pleased."

I had Faith's leash looped around my hand. She'd stopped barking, but when the two men entered the room, she threw herself forward dragging me along behind. Rattigan cast us a withering glance. Since I was pretty much standing in his way, I stuck out my hand.

"Melanie Travis," I said. "I'm Frank's sister. And that's my son, Davey."

Rattigan shook my fingers briefly. He didn't offer his own name. Apparently we were just supposed to know who he was.

Stepping around me as if my presence was immaterial, he made a quick inspection of the room. His survey was fast but seemingly thorough. For the most part he kept moving, stopping only once or twice for a closer look at a fixture or a particular bit of craftsmanship.

I caught Davey's eye, giving him the mother's stare that he knows means business, and beckoned him to my side. When he drew near, I looped my arm around his shoulder. All things considered, it seemed best if the two of us just stayed out of the way.

40

Rattigan paused by the counter, his manicured fingernail scratching at the granite surface. "Who approved this?"

"I did." Frank was nervous, I could tell. He looked down at the spot Rattigan was rubbing.

"Who did the work?"

"Avril Bennett from Norwalk."

Rattigan nodded abruptly and moved on. "Watch your men. If you don't let them know that you're the boss every step of the way, they'll try to take advantage."

"You're right. Of course." Frank was groveling, and it wasn't a pretty sight. If' my brother got any lower, he'd be slithering on the ground.

Rattigan stopped next to the battered snow shovel. Frank had shoved it into a corner and forgotten it. Rattigan nudged the tool with his foot.

"In case of bad weather," Frank said brightly. "It's never too early to be prepared."

If that explanation fooled anyone, I was Mata Hari. Rattigan didn't comment, however. He merely completed his circuit of the room, and walked out the door, Frank trailing behind. A moment later I heard the smooth purr of the Jaguar's engine coming to life.

It wasn't until then that I realized I'd been holding my breath. What an unpleasant man. He'd even managed to silence my son and that was no small feat. I gave Davey's shoulders a reassuring hug.

"Can we go now?" he asked.

"In a minute. Why don't you take Faith out to the

car? I just want to say goodbye to Frank."

As the jag pulled away, my brother reentered the building. He ran a finger under his shirt collar and pulled it away from his neck. His grin was on the feeble side. "Well, that's Marcus."

"So I saw. I'm surprised he didn't have you shine his shoes while he was here. Or maybe just lick them clean."

"Come on. He's not that bad."

"He's rude and obnoxious, for starters. And that's just a five-minute impression. If I actually got to know him, I could probably find more things not to like."

"You shouldn't judge by what you saw today. Marcus is a busy man. He doesn't have time to waste."

"Speaking of which . . ." I let the sentence dangle.

"What?"

"The man's a developer. From what I read in the paper, he's got projects going all over Fairfield County. How come he didn't have one of his own crews renovate this building?"

"Because I told him I'd take care of it, okay?"

Even Frank must have realized how defensive he sounded. I figured I didn't need to add to his troubles by pointing it out. Nor by pointing out how odd this whole setup seemed. Until recently, the sum total of my brother's handyman skills had consisted of doing odd jobs around his elderly landlady's house. Somehow I was quite certain that knowing how to rewire an outlet or unstop a toilet didn't begin to qualify him for a project like this.

Frank was having another look at the countertop Rattigan had inspected. It must have passed muster because he didn't look too concerned. "Don't worry. Everything's going to be fine. Three months from now, The Java Joint is going to be the place to be in north Stamford. You'll see."

"The Java Joint?"

"Yeah." His face reddened slightly. "I changed the name. With the neighbors protesting and all, I wasn't sure Grounds For Appeal was the way to go."

We looked at each other and grinned. At least he hadn't lost his sense of humor.

"You take care of yourself, okay?"

"No problem," said Frank.

I wished I shared his confidence.

Four

That weekend, Faith was entered in her first dog show since she'd turned a year old in May. With most breeds, the only difference that first birthday makes is that the dog is then ineligible to be shown in the Puppy Class. In Poodles, however, the change is enormous.

Before one year of age, they are shown in the puppy trim with face, feet, and base of the tail shaved, and the rest of the body covered with hair. At twelve months, however, Poodles must be dipped into either continental or English saddle, the two approved adult trims. Both involve growing a large mane coat in front, while removing much of the hair on the dog's hindquarter.

Because of this, Poodles usually need time to mature into their new trims. Only Toys, which stand ten inches or under at the shoulder and are the smallest of the three varieties, resume showing in the adult classes almost immediately. Miniatures, whose height is between ten and fifteen inches, often take off a month or two. For Standards, the kings and queens of Poodledom, the wait for a dog to be fully mature can take up to a year.

I had shown Faith about a dozen times when she was a puppy. On each outing I'd been a little less nervous, and Faith had been a bit better trained. As an older puppy she'd usually won her class quite handily, but she had yet to win any points toward her championship.

At every dog show in each breed or variety there are six classes that a dog may be entered in: Puppy, 12-18 Months, Novice, Bred-By-Exhibitor, American-Bred, and Open. The classes are divided by sex, and each of the class winners is brought back into the ring to vie for the awards of Winners Dog and Winners Bitch. Only these two receive points, with the number of points awarded being determined by the number of dogs shown.

The lowest number of points awarded, with competition, is one. The highest is five. It takes fifteen points to make a dog a champion, with the additional qualification that each dog must also win at least two majors, that is, he must pick up at least three points at a single show, a proviso that ensures he has beaten a number of competitors.

Now Faith was seventeen months old and, ready or not, I was itching to get her back in the show ring. On the day she gave her to me, Aunt Peg had made me promise that I would finish Faith's championship. But as much as I enjoyed going to shows, I found I was spending entirely too much time on coat care. The sooner we started showing again, the sooner we'd have a chance to win some points.

Though there were two shows in the area over the weekend, Faith was only entered on Sunday. Aunt Peg had inspected the premium lists mailed out six weeks in advance and declared Saturday's Poodle judge to be an old fool. Practically speaking, that was likely to mean that he'd never put up Aunt Peg's dogs in the past. Sunday's judge was determined to be a fair and knowledgeable man and the entries were made.

The dog show was run by the Ramapo Kennel Club and was held at an indoor location in Suffern, New York, just on the other side of the Tappan Zee bridge. Hard core exhibitors think nothing of driving hundreds of miles to seek out the best venues or most accommodating judges. I'd seen Aunt Peg pick up and leave home for an entire week when there was a circuit of shows in progress. Not me. As far as I was concerned, the closer, the better.

I pulled the Volvo into the unloading zone beside the big building and got out, leaving Davey and Faith to guard each other for a few minutes while I took my equipment inside. Since Davey had spent the entire trip entertaining us with increasingly louder renditions of "Itsy Bitsy Spider," it was a relief to enter the dog show through a side door. Amazingly, with fifteen hundred dogs present, the large room was quieter than my car had been.

The near end of the building had been set aside as a grooming area for exhibitors who needed to make additional preparations to their dogs before taking them into the ring. Even with all the work I'd already done on Faith at home, she, like all the other Poodles in attendance, still fell into that category. I walked along the wide strip between the handlers' area and the rings, my portable grooming table tucked under one arm and a bag of supplies slung over the other. It didn't take long to spot Aunt Peg.

It helped that she's nearly six feet tall and was wearing a red dress. I threaded my way down a narrow aisle bounded on either side by stacked crates until I reached the area she'd staked out. Her grooming table was already set up and a large metal crate was beside it. Inside, I could see Faith's littermate, Hope, snoozing happily.

"You must have gotten here early," I said. Hope was already brushed out, which meant that Aunt Peg was way ahead of me.

Aunt Peg looked up from the catalogue she was

perusing. "I assumed you'd want me to work on Faith's trim. If she hasn't been scissored since I saw her last month, it's going to take some time."

Scissoring is an exacting job. Not only do the lines for the trim have to be set in just the right spot to maximize each Poodle's good points, but the finish of the hair must also be smooth and rounded. It isn't an easy skill to perfect. I'd been practicing for a year now, but I was still happy to let Aunt Peg supply the finishing touches before Faith went into the ring.

I set down my grooming table, kicked its legs into position, then placed it right side up. "Of course Faith's been scissored. I did it myself."

"Heaven help us all."

Peg has been a Standard Poodle breeder for longer than I've been alive. She and her husband, Max, founded the Cedar Crest line based on the theory that knowledge, hard work, and a bit of luck could lead to excellence. The success of the Cedar Crest Standard Poodles in the ring over the ensuing decades has proven them correct.

Max had died of a heart attack just about the time that the litter Faith had come from was born. Now Peg was carrying on alone and she was equal to the task. She's smart, she's shrewd, and she's not above engaging in shameless manipulation if the need arises.

She also has an insatiable sweet tooth, which was why Davey and I had a box of doughnuts in the car. Aunt Peg was right, Faith did need scissoring. And she wasn't the only family member who'd figured out how to get what she wanted.

I went out and parked the car, then Davey and I walked Faith back up the hill to the show site. He was carrying the doughnuts. I had his bag of books, crayons, and drawing paper. With luck, the supplies would distract him long enough for me to get Faith put together and into the ring.

When we returned, Hope was out on her grooming table. The Poodle was lying quietly while Aunt Peg cut the bands holding her topknot hair and brushed through the long strands to straighten them. Like all of Peg's dogs, Hope is very well trained, but when Faith walked into view, her tail began to thump up and down and she whined excitedly under her breath.

"Oh, all right," said Aunt Peg. "Say hello to your sister and get it out of your system."

She stepped back and Hope leapt to her feet. Faith jumped up and placed her forepaws on the rubber-matted tabletop. The two of them touched noses while their hind feet danced in place. Both tails whipped back and forth.

"They say that dogs forget," Peg said, watching the reunion. "But mine always seem to know their own family." Her gaze shifted to Davey and her eyes lit up. "Did somebody bring me doughnuts?"

"We did!" Davey held out the box. "Mom said they were a bribe."

There's nothing like the innocent honesty of a six year old to keep you on the straight and narrow.

"Is that so?" Aunt Peg lifted the box top and peered inside. "If you've got a Bavarian cream in here, it just may work."

When Davey was younger, I used to perch him on top of the big metal crates, because it seemed the best way to keep him in one place. Now that he's old enough to climb up and down, he's decided he still likes having the highest perch for a seat. I handed him his bag of toys, which he dug into eagerly, then hopped Faith up onto her table, laid her down on her side, and began to brush through her coat. Beside me, Aunt Peg went back to work on Hope's topknot.

"Have you heard about Frank's latest scheme?" I asked as I rooted through my grooming bag looking for a greyhound comb.

Peg, who keeps her supplies neatly sorted in a proper wooden tack box, made sure I saw her look of disdain for my less than efficient arrangement. "Heard about it? My dear girl, he's been to my house and shown me blueprints. I've even been asked to make a contribution."

"Frank brought you *blueprints?*" It was easy to see where I fit in on the scale of important relatives.

"He most certainly did. Presumably your brother figured that you'd be easier to convince."

She was probably right. Since our parents had been killed in a car accident six years earlier, every downturn in Frank's fortunes had brought him to my doorstep.

"Well, I wasn't."

"So I heard." Aunt Peg picked up a spray bottle of water and spritzed the flyaway ends of Hope's coat. "He insisted on telling me the whole sad story. By the time the boy got to me, he'd already tried hitting up the entire family."

It couldn't have taken him long. There aren't that many of us.

"Rose and Peter, too?"

Peg nodded. "He thought they might be understanding, I guess, considering their background."

Aunt Rose, my late father's sister, had until recently been a member of the Sisters of Divine Mercy. She'd left the convent and married Peter, who'd resigned from the priesthood at the same time. They were living in New London now, where Peter was teaching college and Rose was doing social work. By all accounts, they were very happy.

"I'm sure they were understanding," I said, laughing. "But they still don't have any money."

"Nobody ever said your brother was the brightest bulb in the box. I gather he tried Bob next and that didn't pan out, either."

"I told him it wouldn't."

"So that only left me."

"I hope you were gentle. Did you at least look at his blueprints before you turned him down?"

"I looked at his blueprints," Aunt Peg confirmed. "And then I lent him the money he needed."

I'd been using a pin brush to sweep long strokes through the hair. Now my hand stilled. "You didn't."

"Indeed I did." Peg was putting in the tight topknot that Hope would wear into the ring. Using a knitting needle to make parts, she banded the hair into a row of ponytails, starting just behind the Poodle's eyes and working back to her occiput.

"Why on earth would you do something like that?"

"Why not? How old is Frank now, twenty-seven? He can't keep wandering in circles forever. Could be all he needs is a point in the direction and a good shove. Maybe this will get him started."

I didn't believe that for a minute. I wondered if she did. "More likely it will end up costing you your investment."

"Now, Melanie. Frank told me just yesterday that you'd been by to have a look at the place. He said you thought things were coming along quite well."

"Did he tell you I was there to help mop up two inches of standing water?"

"No," Aunt Peg said thoughtfully. "I don't believe he mentioned that."

Of course not. Frank never wanted to be the bearer of bad news. "Did he happen to mention that he's gone into business with Marcus Rattigan?"

"Now that he did tell me." Aunt Peg frowned. "He seemed rather proud of the association. I can't imagine why."

"Do you know him?"

"I guess you'd say I know Marcus slightly, although it's been years since we've spoken. Like everyone else, I read about his current exploits in the newspaper. A decade ago he was involved for a short time in showing dogs."

"He was? What breed?"

"Several, actually. He wasn't a breeder, he was a backer."

"Like Cy Rubicov and Austin Beamish?" I asked, mentioning two men she and I had had dealings with over the last year.

Aunt Peg nodded.

According to the American Kennel Club, the purpose of a dog show is to select the best breeding stock for producing future generations of each breed. And in the purest sense, that's still what takes place. Dog shows are also a competition, however, where big money can produce big results.

Many of the top winning dogs, the ones parading around the group rings at Westminster and traveling the country to rack up a record of Best in Show wins, are sponsored by wealthy patrons. Breeders like Aunt Peg do the hard work behind the scenes: studying pedigrees, testing for genetic problems, and whelping litters of puppies, but they often don't have the money to showcase a really outstanding dog. That's when a sponsor is sought to lease a dog or take a co-ownership.

The backer provides the financial support to pay for handling fees, advertising, and travel costs. In return, they receive the satisfaction of being associated with a winner. Having met Marcus Rattigan, I could readily imagine that he would have enjoyed that kind of involvement.

"He had quite a good Pointer," said Aunt Peg. "And an excellent Bearded Collie. But the dog that really put him on the map was Winter."

I kept on brushing and waited for Aunt Peg to continue. When it comes to dogs, past and present, she's a walking encyclopedia. Not that that surprises me. Week after week, that's what people do at dog shows; they gather together and talk dogs.

Davey looked up from his coloring book. I hadn't even realized he was listening. "Winter's a season," he said firmly. "Not a dog."

"Not in this case. Winter was the name of a gorgeous Wire Fox Terrier bitch. Champion Wirerock Winter Fantasy. She was number one all breeds, about ten years ago. Everybody knew her."

I looked at Davey and shrugged. Obviously we were out of the loop.

"Big deal," he said and went back to his coloring.

"Considering he wasn't around very long, Marcus was lucky to have ever gotten his name on such a good one," Aunt Peg sniffed. In her mind, anyone who didn't have an abiding love affair with dogs was considered suspect. "I believe the breeder was somebody local, and if I remember correctly, their luck ran out later. Winter was only able to have a single litter of puppies."

"Do you know why Rattigan stopped showing?"

"No, people come and go all the time, you know. I suppose he just lost interest. I do know that he wasn't the most popular man around. I doubt that anyone was sorry to see the last of him."

"Because he'd been so successful?" I'd encountered enough jealousy among exhibitors to make the guess a likely one. ⬟

"That was probably part of it, but only a small part. Lots of people have top dogs, but some of them handle it more graciously than others. Marcus was the type who liked to gloat. He couldn't resist lording it over people every time he won. Dog shows are really a rather small community. The same people see each other week after week, and that kind of behavior gets old very quickly."

"Hey, look!" said Davey. "There's Sam."

I stopped brushing and turned around eagerly. Faith, sensing my mood, lifted her head to see what was going on. Sam Driver, my friend and lover, was making his way toward us down the congested aisle. Trotting at his side was a gawky four-month-old Standard Poodle puppy. All legs, feet, and curiosity, the youngster stopped to sniff every table and crate they passed, slowing Sam's progress considerably.

"He's got Tar with him!" Davey slithered off the crate top and ran to meet them.

I watched as Sam opened his arms and Davey ran into them for a hug. The two of them were great friends, and had been almost from the moment they'd met. Sam was terrific with children. Actually, Sam was terrific in a lot of ways.

Sometimes I thought of my life as a road filled with twists and bumps. In that context, Sam was the best smooth patch I'd encountered in years.

His blond head bent low over Davey's darker one as the two of them shared a secret. Then Davey leaned down to ruffle his hands through Tar's coat. At the same time, the puppy jumped up to lick his face. Davey straightened too fast, then overbalanced. Boy and puppy went down together, rolling end over end until they landed at my feet in a heap.

"Everybody still alive?" I heard giggling and saw the puppy's tail wag, so I guessed I had my answer. "I thought you had to work this weekend," I said to Sam.

"So did I, but I managed to get things wrapped up last night."

Sam drew close, slipped an arm around my shoulder, and greeted Peg, Faith, and Hope in turn. He has his own line of Standard Poodles, and though he lacks Peg's longevity, he's a true dog man in the best sense of the word. For years, he'd kept and shown only bitches. Tar was his first male. Looking to find an outcross that would nick with his own line, he'd purchased the puppy from Aunt Peg over the summer.

As a baby puppy, Tar had been stunning; enough of a standout that even a relative novice like myself could see and appreciate his quality. Now, half grown and beginning to teethe, he was all mismatched pieces and parts. He extricated himself from Davey's grasp, grabbed the middle of the leash in his mouth, and began to tug on it, growling fiercely.

"Is that how you plan to socialize my puppy?" Aunt Peg inquired. "By letting him pull on his lead?"

"Funny thing about Tar." Sam reached down and removed the leash from between the puppy's teeth. "He's very stubborn. I think he takes after his breeder."

Aunt Peg has a tendency to intimidate people, but not Sam. For one thing, he's one of the few people around who's actually taller than she is. For another, he's equally adept at verbal sparring. But just because she can't push him around doesn't stop her from trying.

She lifted a brow as Tar leapt up and down in place, his long ears rising, then flapping down around the sides of his head. Faith was already on her feet. Now Hope stood up to get a better view of the proceedings and her just completed topknot flopped to one side.

The puppy was wearing out his welcome, and Sam was quick to realize it. "You two have work to do. How about if Davey and I take Tar for a spin around the building?"

"Sounds perfect," I said gratefully.

"We'll come back before judging. If you need anything before that, just holler."

I watched the three of them walk away, Davey proudly holding Tar's leash, his other hand tucked into Sam's much bigger one. Sam's jeans were old and their fit was snug. No doubt about it, it was a pleasure to watch him move.

"We haven't got all day," Aunt Peg pointed out. "Can't you moon over him and brush at the same time?"

I picked up my comb and went back to work. It's not that romance is dead these days, just that mostly we're too damn busy to care.

Five

With Aunt Peg's prodding and some last-minute help from Sam, we made it to the ring in plenty of time. Peg had grumbled incessantly over Faith's coat, complaining as she scissored that there was too much hair under the bitch's body, and not nearly enough on the top where it should have been the longest. From experience I knew it was best to simply nod in agreement and promise to do better next time. But when the preparations were finished and we headed up to ringside, I was very pleased with the way my Poodle looked.

Since neither of our two bitches was ready to compete in the Open Class, I had entered Faith in 12—18 Months. Aunt Peg was taking Hope in Bred-By-Exhibitor. In the ring the breed before ours was just finishing. The classes for dogs would be judged first, followed by those for bitches, so we had a few minutes to wait.

Ever since we'd arrived I'd been concentrating on making Faith look her best. Now as we awaited our turn, I began to feel the familiar dance of butterflies in my stomach. Aunt Peg, who has nerves of iron, was chatting with a fellow exhibitor. Sam and Davey had gone to see the steward about picking up our armbands. There was nothing for me to do but stand off to one side and try not to let any curious spectators with sticky-fingered children come too close to my carefully coiffed Poodle.

When I heard someone come up behind me, I automatically angled my body to block access to Faith.

"Ms. Travis? Is that you?"

The voice belonged to Kate Russo, one of my students at Howard Academy. A shy eighth grader, she had braces on her teeth, and a slender body that had yet to develop any curves. With her creamy skin and big brown eyes, Kate would be a beauty someday, but she hadn't begun to realize that yet.

"Hi, Kate. What are you doing here?"

"A man from my neighborhood does this." She waved a hand to encompass the show. "You know, he has dogs. I've been helping out in his kennel and it's pretty cool. Now he's going to start teaching me about dog shows."

"What's his breed?"

"Wire Fox Terriers. John's been breeding them for years. He's got a new dog coming out that he's really excited about."

I nodded, keeping an eye on the ring over her shoulder. "Are you enjoying the show?"

"It's great! My mom and I both came. She doesn't care about the dogs, but she kind of has a thing for John. . . ." Her face suffused with color and she quickly changed the subject. "That's a Standard Poodle, right?"

"Right. Her name's Faith."

Hearing her name, the Poodle in question preened for effect.

Kate stared at the elaborate trim and the dense coat of black hair now lacquered with hair spray into an upright position. "I never knew you could do stuff like that."

"I never did, either." I laughed. "Actually, I'm still learning. I bet Wire Fox Terriers take a lot of grooming, too."

"They do. John's always out in the kennel working on his dogs. Right now, I mostly pick up the pens and play with the puppies, but someday John's going to teach me all that stuff. He promised."

Faith shifted restlessly, and I slipped a piece of dried liver out of my pocket to give to her. In the ring the Standard Poodle Puppy Dog Class was just ending.

"Hey," said Kate. "Was that your car I saw parked over at Haney's General Store the other day? It looked like yours."

"Maybe. I was there on Wednesday." I glanced around and saw that Sam had Davey and Tar settled in a chair by the ring. He was helping Peg slide her armband on. The entry in dogs wasn't large and the judging was moving quickly.

"That was the day. Some friends and I went by on our bikes. They're really tearing that old place apart, aren't they?"

"That was the first step. Now they're trying to put it back together. Do you live around there?"

"Two streets away. Mr. Haney used to sell penny candy. I was probably one of his best customers."

"Ready?" Sam approached, holding out my armband. "It's just about time."

"Wow," Kate breathed under her breath. "Who's that?"

Smiling, I introduced them. Sam had the same effect on Davey's babysitters. Hell, who was I kidding? He had the same effect on me.

Kate giggled her way through the introductions, and turned beet red when Sam held out his hand to shake hers. If she fainted, he was going to have to take care of it. The steward was announcing my class.

Since Faith was the only one entered in the 12—18 Months Class, I wasn't unduly impressed with the blue ribbon the judge handed us. "Stay around," he told me, in case I didn't know the routine. "You'll be coming right back in."

Peg's class followed mine and consisted of two bitches. I stood just outside the gate and watched. When I was in the ring, I felt awkward and clumsy. Aunt Peg handled Hope with skill and flair and made the job look easy.

"When am I going to learn how to do it that well?" I asked Sam, who had come to stand beside me.

"Give it time. Don't forget, Peg's been doing this for thirty years. Besides, I think you may have a shot at beating her today."

"You do?"

Sam nodded. "Did you see the way the judge went

back and had another look at Hope's chest?" He placed his hands between Faith's front legs to demonstrate. "Hope is still narrow at this age. Her chest hasn't dropped yet. Faith is much more developed. Didn't you see him smile when he went over her front?"

"No," I admitted. "I guess I was too busy resetting her hind legs."

"You've got to keep your eye on the judge all the time. Watch where he is and what he's doing. If he's not worrying about Faith's back legs, then you shouldn't be, either."

"I know."

It was good advice, and Peg had said as much on several occasions. When I stood outside the ring, it all seemed possible. Then I went in and got rattled, and everything I thought I'd learned flew right out of my head.

Peg accepted her blue ribbon and led Hope from the ring. The four bitches entered in the Open Class filed in to be judged.

"Here," said Sam, taking my hand and making a sweeping motion upward over Faith's chest as she stood quietly beside us. "What are you doing when you do this?"

"Lifting the hair." That was easy. Even while they were in the ring, Poodles were constantly being groomed. It was a struggle to keep the hair perfect for any length of time and the handlers fussed over their dogs endlessly.

"That's true, but you're also reminding the judge of what he felt under his hands when he examined her. He was pleased with her front, but now fifteen minutes have passed and he's judged a half-dozen bitches since. Maybe he doesn't remember. It's your job to remind him by drawing his eye back there. When you go in the ring for Winners Bitch and he looks at Faith, I want you to make that same motion."

"But—"

"No buts," Sam said firmly. "Just give it a try."

"That's not the strongest Open Class I've ever seen," Peg mentioned as the judge awarded a weedy looking silver bitch first place. "We may have a shot at this."

"I may," I said blithely as the steward called our numbers. "I'm told your bitch has a narrow front."

Aunt Peg frowned at Sam. "You might have taught her something useful, you know."

"I'm trying." Sam laughed.

In the Winners Class, we were lined up in the order in which our classes had been judged. The silver was in front, followed by Hope, then Faith. The Puppy Class winner was behind me, scampering around at the end of its lead.

The judge stood across from us on the other side of the ring to evaluate his choices. I had Faith posed with her weight evenly balanced, her front legs straight underneath her, her hind legs extended slightly behind. My right hand was cupped beneath her muzzle, supporting her head. My left held up her tail.

The judge's gaze drifted down the line. Where on earth was I supposed to get an extra hand to highlight Faith's front? I glared at Sam. He glared right back and made an impatient motion. Easy for him. *His* hands were free.

At the last second I dropped Faith's muzzle and casually swept my fingers up over her chest hair. The judge's gaze paused for a moment, then continued on to the puppy.

One by one, each of the class winners was moved down and back along the diagonal mat that cut across the center of the ring. As the judge has seen all the entries before, judging in the Winners Class is often somewhat perfunctory. But this judge was taking his time about making up his mind.

When we'd all been moved, the judge looked down the line again and beckoned. I thought he wanted Aunt Peg. She didn't move, at least not with Hope. Instead, she turned around and poked me. The judge was still beckoning.

"Get up there," she said under her breath. "He wants you."

I led Faith forward. The judge placed her at the head of the line, then said, "Take them all around, please."

Blood was pounding in my ears, making me suddenly feel light-headed. I hoped I didn't trip over my feet. I heard a sudden burst of applause—Sam and Davey no doubt. As Faith and I ran by, my son shouted gleefully, "Go, Mom!"

The judge lifted his finger and pointed in my

direction. "Winners Bitch."

I stopped running and stood utterly still. Faith played at the end of her leash, cavorting in time to Davey's delighted cheer.

"Congratulations!" said Aunt Peg, coming up behind me. She gestured toward the marker near the gate where I was meant to stand. "Go get your ribbon."

"I won a point," I said stupidly. After a year of bathing and brushing, of trying to learn to handle and teach Faith how to be a show dog at the same time, a year of coming close but never being quite good enough, I'd finally realized what all the fuss was about.

It felt great to be a winner.

"You won two points," said Peg. "You beat eight bitches. Now go get your ribbon before he decides to give it to somebody else."

That was all the urging I needed to find my way over to the marker. I accepted the purple ribbon for Winner Bitch with a goofy grin that made the judge smile, as well.

"First show?" he asked kindly.

"No, but my first win."

"That's a pretty bitch. You're going to do very well with her."

I made it out the gate, mostly because Sam came and got me. Davey was jumping up and down on his chair, and Tar had decided to add to the general excitement by lifting his nose to the ceiling and howling.

"She was great," I babbled, wrapping my arms around Faith's neck and crushing all her hair. "Wasn't she great?"

Sam gently pried my arms free. "She was, and so were you. But don't mess her up too much, you both have to go back in."

Oh, Lordy, in all the excitement I'd forgotten about that. After Winners Dog and Winners Bitch have been chosen, the champions compete for Best of Breed, or in the case of Poodles, which have three varieties, Best of Variety. Since they are undefeated thus far on the day, the Winners Dog and Bitch are also eligible to compete.

In the ring now, Reserve Winners Bitch was being judged. Sam plucked a long comb out of his back pocket, found a can of hair spray, and made hasty repairs to Faith's neck hair. Thanks to his expertise, by the time the champions were called to enter the ring, she looked almost as good as new. We walked in and took our place at the end of the line.

Ten minutes later Best of Variety was awarded to a beautiful black bitch shown by a professional handler named Crawford Langley. Best of Opposite Sex was the Winners Dog. Faith, who was enjoying her chance to show off, won Best of Winners. The steward picked up her walkie-talkie and placed a call for the photographer.

One by one, each of the winners took a turn at having its picture taken with the judge. The top winning dogs used these win photos for advertising. Aunt

Peg framed her most important wins and hung them on the kennel wall. I hadn't yet decided what I'd do with my first picture, but I was sure I'd find a place to display it prominently.

Back at the grooming area as we wrapped ears, took down topknots and spritzed a conditioner on the hair spray, I asked Sam and Aunt Peg if they had plans for dinner. Peg, who'd recently started seeing someone, did, but Sam was free.

"Nothing fancy," I said, running through the contents of the cabinets in my mind. "Maybe spaghetti."

"Sounds good to me." Sam was easy. I like that in a man.

After extracting a firm promise from me that I would wash the hair spray out of Faith's coat before it was in long enough to do damage, Peg packed up and left. The rest of us soon followed. Three people, two Poodles, two cars. Someday I had to simplify my life.

Davey elected to ride home with Sam and Tar. Sitting on the front seat beside me, Faith whined softly for much of the trip. Every so often she'd reach over and lay a paw on my arm, encouraging me to go back and get Davey, whom she seemed to think I'd forgotten.

In Sam's Blazer just ahead of us, Davey kept turning around to wave out the back window. I showed her where he was, but Faith couldn't make the connection. Standard Poodles are so smart that it's easy to take their superior reasoning ability for granted. Then they miss a trick, and you're left wondering why.

We pulled into the driveway just behind the Blazer. Faith saw Davey get out of Sam's car and erupted into a flurry of excited barking, no doubt meant to inform me that she'd found my missing son and I no longer needed to worry. When I opened the door, she flew out of the Volvo and threw herself at him. Then she noticed Tar, who'd come tumbling out of the Blazer behind Davey, and stiffened.

Faith had met the puppy at the show, but that was neutral territory. This was *her* house, and she wanted to make sure everybody knew it, especially any furry little interlopers with big eyes and clumsy feet. She cuffed him once with a front paw and growled just to set matters straight. Obligingly Tar lowered his head and adopted a submissive position.

"All right," I said to Faith. "He's just a baby. Lay off."

She gave me that innocent "Who me?" look, that all dogs perfect the first time they pee on the floor as puppies.

"Yes, you," I told her.

Faith lowered her front end to the ground and lifted up her hindquarter, tail wagging, a classic invitation to play. Tar accepted by leaping to his feet. Together, they ran across the yard.

"I guess that's settled." Sam kept an eye on them while I unlocked the door. "Too bad, people can't be that sensible."

We ushered the Poodles through the house and into the fenced backyard, then unloaded the car. Davey was angling for Sam to try out a new Nintendo game with him; I was hoping Sam would spend some time with me. The only thing we agreed upon was that we were all ravenous.

By way of a compromise, the two of them played video games while I threw dinner together. Threw being the operative word. I found a loaf of French bread in the freezer, and lettuce and tomatoes in the crisper. The rest of the spaghetti dinner came mostly from boxes and cans, but what the hell. When I was finished you could hardly tell. Sam, gentleman that he is, never mentioned a word.

Davey usually goes to bed early after he's spent the day at a dog show. All the activity wears him out, and since he had school the next morning, I was happy to opt for a quick story and turn out the lights. Faith climbed up on the bed, turned two circles, then lay down beside him. I rubbed her muzzle and she sighed softly. Before I'd even reached the door, all four eyes were shut.

When I got back downstairs, Sam was in the kitchen finishing the dishes. Tar was sprawled in a boneless heap at his feet.

Coming up from behind, I wrapped my arms around his waist and rested my head on his shoulder. "You didn't have to do that."

"Why wouldn't I?"

I lifted my head. "What do you mean?"

Sam plucked a dishcloth off the counter and dried his hands. "I think we should talk."

That sounded ominous. Maybe it was my imagination. "Sure. What do you want to talk about?"

Sam took my hand and led the way into the living room. We sat down on the couch. I decided to take the hand holding as a good sign. But as he turned to face me, I wondered why he looked so serious.

"I love you, Melanie."

My breath caught in my throat. Sam had never said those words before. I wasn't sure I was ready to hear them.

I cared for Sam deeply. I knew we were a good match. That was as much as I'd allowed myself to feel, and it was enough. More than enough.

I'd been in love before. I'd experienced that heady rush that makes your feet float above the ground, and blinds you to all but the best possibilities. And I'd lived through the long hard fall that came when it ended.

I squeezed his hand, but didn't speak. I couldn't quite think what I wanted to say.

Sam gazed down at our joined fingers. "You know how I feel about Davey. He's terrific. But what we're doing now isn't working. It isn't enough. You're here, I'm in Redding. It feels like we talk on the phone more often than we see one another. Between your job, my job, the travel, the Poodles . . ."

His voice trailed off, but I knew what he meant. With all our other obligations, there never did seem to be enough time just for us. Sam designed computer software and was mostly self-employed, though in the last month he'd taken two consulting jobs on the side.

Weekdays, Davey and I needed to be in Stamford. Lately, weekends had often found Sam on the road. Aside from Tar, he had four other Standard Poodles at home. He'd found a local pet-sitter, but the only way he could spend the night at my house was if we made arrangements in advance. Welcome to life in the nineties.

"I'm a little confused," I said. "Are you proposing, or breaking up with me?"

I'd been half kidding, but his expression was suddenly sober. "I think I'm proposing."

A dozen different thoughts rocketed through my brain, the tumult fast and furious, and much too tangled to sort out.

Sam was looking at me intently, his eyes the color of an early morning sea. His hand came up and cradled my jaw, thumb rubbing softly over my cheek. Then he dipped his head down and kissed me. His lips were warm and tasted of the red wine we'd had with dinner.

I breathed in deep and drank him in. I wanted to go somewhere beyond thought. I wanted to lose myself in the moment, in the man. For now, it was the only answer I had to give.

After a day like that, going back to work on Monday seemed dull by comparison. Unfortunately, it's just when I'm in that kind of mood that the day seems to stretch on interminably. My last session of the day was with Kate Russo and her best friend, Lucia Thornton, both of them further behind in their schoolwork than they ought to be, and paired in my sessions so that they could support each other in their struggles to catch up.

Like Kate, Lucia was tall and slender; unlike Kate, she watched her weight religiously. Lucia was an equestrienne. She showed her Thoroughbred hunter, Remarkable, in weekly horse shows ranging from Connecticut to Palm Beach; and she'd explained the first time we met that the skin-tight, buff colored riding breeches worn for competition showed every extra ounce. My opinion—unsolicited by the head-master and therefore unoffered—was that if Lucia spent half as much time on her studies as she did on the back of her horse, she wouldn't have had any need of my services.

As they packed up their books at the end of class, Lucia looked out the window at the parking lot below. She flipped her blond hair behind her shoulders and glanced at me slyly. "Looks like Ms. Travis has a boyfriend."

"Let me see." Kate leaned over and had a look. "I hope it's the one I met yesterday. He's a real stud."

"What are you two talking about?"

"Down there." Lucia gestured. "There's a guy leaning against your car, like he's waiting for you to come out."

Sam? I thought, then quickly discarded the idea. If he'd needed me for something, he would have called. "I'm sure it's a mistake," I said, walking over to see.

"Look!" Kate giggled, waving her hand in a broad motion. "He's waving back."

I should have known, I thought when I reached the window. Who else would hang around the school parking lot, embarrassing his sister and drawing attention to himself by waving at students in their classrooms?

No one but my brother, Frank.

Six

I gathered up my things and walked out to my car. "Now what?" I demanded.

You have to understand, Frank and I are not buddies. In the course of a normal month, we'd be lucky to see each other once, and more likely not to cross paths at all. All this hanging around together was beginning to get on my nerves. Besides, whenever Frank shows up it's pretty much of a sure bet that he needs something.

"Is that any way to greet your favorite brother?"

Judging by recent experience, I'd have to say it was the only way.

"Actually," said Frank. "I have a problem."

Everyone had problems, but he'd never figured that out. In Frank's mind, other people's worries were insignificant, while his own loomed large enough to require the assistance of everyone in the vicinity.

I reached around him, opened the car door, and threw my things on the seat. "Yes?"

"There's been an accident at the store."

"More water?"

"Mel!" Frank was agitated enough to rake his fingers through his carefully styled hair. "This is serious."

I'd headed out a minute early, but now the school doors were open and kids had begun to pour out. Whatever my brother wanted, I had no desire to discuss it in front of my ever curious students. I had a half hour until Davey's school got out, then another twenty minutes while he rode the bus. That should give me enough time to deal with Frank.

"The store's on my way home," I said. "I'll meet you there."

Frank's Eclipse hugged my bumper for the duration of the short drive. From the outside the store looked just the same as it had the week before. Before I was even out of my car, Frank had hopped up onto the porch and unlocked the door. Once again, there were no workmen in sight.

I started to follow him into the store, then stopped abruptly. There was a gaping hole in the floor near the back counter.

"It's all right," said Frank. "As long as you don't go too close, the floor's sturdy enough."

"What happened?"

"Damned if I know. Some of the guys were working earlier and the floor just gave out. One minute Andy was standing there drinking a cup of coffee. The next, he fell right through to the basement."

"Was he hurt?"

"A broken leg and some cuts and bruises. Must have hurt like hell, though. He was swearing in three languages. The ambulance crew from the hospital responded right away and two of the other guys went with him. I checked with the emergency room before I went to meet you. Andy's already been patched up and sent home."

I stepped forward gingerly and peered down into the dark opening. The basement floor was visible eight feet below. "You're lucky it wasn't a lot worse."

"Tell me something I don't know. I hope he's not planning to sue."

"Are you covered?"

"You mean insurance? Yeah. Marcus took care of all that stuff. And of course we'll pay Andy's medical expenses. But the last thing I need is a claims adjuster hanging around asking what went wrong."

"What did go wrong?"

Frank looked pained. "All I can think is that the water leak last week must have weakened the supports, and one of them gave out. The building was supposed to be structurally sound. Marcus had it checked out before we started construction."

I backed up, walked around the hole, and headed for the basement stairs. "Sounds to me like you rely on Rattigan for an awful lot."

"He's my partner, remember? Besides, he's done plenty of conversions, all of them much bigger than this one. He knows what he's doing."

Too bad the same couldn't be said of my brother. If

he knew what he was doing, I could be home right now changing into my jogging clothes so Faith and I could take a run. Instead, I was about to have a look in a musty, old cellar.

The basement door was already open. The steps were narrow and dark. I gripped the spindly handrail and navigated my way down the stairs with care.

Frowning, Frank followed. "What are you looking for?"

"I don't know." I reached the bottom, found the string dangling from the lightbulb, and turned it on. "I'm just wondering why this place seems so accident prone."

"It's old, that's all. It's probably been years since Haney did any repairs."

I stepped beneath the hole and had a look. "Those boards look pretty rotten."

"It wasn't just the floorboards, it was the joists underneath, too." Frank pointed to the beams he was talking about, displaying his newfound knowledge proudly. "The whole thing gave out."

"That seems odd."

"What does?"

"You'd already installed the counter in the back of the room, and with that granite top, it's got to be heavy. I would think that if the floor was going to cave in, it would have happened there."

"Maybe the boards are okay back there."

"Maybe." I stepped back to the swinging bulb, grasped it by its base and directed the meager light toward the support column nearest the hole. Something didn't look right.

"Come here and hold the light," I said to my brother. "There's something I want to show you." I reached up and ran my finger along a jagged wooden edge. "It looks like this support post broke, too."

"So what? The whole thing broke. It's all going to have to be replaced."

"But this support column doesn't look rotten." I stepped around into the shadows and looked at the post from the other side. "And the break looks different back here. The edges are smooth, not uneven, like you'd think they'd be if the thing just snapped."

"Let me see that." Frank came over and joined me.

I looked down at the dirty wooden floor, pushing some of the debris around with my toe. "What's this?" We knelt down and had a closer look.

"Sawdust," said Frank.

I swallowed heavily. My brother and I looked at each other. For once I could read his mind, and we were both thinking the same thing.

"Your floorboards may have been rotten, but they didn't break from old age. Somebody sawed this support post nearly in half."

Frank was already shaking his head. "That's crazy. Who would do a thing like that?"

I stood up and dusted off my knees. "You tell me."

"Nobody." Frank headed for the stairs. "There's no reason anybody would want to sabotage the coffeehouse."

"What about the neighbors? You told me they were unhappy about the conversion." I turned off the light and followed. All at once the dank, gloomy basement was giving me the creeps. It was a relief to step up into the sunlight and close the cellar door behind us.

"Sure they've shown some concern, but it's a big leap from nailing up posters and arguing with the zoning board to rigging a building so that somebody gets hurt."

"All right, then let's look at it another way. Who had access to the building?"

"Probably half of Stamford." Frank grimaced. "Most of the guys have keys because I'm not always here. Usually they lock up, but they don't always remember. And sometimes they leave the place open on purpose so deliveries can be made."

"You're not helping any."

"Don't you think I know that? But damn it, Mel, this is crazy. I don't care what it looked like down there. It had to have been an accident, because nothing else makes any sense."

"What about your broken water pipe? Do you still think that was an accident, too?"

Stubbornly Frank nodded.

"I think you should call the police."

"No."

"Frank, listen—"

"I am listening." My brother held up a hand. If we were younger, he'd have probably covered my mouth with it. "Now you listen to me. I'm not calling the police. Marcus put me in charge of this project because I told him I could handle it. Handling things does not involve bringing in the police."

My brother can be incredibly pig-headed at times. Usually I don't hold it against him since I suffer from the same trait myself. But this time I had to argue.

"What if somebody else gets hurt?"

"Nobody will. Trust me, Mel. Now that I know we need to be more careful, we will be."

It wasn't much of a concession, but it was probably all I was going to get. "Speaking of Rattigan, does he have a key, too?"

"Of course he has a key. He's the owner."

"Have you talked to him about what happened today?" Frank's gaze skittered away. "Not exactly."

"Which means?"

"I called his office, but he wasn't in."

"You didn't leave a message?"

"No."

"Why not?"

"Jeez, give it a rest, will you? Can't you ever just leave anything alone?"

"You want to be left alone?" I straightened my jacket on my shoulders and began to button it. "Be my guest. You were the one who brought me here. I thought you wanted my opinion. But since you don't . . ."

"All right, look. The last time I saw Marcus, he and I had a bit of an argument, okay?"

"About what?"

"It wasn't a big deal," Frank said vaguely.

He was lying and we both knew it. I kept right on buttoning.

"I guess he's unhappy about the protests."

That was better. Now we were getting somewhere. "If you can believe what you read in the paper, people protest just about every time he builds something."

"Well, this time he seems to think it's more hassle than the project is worth. He's unhappy about the cost overruns, too."

"That's why you went to Aunt Peg when you needed more money. So he wouldn't find out about it."

"She told you about that?"

I nodded. "She was pleased to see you involved in something worthwhile. She thinks you have a future in coffee bars."

"I do have a future here." Frank slapped his hand down hard on the granite countertop. The hollow sound echoed in the empty room. "I'm doing everything I can think of to hold this project together. Marcus has handled enough construction to know that nothing ever proceeds without a hitch. If he'd just cut me some slack, I'm sure I could get everything back on track."

"And if he doesn't?"

"Then he terminates the project, and puts the building back on the market. Hell, in his tax bracket, he could probably just raze the place and take a loss. Either way, I'm out a bundle of money. I'd owe the bank and Aunt Peg both, and I wouldn't have a thing to show for it."

I stared at him in dismay. I'd been afraid my brother

might get in over his head, but things were much worse than I'd realized.

"What about the long-term lease you said you had? That must give you some rights. Surely he can't just sell the building out from under you."

"Yeah, well . . ." Frank flushed. "We haven't exactly signed the papers yet."

"Why *not?*" Now I was growing angry.

"Marcus was having his lawyers draw them up. In the meantime, we went ahead and started the construction. He said I shouldn't have to pay rent now, when I wasn't making any income. The lease was for later, when the coffee bar was up and running."

An old expression flitted through my mind. Lie down with dogs, get up with fleas. Except that all the dogs I know would have treated my brother a whole lot better than Marcus Rattigan had.

"You need to sit down with Rattigan and find out exactly what his plans are. There's no use in proceeding here until you know what he has in mind."

Frank nodded glumly.

"And you have to tell him about what happened to Andy. He's going to find out anyway. It'll look a lot better if he hears it from you."

"I guess you're right."

Of course I was right, but that didn't necessarily mean that Frank would listen to me. My brother was an expert at evading responsibility. And right now I didn't have any more time to spend trying to convince him to act like an adult.

"Look, I've got to go. Davey's bus will drop him off in ten minutes and I have to be there." I leaned forward and gave my brother's cheek a quick kiss. We're not usually a demonstrative family, but he seemed to need the reassurance.

"Go home, call and check on Andy, and then talk to Rattigan and get everything straightened out. And let me know what happens, okay?" Actually I wasn't at all sure I wanted to know, but the threat that I might call to check up on him was probably the only thing that would make him follow through.

"Okay," said Frank. "And thanks."

When I left he was standing on the porch, locking the front door carefully behind him. Already I was late enough to have to speed all the way home. For once, luck was with me. I didn't trip over any radar-traps, and Davey's bus was late, too.

As I turned onto our road, the school bus lumbered down the block just ahead of me. I waited behind the flashing red lights while Davey got out at our driveway, then pulled in behind him as he headed for the front door. Together we went in and liberated Faith from her day's confinement.

Frank didn't call that evening to tell me how things had turned out, but then I didn't really expect him to. In his case, no news was usually a good thing, so I was just as happy not to hear.

The phone did ring the next morning just after I'd put Davey on the bus. As soon as I lifted the receiver, I heard screaming.

"Frank?" I barely recognized my brother's voice. It was high and edgy with panic. "What is it? What's the matter?"

"It's Marcus! I'm at the store. I don't know what to do. Mel, he's here on the floor, and there's blood everywhere. He's dead, Melanie. Marcus is dead."

Seven

Dead?

"Frank, are you sure?"

"Hell, yes! And you would be, too, if you saw what this place looked like."

"You've got to call the police."

"I did that first thing. Nine-one-one. They said someone's on the way. Mel, you've got to get over here. You've got to help me."

Help him what? I wondered. But Frank was so rattled, there was no point in asking for any explanations over the phone.

"I'll be right there," I said. "Don't touch anything."

"Touch anything? Shit, I'm not crazy. Just hurry up, okay?"

I took a minute to call Howard Academy and lie to Lily, the receptionist, telling her that I was sick. Lily promised to report the reason for my absence to the headmaster, see that my day's appointments were rescheduled, and told me, ever so sweetly, that she hoped I'd be feeling better soon.

So did I, though it was beginning to look doubtful.

I grabbed my jacket and purse and loaded Faith into the car. She was so pleased to be included that she didn't even question the break in routine. I made good time to the store, but the police and an ambulance had beaten me there.

Faith stood up on the backseat and woofed softly at all the excitement. I pulled past the vehicles blocking the front of the store and parked around the side. Cracking all four windows for air, I left her to watch the show.

Though the back of the ambulance was open, nobody seemed in any hurry to load a passenger. Two EMTs were standing near the front of the vehicle, talking. They watched as I strode up onto the porch.

I pushed the door open and was stopped almost immediately by a uniformed officer, who blocked my path. "Sorry, ma'am, you can't come in here."

He was big, six two, six three, minimum. My eyes were level with a name tag on his chest, which identified him as Officer Pickering. I tried looking around him.

"Is my brother in here?"

"Mel!" Frank hurried over. "It's all right. I asked her to come."

"It's not all right," Pickering said firmly. "This is a crime scene, and nobody's coming in until the detective gets here."

"Come on." I took Frank's arm. "Let's go outside. We can wait on the porch."

Pickering nodded and stepped aside, and I saw what he'd been guarding. I wish I hadn't looked. But once I did, I couldn't seem to do anything but stare.

Marcus Rattigan's crumpled body was lying on the wooden floor. There was a pool of blood beneath him, and more splattered like red slash marks over the worn floorboards around him. A wooden framework of some sort lay half on top of him, and the back of his suit jacket had been pierced by a large, jagged piece of glass. There was more glass, sharp shards of it, everywhere.

It took me a moment to realize what the frame was. When I did, I looked up. The skylight that should have been in the roof, wasn't.

"I think I'm going to throw up," I said.

Frank grabbed my shoulder and turned me away. Pickering pushed us both out the door before I could pollute his crime scene. The cool air felt good on my heated cheeks. I dragged in one deep breath, then another, and began to feel a little better.

"You okay?" asked Frank.

"I think so." The urge to retch was passing. I staggered over to the porch railing and sat, half slumped, on the narrow perch. "Frank, what happened?"

"How should I know? I got here this morning and there he was."

"Were you the first?"

Frank nodded. "The crew usually rolls in around nine-thirty. After I spoke with you, I called Avril, gave him the day off, and told him to spread the word. I didn't say anything about Marcus, I just told him not to bother coming in."

"Didn't he ask why?"

"Maybe. Who knows? To tell you the truth, I'm not really sure what I said. I just wanted the police to hurry up and get here."

I could certainly understand that. "What about Rattigan? Did you talk to him yesterday afternoon like you said you were going to?"

"No, I couldn't get hold of him."

Frank was squirming. It wasn't a good sign. More likely he hadn't tried to get hold of Rattigan.

"You talked to his secretary?"

He half shrugged. It wasn't the answer I was looking for, but before I could press him on it, two more cars pulled up in front of the building. Both were late models, dark colored, and American made. The two men who'd arrived greeted each other briefly, then walked past us and went inside.

"The troops have begun to arrive," said Frank. "I wonder what happens now."

After a few minutes, the door opened again and one of the new arrivals came out to talk to us. He was a tall, spare black man with a solemn expression and a deliberate stride. His dark brown eyes examined the two of us thoroughly before coming to rest on Frank.

"Detective James Petrie," he said. "I understand you were the one who found the body?"

"That's right."

I glanced at my brother. He sounded nervous, and

was threading his fingers together as if he couldn't figure out what to do with his hands. Even to me, he looked as though he had something to hide.

"What time was that?"

Frank looked at his watch. "About half an hour ago?"

"You called me at eight-thirty-five," I said.

"You're his sister?" Petrie asked, and I nodded. "Name?"

"Melanie Travis."

"Mind telling me why you're so sure of the time?"

"My son's school bus comes at eight-thirty two, and if he misses it, it's a hassle so we're always out there on time. I'd just come back inside when Frank called."

Now that the detective had turned his gaze on me, I saw why my brother was wringing his hands. I hadn't done anything wrong. Even so, being interrogated by the long arm of the law made me feel jumpy.

"What was your relationship to Mr. Rattigan?" Petrie asked Frank.

"We were business partners."

This was no time for my brother to start overstating his involvement. "Just here," I interjected. "Not in general. Rattigan owns this building, and Frank was renovating it."

Petrie paused for a long moment. "It would be better if you'd let your brother answer the questions himself."

Not really. Actually, I was quite certain it would be better if I answered for him. Not that I had any choice.

"Okay."

"Now, then," said the detective. "You arrived at about eight-thirty. What was your reason for coming here?"

"To open the building. To get things started for the day."

"The door was locked when you got here?"

"Yes."

"Did you notice anything unusual upon your arrival?" Frank thought for a moment, then shook his head.

"Had you planned to meet Mr. Rattigan here this morning?"

"No, usually he works in his office downtown. He's only stopped by here once or twice."

Was that true? I wondered. Or was Frank shading the truth to make it sound better? When I'd met Rattigan the week before, Frank had been expecting his visit; he'd implied that it was something that happened regularly.

Don't blow it, I thought, sending my brother a mental message to be careful. Get your facts straight!

Step by step, Detective Petrie led Frank through the events of the morning thus far. He questioned him about the details of his relationship with Rattigan, asked who'd installed the skylight and when the work had been done. They discussed the hole in the floor and the worker who'd fallen through. Then Petrie requested the names and addresses of all the other men in the construction crew. Carefully he recorded each of Frank's answers in a small notebook.

Finally the detective recapped his pen and slid it into a pocket. The interview was drawing to a close. "Has anyone been on the roof in the last couple of days?"

"Maybe. I'm not sure," Frank waffled. "I'm not here all the time, you know. I don't think so."

With answers like that, it was no wonder Petrie was ready to take a break. Instead of trying to pin Frank down, he merely said, "You live in Cos Cob, right? I want you to stay available. I'm sure I'll have more questions at a later date."

While we'd been talking, the medical examiner and a team of technicians had arrived. Petrie left us and went back inside to confer with them.

Frank swore loudly when he'd gone. "What's with that guy? You'd think I was a suspect or something."

I stared at my brother. "Wake up, Frank! You *are* a suspect."

I looked around to make sure no one was close enough to overhear what I was about to say. The ambulance had long since left, and everyone else was inside. "You and Rattigan were partners together in the building where he was found dead. Not only that, but according to what you told me yesterday, there was a good chance he was about to screw you out of a lot of money."

Frank's tongue nervously moistened his lips. "The police don't know that."

"Maybe not now, but they will soon enough once they start asking questions and going through his records. I think you ought to get a lawyer."

"But I didn't do anything! Besides, nothing would make me look guilty faster."

I stepped away from the railing and looked inside the window. Rattigan's body had been removed, and the police seemed to be finishing up.

"You told Detective Petrie that you weren't planning to meet Rattigan. Do you know what he was doing here?"

Frank shook his head. "I've wondered about that, too. Usually when he was going to stop by, I'd have some notice. As far as I know, he's never been here when everyone else is gone."

I gazed through the window and up at the hole where the skylight had been. "Do you suppose it could have been an accident? Maybe the thing wasn't installed correctly and it was just Rattigan's bad luck to be standing under it when it fell."

"Nice try," said Frank. "But no way. There's some sort of copper lip around the frame to hold it in place, so they can't just fall. Besides, I know for a fact that both those skylights were bolted in solid."

"What makes you so sure?"

"Because I was up there two days ago, checking on the gutters. Some leaves had blown down onto the skylights and I went over and brushed them off. Everything was tight as a drum then."

I strode back to his side. "What did you say?"

Frank looked at me innocently. "What?"

"I could have sworn that when Petrie asked you if

anyone had been on the roof recently, you said no."

"Not exactly. I said I didn't know. Don't make a big deal out of it, Mel. Nobody else was here at the time."

"Are you certain one of the neighbors didn't see you? Were you wearing gloves?"

Frank's silence said it all.

I threw up my hands eloquently. "You'd better go back in and talk to Petrie again. Tell him you just remembered something he ought to know."

"No way. I'm innocent, remember? I didn't do it. And I'm not going to give these guys any information that makes it look as though I did."

"The thing that makes you look guilty is lying, Frank. Especially if you get caught."

My brother stared off into the trees on the other side of the road. I hoped he was thinking about what I said. But when he spoke again, it was clear he'd had something else entirely on his mind.

"You've solved a couple of murders."

"No." I wasn't denying his statement. Rather, I could guess where this conversation was heading and I didn't want any part of it.

"Yes, you did. There was Uncle Max, remember? And that Poodle guy last summer. I hate to say it, Mel, but maybe you have a knack for that kind of thing."

"Frank, Marcus Rattigan was an important man. The police are here, they're mounting an investigation, and they're going to do everything they can—"

"Bullshit! They're going to try to pin this on me, Mel. I can see it coming. Even though I had nothing to do with Rattigan's murder, I'm the easy choice, the obvious choice. You and I know it, and so do they."

"What do you think I can do?"

"Poke around. Ask questions. Isn't that what you did before?"

"Yes, but—"

"But nothing," said Frank. "You're my sister. You have to help me."

I turned my back on him, fuming silently. Over the years I'd heard many variations on that same plea. *You're my sister, you have to share your cupcake with me. You're my sister, you have to type my term paper. You're my sister you have to help with my rent.* But those instances paled beside what he was asking now.

Was he right? I wondered. Would the police settle upon him as the obvious suspect and look no further? If so, my brother was in a lot of trouble. I'd been acting as Frank's protector for years; but by now the role was wearing thin. Why was I the one who always had to be the family watchdog?

"Well?" he prodded.

"I suppose I could ask some questions," I conceded. "But I'm not making any promises. Deal?"

"Deal," Frank said grudgingly.

"In the meantime, you better go inside and clear up a few things with Detective Petrie."

"No way." He held up a hand. Behind us, the door opened and several policemen emerged. "I'm outta here."

Frank braced a hand on the railing, hopped over

lightly, and strode to his car. Before I could follow, Detective Petrie emerged from the building. "Your brother was sure in a hurry. Anything wrong?"

"No, everything's fine." The glib answer shot out of my mouth before I'd had a chance to think. I felt my face redden. "I mean, as fine as things can be under the circumstances . . ."

Petrie nodded, letting me off the hook.

He came over and stood beside me, his bearing rigidly erect. I figured that meant either the Marines or Catholic school. In my experience it takes a drill sergeant or an order of nuns to have that effect on posture. But despite Petrie's stance, he looked friendly enough.

"What will you do now?" I asked.

"Get the investigation started. Talk to anyone and everyone who had dealings with Marcus Rattigan. Then we'll try to narrow down how he spent his last few days, where he was, who he was with."

"Do you know when he died?"

"When did you leave here yesterday?"

"Close to three-thirty."

"You and your brother left together?"

"Yes." I hesitated slightly before answering. Surely Frank had been only a step or two behind me.

"All we know now is that he died sometime between then and this morning. The medical examiner will probably be able to fix it closer than that, and we'll check with his home, his office, try to nail down what time he was last seen."

"I would think there'd be plenty of suspects," I said. Petrie's eyes narrowed. "Would you? Why?"

"Judging by what I've read, he sounds like the kind of man who must have made some enemies."

"Not everyone agreed with what he wanted to do, that's for sure. On the other hand, he knew how to make money. Your brother seemed happy enough to be involved with him."

Warning bells went off like a siren in my head. So much for friendly. I'd thought I was the one fishing for information. So why was I suddenly standing here with Petrie's hook dangling in front of me?

"I guess he was," I said, declining to elaborate.

A uniformed officer came out onto the porch and began to unroll a spool of bright yellow crime scene tape around the railing. Obviously the renovations would have to stop. I wondered who Rattigan's heirs were, and who owned the building now.

Detective Petrie reached in his pocket and pulled out a card. "You think of anything I ought to know, you call me, okay?"

"I will," I said, biting back the things I thought needed saying, and silently cursing my brother.

I didn't like the idea of lying to the police. I hoped I wasn't going to have to make a habit of it.

Eight

Since it was barely ten o'clock I briefly considered driving to school, claiming I'd had a miraculous recovery, and working the rest of the day. That notion lasted just about as long as it took me to walk to the Volvo.

The trees around me were brilliant with color. Though there was a chill in the air, the sun was warm on my back. Connecticut is known for its cold, snowy winters and short, humid summers, but October is a month that it handles superbly. I breathed in deeply and acknowledged that it was going to be a gorgeous day.

Faith had been dozing on the seat, but she jumped up as I approached. Tail wagging, hind feet dancing, she pushed her nose through the opening I'd left at the top of the window and wuffled a greeting. To go to school now I would first have to take her home and drop her off.

Faith and I made eye contact and she whined softly. I recorded her vote and added my own. Hooky, it was.

I got in the car, wrestled forty-five pounds of effusive Standard Poodle into the passenger seat, and drove myself to Aunt Peg's. She lives in Greenwich, north of the Merritt Parkway, in a big old farmhouse. There's a small kennel building out back, and enough acreage that the occasional barking dog doesn't usually bother the neighbors.

Now that Max was gone, Aunt Peg had been slowly

cutting down on the number of dogs in residence. Poodles are people dogs. They can adapt to almost any situation, but they thrive on human companionship.

Keeping only the best with which to continue her breeding program, Aunt Peg had placed some of her young adults in new homes. As these Poodles went to families who might not have had the time or energy to take on a rambunctious, untrained puppy, the situation worked out well for everybody.

At the moment Peg had three Standard Poodles "in hair" in her kennel, and five house Poodles, all retired champions, and all maintained in sporting trim with short curly hair and rounded topknots and tail pom-pons. Aunt Peg would have considered the notion heresy, but I thought her house dogs looked a lot more sensible than my show dog did. I couldn't wait until Faith finished her championship and I could cut off all her hair, too.

Nobody bothers to ring the doorbell at Aunt Peg's. As soon as a car turns into the driveway, the Poodles race to the windows and announce that visitors have arrived. By the time Faith and I reached the front door, Peg already had it open.

"Why aren't you in school?" she demanded, angling her body so that her dogs couldn't slip out while Faith and I came in. "Are you sick? Is Faith all right?"

Her gaze slid past me and focused with concern on Faith. Typical.

"We're both fine. Your nephew is the one who's in trouble."

"Frank?"

As if she had more than one. As if the notion of Frank in trouble should come as any surprise.

"I thought I just bailed that boy out," said Peg. "What's the matter now?"

I knelt down and let the Poodles swarm over me for a minute. We were old friends and they'd have been highly insulted if I neglected to greet them properly. "Frank's partner, Marcus Rattigan, is dead."

"Heart attack?" Aunt Peg asked hopefully. "Plane crash?"

"He was crushed by a falling skylight."

She'd seen the blueprints. "Don't tell me it happened at the coffee bar."

So I didn't. Instead I stood up and took myself into the kitchen. A conversation like this was going to require fortification.

Aunt Peg's a tea drinker. Her meager concession to those who don't share her preference is to keep a jar of instant coffee in the freezer. I filled the kettle with water and set it on the stove.

"When?" asked Peg.

"The police don't know yet. Sometime between late yesterday and early this morning."

"I take it this wasn't an accident?" Her voice floated out from the pantry. In Aunt Peg's mind no snack, however small, is complete without sweets. No doubt she had something stashed away for just such an emergency.

"Frank says no. He's sure the skylight was installed

properly. The police are investigating it as a murder."

She emerged carrying a box of cupcakes, strawberry with white icing and orange candy pumpkins on top for decoration. Just looking at them made my teeth hurt. "Don't you have anything healthy to eat?"

"Cupcakes are perfectly healthy. They're made from eggs and flour." She opened a drawer and took out a bag of rice cakes, holding them away carefully between thumb and forefinger as if their mere presence might contaminate. "You can try these if you want. Douglas brought them by. He claimed they're edible, but I'm not so sure. I think they're made of Styrofoam."

Douglas Brannigan was Peg's new male companion. He was charming, intelligent, and probably much too tolerant of my aunt's domineering ways. It seemed far more likely that he'd be adding cupcakes to his diet than he'd have her eating rice cakes any time soon.

"Do the police have any suspects?" Aunt Peg asked as we took our mugs and sat down at the kitchen table.

"At least one. Frank."

"They can't be serious." Peg sipped at her tea. "Frank wouldn't be my choice for relative of the year, but anyone can see that he's perfectly harmless."

"He and Rattigan have a business relationship that's falling apart. Rattigan was killed at the building they're arguing over, crushed by a skylight that Frank approved the installation of, and Frank's the one who found the body.

"In case that isn't enough, Frank was up on the roof

two days ago fooling around with the skylight, so his fingerprints will probably be all over it. Since he lied about that to the police, he figures it won't be a problem. By the way, Rattigan's death is the third accident at the coffee bar this week. A member of the construction crew fell through the floor yesterday and broke his leg."

"Is that all?" Peg asked dryly.

"Actually, no. Frank thought the floorboards had been weakened when the pipe burst, but we went down to the cellar and had a look. The support column had been sawed nearly in half. The floor was sabotaged, just like the skylight."

Plenty of people would have been horrified by such a blunt summation of the facts. Not Aunt Peg. She rose to the occasion like a trouper. To shore up our strength, she started by breaking out the cupcakes.

"I've heard that Marcus Rattigan's ex-wife refers to him as 'The Rat,'" she mentioned as she passed one my way. "I wouldn't be surprised if it's an accurate assessment."

I plucked the noxious looking orange candy off the top and set it aside. "Rattigan's divorced?"

Peg nodded. "There was one marriage, quite a long one I believe. No children. The divorce was rather nasty."

"How do you know?"

"The man showed dogs, Melanie."

Her tone clearly conveyed the belief that this simple fact explained everything. Actually, it probably did.

When exhibitors have finally exhausted all there is to say about their dogs, they talk about each other. Aunt Peg might not have kept up with Marcus Rattigan, but obviously there were other exhibitors who had.

"What else do you know about him?"

She sat back and thought. The pause gave her the perfect opportunity to finish off her cupcake. When she let her hand drift down below table height, two obliging Poodles licked her fingers clean.

"Mostly just that he had Winter." The thought of the pretty Wire Fox Terrier bitch made Aunt Peg smile. "She did so much winning that Marcus got himself known rather quickly. The year that she was number one, he came to quite a few shows."

I nibbled at the icing around the edge of my cupcake. It was definitely too sweet to bite into. "Didn't you say that Winter's breeder was a local man? What was his name?"

"You know, I don't remember. Marcus was such a large presence, always right on hand to take all the credit. The other man, whoever he was, just faded into the background."

"It seems a shame, considering that he was her breeder."

"It does, doesn't it?" Aunt Peg stood. "Let's go look it up."

"How?"

"Winter showed at Westminster several times. The information would have been listed in the catalogue."

"You keep dog show catalogues going back ten years?"

"From Westminster, I do." Aunt Peg left the kitchen and started down the hall toward her office.

I placed my cupcake in the center of the table, where it would be less of a target for any long pink tongues in the vicinity, and got up and followed. The shelves of Aunt Peg's office were filled with Poodle books and magazines. Old and new issues of *Poodle Review* and *Poodle Variety* sat side by side with *The New Poodle*, *The Book of the Poodle* and *Poodles in America*, a multivolume set that listed the pedigrees of every champion Poodle bred in the United States since 1929.

Still, she didn't have any trouble finding what she was looking for. By the time I reached the room, Peg was already thumbing through a thick purple catalogue with the silhouette of a Pointer on the front, and gold lettering on the spine.

"Here it is," she said. "Champion Wirerock Winter Fantasy. Breeder, John Monaghan. By Champion Galsul Excellence out of Champion Wirerock Ramada. Owner, Marcus Rattigan."

She flipped to the pages in the back and looked up the address. "Care of Anaconda Properties in Stamford. That's no help. I'm sure Mr. Monaghan lived around here somewhere."

"I wonder . . ."

"What?"

"At the show last week, I ran into one of my students. A neighbor of hers shows Wire Fox Terriers, and Kate was there to help him out. She said his name was John."

"That's probably him," said Peg. "There aren't many Fox Terrier breeders in the area. Why don't you ask her about it tomorrow? If it is the same man, I would imagine there's plenty he could tell us about Marcus Rattigan."

She left the catalogue on top of a tall stack and we walked back to the kitchen. The cupcake I'd left on the table was gone. All that remained was a long smear of greasy white icing on the floor. The Poodles looked up innocently as we came in. With eyes like that, no jury in the world would ever convict them.

"Another cupcake?" asked Peg, digging a second out of the box for herself.

"No, I'll pass."

I glanced at the Poodles. Thanks to me, one of them was now courting tooth decay. Since they weren't tempted to confess, I decided to keep mum, too. I sat down and picked up my mug. At least they hadn't finished off my coffee.

"So what are you going to do about this mess?" asked Peg.

"What am I going to do? Why does everyone assume I'm going to do anything?"

"Because you're good at it. And because if your description of your silly, misguided brother's involvement is anywhere near accurate, it looks as though he needs you."

Family responsibility. That made twice in one day that it had been thrust upon my shoulders. At times like this I could only think it was a damn good thing I didn't have a bigger family.

"I told Frank I might ask a few questions," I admitted.

"Good." Peg looked pleased. "If I were you, I'd start with the obvious."

"Which is?"

"Gloria Rattigan, of course. The bitter ex-wife. I should think she'd make a dandy suspect."

"I don't suppose you know where she lives?"

"No, but I can find out." Aunt Peg opened a cupboard and pulled out a Greenwich phone book. "When she and Marcus were together, they lived in Belle Haven. If she kept the house, the address should be listed. Yes, here it is." She wrote the information on a slip of paper and handed it over.

"Do you think Gloria's heard about what happened?"

"I would imagine so. After all, she is his next of kin."

"Ex next of kin," I pointed out.

"All the better," Peg said briskly. "She won't be in mourning. Let's see if she's home." She walked to the wall phone, picked up the receiver, and punched out a number. "Mrs. Rattigan? This is Susie Smith calling on behalf of Save the Manatees and we're hoping we can count on you for a generous donation to our cause."

The click was so loud I could hear it where I was sitting. Aunt Peg grinned. "The generous donation is out, but Gloria Rattigan is in. You've already taken the day off from school. Why don't you go over there now?"

In her rush to manage life to her own satisfaction, Peg has a way of overlooking the small details. "Don't you think it's a little soon? What if she doesn't want to talk to me?"

"Then she'll tell you so. Marcus Rattigan was an important figure in Fairfield County. His death is hardly going to go unnoticed. Ten to one, a reporter will already have beaten you there."

To nobody's surprise, Faith and I found ourselves being hustled out the door only a few minutes later. Aunt Peg requested frequent updates and gave me another cupcake for the road. Because it seemed easier than arguing, I got in the car and drove to Belle Haven. Faith ate the cupcake on the way.

The town of Greenwich encompasses fifty square miles, bordering New York state in the north and Long Island Sound to the south. Much of the residential area along the coast is an exclusive enclave known as Belle Haven. Waterfront estates routinely fetch prices in the millions, and even a distant water view could increase the value of property significantly. Land values here are impervious to dips and surges in the economy. Like the old saying goes, if you have to ask how much, you probably can't afford it.

So as I drove beneath the thruway and turned up onto Fieldpoint Road, I was thinking that no matter how nasty Gloria Rattigan's divorce had been, she couldn't have come off too badly if she still had a house in Belle Haven. After only two wrong turns, I found the address. The house wasn't a beachfront mansion but it was large nonetheless, a three-story Tudor with an expansive lawn and a circular gravel drive. And yes, I realized as I parked the Volvo in the shade and got out, I could see the Sound in the distance above a low band of trees.

If any reporters had come to see Gloria Rattigan, they were gone now. The house looked quiet, almost serene, in the golden October light. At this time of day in my neighborhood there would have been toddlers riding tricycles down the sidewalk, a garbage truck making pickups, perhaps a teenager playing hooky with a boom box attached to his ear. Here there was only silence; as if wealth, the great protector, had cushioned the owners of these homes from the noise and mundane hassles of everyday life.

I left Faith in the car, her nose pressed mournfully against the window, walked to the front door, and rang the bell. After a moment Gloria Rattigan answered the door herself.

She was a slender woman in her mid-forties, with a long, bony face and hands to match. Her hair was the shade of frosted blond favored by women who need to camouflage a lot of gray, and her suit was from Chanel. Manicured fingers toyed with the equestrian themed scarf at her throat as she arranged her somewhat blank expression into a tentative smile.

"Yes? Can I help you?"

"Hi, my name is Melanie Travis. I was wondering if you might have a few minutes to speak with me?"

Gloria closed the door ever so slightly. "Are you a reporter? The police told me the press would probably come."

"No, but I am here about your ex-husband. My brother, Frank, was in business with Mr. Rattigan."

"Many people have business dealings with Marcus. What does that have to do with me?"

I searched her face for signs of grief before continuing. For someone who'd just lost her ex-husband under suspicious circumstances, she looked remarkably composed.

"For the last six weeks Frank had been renovating a building in north Stamford that was owned by your ex-husband."

A small line furrowed between her brows. "Is that the place where Marcus was killed?"

"Yes, that's what I'd like to talk to you about. You see, the police seem to view my brother as a suspect—"

Unexpectedly, Gloria Rattigan smiled. "Your brother is the one who murdered Marcus?"

"No, he didn't. I'm sure of it. But the police—"

"Why don't you come in?" Gloria stepped back and opened the door. "I imagine I can spare a few minutes."

Let me get this straight, I thought as I followed her through an ornate foyer into a large living room. When I was the sister of a business partner, I could stand on the front step. As the sister of a potential murderer, I'd been invited inside.

"Please sit down," said Gloria. "Can I get you anything? Coffee? Tea?"

Confused, I shook my head and sat. Gloria chose a spot on a love seat opposite.

"If you don't mind my saying so, you seem to be handling the news rather well."

"Only on the surface. Inside, I'm jumping up and down with glee."

Times like these, I can only wish I'd learned how to cultivate a poker face. Unfortunately, everything I was feeling was right there in my expression.

"I see I've shocked you," said Gloria. "There was no love lost between Marcus and me. If your brother's the person responsible for his death, I'd be pleased to thank him personally."

I couldn't see the point in declaring Frank's innocence when his presumed guilt was buying me so much goodwill. "I understand that you were married to Mr. Rattigan for a number of years."

"Fourteen. And some of them were even quite happy." Gloria reached over to an end table, picked up a pack of menthol cigarettes, shook one out, and lit the tip with a silver lighter.

"And the divorce?"

"That happened last year. It was Marcus's idea. If you ever met him, you'll know that he was the sort of person who always did exactly what he wanted to do, and the rest of the world be damned."

"Someone told me . . ." I paused uncertainly, then pushed on. "That you refer to him as 'The Rat'?"

Gloria laughed, exhaling small puffs of smoke with each breath. "Why not? If I do say so myself, it was the perfect name for him. I can't say that he liked it much, though. Bastard asked if that meant I thought of myself as a sinking ship."

I couldn't help myself; I laughed along with her. The interview might not be going the way I'd planned, but it was certainly making me feel better. Obviously Frank was simply the first person the police had stumbled over, suspect-wise. Once they got hold of Gloria Rattigan, they would have to concede there were other possibilities.

"The reason I came to see you was because I was hoping you might be able to tell me if there was anyone who might have wanted to harm your ex-husband."

Gloria tipped a long wand of ash into the ashtray. "Aside from me, you mean. How many names do you want?"

I thought she was kidding. "How many do you have?"

"Probably dozens. Marcus could be a real shark and it didn't take most people long to figure that out. You can start with just about anyone who ever tried to do business with him. Marcus was tight with money and fond of iron-clad contracts. I doubt if anybody ever came out on the winning end of a deal with him."

Gloria drew in a deep drag of smoke and slowly let

it out. "It's no secret who belongs at the top of the list, though. Anyone could tell you that. Her name is Liz Barnum."

"Who is she?"

"His secretary. And the bitch he was sleeping with throughout most of our marriage."

Nine

Oh.

That question had worked so well, I decided to try a follow-up. "Why would she have wanted to murder him?"

"Because after working for Marcus for years, slaving for him actually, she finally discovered what a lying, conniving bastard he really was."

"When was this?"

"When our divorce became final last year. My guess is that he'd been stringing her along, probably feeding her that nonsense men spout. You know, about how she was the only woman he'd ever really loved, and if only he were free . . ."

"Until he got himself free."

Gloria smiled tightly. "And dumped Liz like yesterday's news. She thought she'd be getting a ring. Turns out she was lucky not to have gotten a pink slip."

"You mean she still works for him?"

"Yes, crazy isn't it? Supposedly she thinks he's undergoing a period of emotional turmoil. That once he gets things straightened out, he'll realize how much he misses her and come running back."

For someone who'd divorced her husband a year earlier, Gloria seemed remarkably well informed. "How do you know all this?"

"Do I look stupid to you? Marcus has his spies. I have mine. That's one thing living with him taught me. Always cover your back."

"You think your husband was spying on you?"

"I don't think so, I know so. He wasn't what you'd call the trusting type. When Marcus was here, we had live-in help, a couple. The wife did the general house-keeping; the husband, the gardening and occasionally some driving. I found out later that their other duty was to report back to Marcus on my activities during the day."

"Is that what led to the divorce?"

Gloria's fingers brushed at the chintz covered cushion, whisking away an imaginary spot. "That was probably part of it. After a while it seemed foolish for me to adhere to my marriage vows when Marcus was so blatantly abusing his. Unfortunately, it turned out that his views on the subject weren't nearly as liberal as mine."

I glanced around the room, noticing for the first time that one of the reasons it seemed so large was because it wasn't fully furnished. "So the divorce was his idea."

"It certainly wasn't mine." Gloria ground out her cigarette in the ashtray. "Marcus thought he'd walk away with everything. I got myself a good lawyer and he fought like hell. Not that it did much good."

"You don't seem to have done too badly."

"Looks can be deceiving. Do you have any idea what it costs to run this house? The mortgage and utility bills alone eat up half the payments I get. Not only that, but the judge went for rehabilitative alimony. It only runs for five years. At the end of that time, I'm supposed to have figured out another way to support myself, and the payments stop."

"Are you looking for a job?"

Gloria's hand fluttered to her throat. She laughed out loud as if I'd said something funny. "Oh, honey, you are young, aren't you? Me, work? What would I do with a job? I'm looking for another husband."

Out in the car Faith was delighted to see me. She pounced, and licked, and even yipped a few times, just in case there was any doubt. That's one of the things I like best about dogs. You always know where you stand.

When a dog loves you, he shows it. When he hates you, he's equally clear about portraying that emotion. And when a dog's lying to you . . . well, it just doesn't happen.

As for where Gloria Rattigan stood, I had to wonder. On the surface it seemed as though I'd been treated to her honest reaction; her ex-husband was dead, and she couldn't have been happier. Presumably that meant his demise hadn't affected their financial arrangement, and his estate would now pick up the tab for the remaining alimony payments. But could it really be that simple?

And what about the rest of the assets? Marcus Rattigan appeared to be a very successful man. So who inherited everything else?

Back at home I changed my clothes and took Faith out for a jog. As usual, she enjoyed the experience more than I did. Her stride was strong and even, and her ear wraps bobbed jauntily in the breeze. She ignored a fluffy little white dog that chased us, barking madly, for half a block, and curled her lip at a large mutt who harbored thoughts of joining the game.

In the beginning when I could still speak, I told her what a wonderful companion she was. Toward the end, when my legs felt like rubber and just the act of breathing was painful, I could only manage an encouraging pat. She seemed to understand.

As we turned back onto our own block, Davey's bus was just arriving. It stopped at our house and my son emerged, laughing, swinging his backpack, and waving goodbye to his friends. A rush of maternal love carried me the final hundred yards.

Davey saw us coming and held out his arms. I dropped Faith's leash and she ran on ahead. Her greeting just about knocked him over but Davey didn't seem to mind.

"What about me?"

A year earlier my son would have given me a hug.

Now he turned a critical eye my way and said, "You don't look so hot."

"I've been jogging. I looked better two miles ago."

We trooped inside and had a snack, then Davey sat down at the kitchen table to do his homework. This is a new development in his life and he takes the responsibility very seriously. While he was working, I went upstairs and gave Sam a call. From his preoccupied tone I could tell he was working when he picked up the phone, so I kept it brief.

Though he's too liberal to say so, Sam doesn't like the idea of my getting mixed up with murder. Bearing that in mind, I glossed over most of the details of what had happened. Sam asked about police involvement and sounded relieved when I told him they were on top of things. I figured we could sort out the rest the next time we saw each other and we made plans to get together at the end of the week.

The next morning Davey and I actually got up and went off to school like normal people. No last-minute phone calls, no unexpected dead bodies. This, I thought, must be how the other half lives.

I pulled into the Howard Academy parking lot right on time, stopped to pick up a cup of coffee in the teachers' lounge, and still made it to my classroom with a few minutes to spare. As I was getting things set up for the day, there was a light tap on the classroom door. I pulled it open to find the school's headmaster, Russell Hanover II, standing on the threshold.

"Do you mind if I come in?" he asked.

In a school where children come barreling through doorways all the time, the request seemed needlessly formal. Maybe he was trying to set a good example.

"Please do."

Russell cast a withering glance at my outfit, which consisted of a turtleneck sweater and corduroy slacks. It hadn't escaped his notice, or mine, that I was the only woman teacher at Howard Academy that dared to dress in pants. As for his appearance, I'm sure that even Honoria Howard herself would have approved.

He was dressed in a lightweight wool suit, which looked to be of English origin. His tie was a somber shade of blue and his conservative button-down shirt bore a muted stripe and a discreet three letter monogram on the pocket. Ralph Lauren makes people pay a mint to dress in the clothes Russell Hanover was born to.

"I just wanted to make sure everything was all right," he said. "I understand that you were absent yesterday. I trust it was nothing serious?"

"No, nothing serious," I said blithely.

First Frank had me lying to the police. Now I was lying to the headmaster. Somehow I was sure this was not the direction my life should have been heading.

"Good. Bitsy wanted me to check. She gets concerned, especially about people who haven't been part of our little family for very long."

Bitsy was Russell's wife, not an employee of the school per se, but an active alum and a very vocal fundraiser. She was also the former Bitsy Paynter whom the press had lauded as "Deb of the Year" in 1970. She'd told me that the first time we met. As far as I was concerned, that pretty much summed up everything I needed to know.

"It's very kind of you to inquire," I said, then gave myself a mental kick. One minute's exposure to Russell and I was talking like a character out of Jane Austen. "Please give Bitsy my best and tell her I'm fine."

"I'll do that. I'm pleased to note that you seem to be settling in quite well. I've had nothing but good reports on your behalf."

"Really?" The praise made me smile. "That's great."

"Yes," Russell agreed. "It is. You've quite lived up to the confidence I had in your abilities. One always finds that reassuring."

Yes, I thought, I'm sure one does.

"Hey, Ms. Travis!" The classroom door, which had swung partway shut, flew open wide. Spencer Holbrook, cocky grin firmly in place, started to enter the room. Then he saw the headmaster and stopped. "Mr. Hanover."

"Mr. Holbrook. Working on bringing those grades up, are we?"

"Yes, sir."

"See that you do. One wouldn't want to have to call your parents."

"No, sir." Spencer pulled out a chair and sat down as Russell Hanover let himself out.

I opened Spencer's folder and pulled out his most

recent test. It was social studies this time. We stared at the C- together.

"What I don't understand is how you can do so well on your homework and so poorly on your tests."

"Maybe I'm just not good at taking tests. Maybe I get nervous."

I didn't think so. Not this kid.

"What's to be nervous about? I've seen your homework. You know the material. All you have to do is write it down."

"In the heat of the moment, I guess I forgot it."

Heat of the moment, my fanny. Spencer was up to something. I just had to figure out what it was.

I pulled out the chair beside him and sat. "Let's try and refresh your memory. Mr. Duncan is willing to let you take a make-up test this afternoon during recess. Why don't we see if we can get some of these facts in there to stay."

Between my normal Wednesday classes and the rescheduled ones from the day before, I was busy all day. I didn't get a chance to talk to Kate Russo until afternoon when she and Lucia showed up to work on their book reports together. Their English class had just finished reading *Animal Farm*, but judging the girls' lack of familiarity with George Orwell's style, I suspected that skimming the Cliffs Notes was about as much of a literary experience as they'd enjoyed.

When they were packing up their things at the end of the period, I drew Kate aside and asked if her dog showing neighbor's name was John Monaghan.

"That's right."

"Do you happen to know if he ever co-owned any dogs with a man named Marcus Rattigan?"

"Marcus Rattigan, the builder? Isn't he the guy that got killed? I read about it in the paper this morning."

"Right. Apparently he used to show dogs and he had a really good Wire Fox Terrier bitch named Winter." Kate shoved a notebook into her backpack and looked up. "Winter was John's bitch. She's been gone for a while now but he still talks about her all the time."

"Good. Then he's the man I'm looking for."

"For what?"

"I need to talk to him about . . . things," I finished lamely. Kate was bright and curious and she looked entirely too eager to find out what was going on. "Dog things?"

I nodded. It was close enough.

"I'm sure he'd love to meet you," said Kate. "John *lives* to talk about his dogs. He's totally addicted, if you know what I mean."

I could imagine. John Monaghan sounded like most of the people I'd met at the shows. Devoted to the sport of dogs and fanatic in their dedication to the betterment of their breed.

"I'll probably see him this afternoon. Do you want me to ask if you could stop by sometime?" Kate asked.

"Thanks, that would be a big help."

As Kate started to close her backpack, a telltale yellow-and-black-striped book caught my eye. I reached in and pulled it out.

Kate's cheeks grew pink. "I read the book. Honest. But it's an allegory, you know? I wanted to make sure I didn't overlook any of the subtle nuances."

"That's what I figured." I slipped the Cliffs Notes back under cover. "And since you brought it up, the subtle nuances of Orwellian symbolism will be our discussion topic for Friday."

"Great." Lucia rolled her eyes. This was probably the first time she'd realized that she, too, was going to have to read the actual book.

"Do you have a horse show this weekend?"

"Of course," Lucia replied loftily. "I'm leading Zone One in Small Junior Hunters. I go every weekend."

"Think how much better you'll feel if you get this out of the way first. Friday we'll work on those book reports and Saturday you can go off to your show with a clear conscience."

They left the room together, grumbling under their breath. At Howard Academy good manners are considered paramount. If I'd actually been able to hear what they were saying, it would have been my duty as a teacher to file a report. Luckily, my hearing tends to fade at just such moments. I was spared the necessity of doing more paperwork, and the girls were freed from the need to explain to their parents why they had to stay for detention.

After school I drove over to Hunting Ridge Elementary and picked up Davey and Joey. Amazingly, they were once again talking about teeth. I hoped Joey hadn't lost any more; Davey was already feeling left behind as it was.

"The tooth fairy left me a dollar," Joey was bragging as they climbed in the car. "It was awesome."

"A whole dollar. Wow." Davey reached in his mouth and poked around experimentally. "I wish my teeth would hurry up and fall out."

"Some tooth fairies are richer than others," I said, mindful of his full set of baby teeth. "I think yours will hand out quarters."

"I doubt it," said Joey, the voice of authority. "I bet the same tooth fairy will come to your house that comes to mine. She probably does the whole block."

"You think so?" Davey asked hopefully.

"Sure, you'll see."

It would have taken a bigger ogre than me to burst that bubble. All right, so I'd have to spend a bit more when the time came. Balancing that was the realization of how great kids are at reminding you of the small absurdities of life. Who else would even consider debating how much territory a single tooth fairy might reasonably be expected to cover?

Joey stayed for the rest of the afternoon while his mom took his little sister to the doctor. It meant that Faith and I couldn't go out jogging, but we managed to hide our disappointment. Alice and Carly returned with the news that Alice's husband was working late and we all agreed that was the perfect excuse to order in pizza and a Greek salad.

If you didn't count the fact that the boys thought the

olives made better missiles than food, the evening went quite well. Faith ate seven pizza crusts before I stopped counting. I figured that just about made up for the nutritious dinner of dog food that she'd turned her nose up at earlier.

The Brickmans left early so that Alice could put Carly to bed. I sent Davey upstairs to take a bath and was just finishing up the dishes when the phone rang. It was Frank.

"I'm screwed," he said.

What a pleasant way to begin a conversation. I turned off the water and pulled up a chair. This could take awhile.

"Is this new trouble? Or the same as yesterday?"

"Both."

Good old Frank. Clear as mud. "What happened?"

"The police called this morning. You know, that detective, Petrie? He said he had a few more questions and asked me to come down to the station so we could discuss a few things."

"Discuss a few things? Who does he think he is, Columbo?"

"Mel, get serious! I'm telling you I'm in trouble. How are you at raising bail money?"

"That's not funny."

"Tell me about it. Apparently after he left the store yesterday, Petrie went to Marcus's office. He spoke with Marcus's secretary."

"Liz Barnum."

"Liz, right. How did you know that?"

"Rattigan's ex-wife told me. She seemed to think that the secretary might have had a motive for wanting to murder her boss."

"Let's hope somebody did. Because Liz gave Detective Petrie Marcus's calendar and Petrie showed it to me. Damn it, Mel, it was marked there plain as day. According to Marcus's calendar, he and I were supposed to meet at the coffee bar Monday night."

Ten

I sat up abruptly. "Monday night? That's when Rattigan was murdered."

"No shit, Sherlock! And the police think I did it."

"Did you tell them you didn't know anything about any meeting?"

"Of course, but I could tell they didn't believe me. I mean, my name was right there. What were they supposed to think?"

"Okay, back up a minute. Did Detective Petrie ask the secretary how the appointments got listed in Rattigan's calendar?"

"Liz said that usually she wrote them in. She told Petrie that I'd called that afternoon."

"You did," I said, remembering. "You were going to tell Rattigan about Andy's accident. You told me that you'd called but he wasn't in."

"Right. And I didn't leave a message. I certainly didn't say anything about meeting later at the coffee bar. With that great gaping hole in the floor, that's the last thing I would have wanted."

"So how come Liz Barnum thinks you did? Have you ever met her?"

"A couple of times," said Frank. "And we've spoken on the phone."

"Enough that she'd recognize your voice?"

"Hell, who knows? And if someone did call up and say they were me, why would she have doubted it?"

For once my brother and I were actually in agreement. He was screwed.

"You know, there's another possibility," I said. "Rattigan's ex-wife seems to think that Liz had a pretty good motive for wanting to kill Rattigan herself. What if she knew there wasn't any message, but told him that there was?"

"You mean Liz tried to frame me?" Frank's skepticism came through loud and clear. "Why would she have wanted to do that?"

"Maybe she wanted to divert attention away from herself, and you were the most convenient person."

"Sure, Mel." Frank snickered. "I can see that. Liz followed Marcus out to the coffee bar, climbed up on the roof, cut the skylight free, and bopped him on the head with it."

"What's the matter with that?"

"For starters, she's a thirty-five-year-old woman, not some gymnast."

I debated commenting on the sexist nature of that remark but decided to let it pass. My brother had enough problems. "Neither are you, Frank, but you managed to get yourself up on the roof. I imagine she could have done the same. How did you leave things with the police?"

"Petrie said that he was sure he'd have more questions for me as things went along. He told me to keep myself available, whatever that means."

"What it means is that you should go out first thing tomorrow and hire a lawyer. Tell him everything that's happened and let him decide what your next move should be. By the way, I forgot to ask the other day. Where were you Monday night?"

"You mean, do I have an alibi?"

"Exactly."

"No such luck. I was here by myself. I picked up a sandwich at Subway and watched football on TV."

I'd figured a date on Monday night was probably too much to ask. "How about phone calls? Did you call anyone? Did anyone call you?"

"No. Mel, I've been all through this with Detective Petrie. There's no one who can verify where I was until we met up again the next morning."

"Look on the bright side. At least there's no one who can place you at the store, either." I waited a beat for him to agree with me. When he didn't, I prodded. "There's isn't, is there?"

"Of course not," Frank said angrily. "Damn it, Mel, if you're not sure I'm telling the truth, how am I ever going to be able to convince the police?"

Good question.

• • •

The next day at school, Kate Russo relayed a message from John Monaghan. He'd be happy to meet me that afternoon.

"Boy, you work fast," I said.

"Will it help my grades any?"

"No."

Kate grinned. "I didn't think so, but it was worth a shot."

During lunch I called Alice Brickman, who said she'd grab Davey when he got off the bus and keep him until I got back. Then I asked Kate if she wanted a ride home since we were going in the same direction. She accepted happily and offered to make introductions.

John Monaghan lived in a traditional New England colonial about a mile from Frank's store. Like most of its kind in Connecticut, the house was painted white with black shutters. It sat on a hill overlooking the neighborhood and was large enough to convey an air of solid affluence. Kate's house was smaller but similar in style. She pointed it out as we drove by.

"Nice neighborhood," I said as I pulled into John's driveway and parked the Volvo next to the garage.

"Yeah, it's pretty." Katie gathered up her backpack and climbed out of the car. "My mom likes it here. And she sure doesn't mind being right around the corner from John."

Alerted by something in her tone, I glanced over. "Is that a problem?"

Kate's shrug was a deliberate display of adolescent indifference.

"Do you like John?"

"He's okay, if you don't mind someone who's totally wrapped up in his dogs. It's nice of him to let me come over and help out. It's just that . . ." Kate walked to the edge of the driveway and stared off into the distance.

"What?" I went over and stood beside her. Behind the house was a small kennel building, also painted white with black trim. A row of wire fenced runs extended outward on the far side, all of them now empty.

"I just wish Mom didn't think she always had to have a man around. We do all right on our own, just the two of us. But she can never see that. She was the one who got me started coming over here."

Kate tossed her head angrily. "I guess she figured it would be a good way for her to get to know John better. She thinks he's some great catch because he's single and has some money, and is retired and all. It never even occurred to her that I might actually like the dogs."

I thought about how to respond. Single motherhood wasn't easy, but I was sure that wasn't what Kate wanted to hear. I wondered if she'd ever told her mother how she felt.

"I'm sorry—" I began, but Kate cut me off.

"Don't be." She spun on her heel and headed back toward the house. "Forget I said anything, okay? Let's go inside."

By the time we reached the front door, it was already open and John Monaghan was standing on the brick step. "Here you are. Becca started barking so I knew someone had arrived."

Becca was the trim Wire Fox Terrier at his heels. She greeted Kate first and then me, jumping up on each of us and sniffing us thoroughly before John called her back to his side. "You must be Kate's teacher."

"Melanie Travis." I took his hand and had my arm pumped up and down vigorously.

John wasn't tall, but he was strong. With a hairline that had receded to the middle of his head, and a pair of wire-rimmed glasses balanced on his nose, I judged him to be in his fifties. His features were unremarkable, but he had a wonderful smile.

"Kate tells me you're interested in my dogs," he said. "Are you looking for a puppy?"

"Not exactly. I'm actually hoping to get some information."

"I'm heading back to the kennel," Kate announced. I wondered if she was embarrassed at having revealed so much of herself. She couldn't seem to escape my presence fast enough. "You two can take it from here, right?"

We agreed that we could and John ushered me inside as Kate disappeared around the side of the house. "Come this way," he said. "We'll talk in the library."

We walked down the hall with Becca trotting along behind. As we reached the arched doorway, I heard the scramble of nails and a low growl. I glanced back in time to see the Fox Terrier emerge victorious from beneath a table, a small stuffed animal clutched between her teeth. Carrying it proudly, she ran to catch up.

The library was a spacious room with dark paneling, two leather couches and a wonderful old cherry wood desk. Everywhere I looked there were pictures, framed eight by ten glossies of the Wirerock Fox Terriers winning top awards at various dog shows.

Aunt Peg has a collection of win photos that spans more than three decades. This selection was perhaps more recent, but certainly no less impressive. One dog in particular had been showcased, with an entire wall devoted to her achievements.

Picture after picture showed an alert, beautifully balanced little dog whose crisply styled wire coat was white save for a black saddle and the tan markings on her head. In nearly every photo the judge was holding a big red, white and blue ribbon indicating that the Wire had won Best in Show.

"This must be Winter," I said.

"You've heard of her?" John sounded pleased.

"My aunt told me she was a beautiful bitch and, coming from her, that's high praise." I turned to face him. "Actually, I have to admit my interest in Fox Terriers is somewhat peripheral. I was hoping you might be willing to talk to me about Marcus Rattigan."

"Marcus?" John walked over to a couch and sat

down. Becca immediately jumped up beside him. "What a terrible tragedy. A senseless and unexpected loss."

"You and he were friends?"

"Indeed." John waved me to a seat. "We'd known each other for years. We campaigned Winter together. Without his support I never would have been able to give that bitch the career she deserved."

I'd heard Gloria's version of what Rattigan was like. Here, perhaps, was someone who could show me another side.

"Are you talking about financial support? Or was Rattigan a breeder, as well?"

"No, not at all. Marcus knew where his strengths lay, and he played to them. He left breeding to the experts, which is how it should be. He was listed as co-breeder of Winter's lifter because of the lease arrangement, but that was a name-only thing. He left all the details to me."

"I heard that after Winter's career was over, he dropped out of the dog show scene. Why was that?"

"Why not?" John grasped the toy in Becca's mouth and wrestled with her playfully. "Marcus had nothing left to prove. He'd been to the pinnacle, and there aren't many people who can say that. After Winter retired, I gather the sport lost much of its appeal for him."

"What about Winter's puppies?" I asked, enjoying the byplay as Becca made throaty noises and batted at his fingers with her front paws. "My Aunt Peg breeds

Standard Poodles. She always tells me that the true measure of a dog's value is not what it can win today but what it can produce for tomorrow."

"Your aunt sounds like a true dog person. But there you have the difference. Marcus was my friend, but even I have to admit that for him the dogs were merely the means to an end. He thought of them in terms of immediate gratification, not long-term results.

"Unfortunately, Winter was only able to have one litter. Three puppies, all boys. After they were born, she developed acute metritis and I had to spay her to save her life. It was a terrible blow. After that, Marcus's level of interest was never quite the same."

"Tell me about the puppies," I said because I knew he would have been disappointed if I hadn't. "Were they as gorgeous as their dam?"

"No, they weren't, but that was hardly to be expected. Winter was a once in a lifetime bitch. I was truly sorry never to have gotten a girl from her. Still, it was a sound, healthy, attractive litter and I kept all three. Once it became clear that they were the only progeny Winter would ever have, I didn't want to part with any of them."

John glanced out the window, toward the kennel. "Every Fox Terrier I have today traces his or her pedigree back to Winter through that single litter. Even better, I have a young grandson of hers that's about to make a big splash. Wirerock Summer Dreams. Watch for him."

"I will," I said, smiling at his enthusiasm. "Had you

thought of asking Marcus Rattigan to sponsor this dog, too?"

"No. Marcus's interest in the dog game was over a long time ago. Summer will be all mine to campaign and enjoy. I'm really looking forward to having fun with him."

"Have Wire Fox Terriers always been your breed?"

"For the most part. I dabbled briefly in Welsh Terriers about a decade ago, but Wires were always my first love." John ran a hand down Becca's back and scratched in front of her tail. The little dog wiggled her body in appreciation. "It's not hard to see why."

It was time for a graceful segue. Dog people can talk about their dogs forever, but I needed to get the conversation back on track. "Since you and Rattigan were close, I hope you don't mind my asking, but do you have any idea why someone might have wanted to kill him?"

"None," John said firmly, then recanted. "Well, Marcus could be a bit of a bully at times, but murder? I'd never have anticipated anything like that. Why are you so interested in what happened?"

"My brother was involved in a business venture with Marcus Rattigan. He was doing the renovations on the building where Rattigan was found."

"The proposed coffee bar."

"You know about it?"

"In this neighborhood, it's hard not to," John said, frowning. "The project has generated a fair amount of local unrest."

"So I've heard. Do you know any of the protesters?"

"I imagine I know just about all of them. I've lived in this house for twenty years."

"Did any strike you as angry enough to resort to violence?"

"Over a zoning issue? That seems a little far-fetched to me. Although nobody around here is pleased with that conversion. You say that's your brother's doing?"

"Yes," I admitted unhappily. "It's the first time he's been involved with anything like that, and he's gotten himself in way over his head."

"I can see why you'd want to help him then." John set Becca aside and rose. "You let me know if there's anything else I can do for you."

"Thanks, I will. Maybe we'll run into one another at a dog show someday. I have a Standard Poodle bitch that just got her first two points last weekend."

"With you handling?" John asked as he escorted me to the door. "You must be good. That's a tough breed for an owner-handler."

"I have a couple of very experienced coaches," I said modestly. "Faith is my first show dog. I'm a long, long way from accomplishments like yours."

"So was I, once. It took a lifetime of hard work to get where I am today in dogs. You just have to stay focused on your goals and work on taking things one step at a time."

I picked up Davey from the Brickmans and Faith from home, then drove downtown to run some errands. We stopped at the supermarket and the dry cleaner. On the way back I let Davey convince me that one scoop of ice cream apiece wouldn't ruin our dinners.

Faith took hers in a cup, which she balanced neatly between her front paws on the seat. She didn't spill a drop. Davey's cone, meanwhile, dripped from the top, the sides, and finally, a hole in the bottom. It's a sad thing when your dog has better eating habits than your son.

Back at home I was putting the groceries away when Gloria Rattigan called. "I'm glad I got you," she said. "I thought of something I probably should have mentioned the other day. We were talking about people who weren't too happy with Marcus, remember?"

"Sure." I shoved an armload of frozen vegetables into the freezer and pushed it closed with my hip. "Did you think of someone else?"

"Roger Nye. He's our next door neighbor here. Has been for years. He and Marcus got into a huge fight summer before last. And I mean, huge. Roger's normally a pretty mild mannered guy, so this made a big impression on me. I don't know what Marcus did, but whatever it was, Roger swore up and down that he'd never forgive him. As far as I know, they never spoke again."

"Do you think Mr. Nye would be willing to talk to me?"

"I don't see why not, especially if I call and ask him to. You haven't forgotten about Liz Barnum, have you?"

131

"No." The secretary was next on my list.

"If I think of anyone else, I'll be sure and let you know."

"Thanks, I appreciate it."

It was nice of her to be so helpful, but I couldn't help but wonder why she was bothering. Considering how pleased she'd been by her ex-husband's death, Gloria Rattigan hadn't struck me as a particularly *nice* person.

"Just one more question," I said. "Do you happen to know who will inherit Marcus's estate?"

"I'll say I do."

A burst of raucous laughter assaulted my ear and I held the receiver away as Gloria continued.

"The lawyers contacted me yesterday. Bastard never got around to changing his will after we got divorced. Probably figured he'd live forever, that's just the way Marcus would think. Aside from a few bequests, the rest of it comes to me. Isn't that a hoot?"

It was a hoot, all right.

"I guess that means the search for a new husband is off?"

"Are you kidding? I'm still looking, I've just changed the parameters. Thanks to my newfound prosperity, I'm going for less money and more muscles."

I hung up the phone and had a good laugh. It's hard not to admire a woman who knows how to roll with the punches.

Eleven

On Fridays Howard Academy has early dismissal. According to the school brochure, which stressed the importance of family values, this was to enable students to get an early start on their homework so they'd be free to spend the rest of the weekend with their busy, hardworking parents. I didn't believe it for a minute.

Seven weeks into the school year, I was pretty certain that the real reason we got out early was to give Russell and Bitsy a head start on their getaway weekends to sun and snow. Not that I was complaining, mind you. Any system that allowed me to be finished with the week's work by 2 P.M. on Friday afternoon was perfectly all right with me.

Unfortunately, the weather that day was damp and drizzly. The chill of winter-to-come was in the air. I was supposed to go out jogging but, not surprisingly, I couldn't seem to muster any enthusiasm for the chore. Instead I got in the car and drove to Marcus Rattigan's office in downtown Stamford.

Anaconda Properties was located in a new high rise office building, one of several that had sprung up near the railroad tracks during the development boom of the mid-eighties. The building was twelve stories of concrete and reflective glass and offered underground parking. A sign out front announced that office space was still available.

I skimmed the directory, found Rattigan's company listed on the tenth floor, and rode the elevator up. The office suite devoted to Anaconda Properties was on the south side of the building. Double doors were flanked by frosted glass windows and bore a small brass plaque with the company name and logo, an image of a coiled snake, ready to strike. How appropriate.

The doors were unlocked and led directly into a small reception area that was sparsely furnished in modern, high-tech style. A woman with delicate features and lustrous chestnut hair was sitting behind a desk, talking on the telephone.

"Please hold a moment," she said as I walked in. She pressed a button on the phone and looked up. "Yes, may I help you?"

"I'm looking for Liz Barnum."

Her carefully tweezed eyebrows lifted slightly. "I'm Liz Barnum. May I ask what this is in reference to?"

"I'd like to talk to you about Marcus Rattigan."

"Are you a reporter?"

"No, I—"

"You're not with the police."

"No."

"Then I have nothing to say." Liz glanced at the door expectantly, her hand hovering above the phone console as she waited to resume her call.

I wasn't about to give up that easily. "I think you've met my brother. Frank Turnbull? He was working with Mr. Rattigan on the conversion of an old general store in north Stamford."

"You're Frank's sister?" She looked at me carefully, as though searching for a family resemblance. What she saw must have been good enough, because she punched a button, said, "I'll have to call you back," and hung up the phone. "How is Frank?"

It seemed I'd said the magic word. Interesting.

"Naturally he's very upset about what happened. He's even more concerned about the fact that the police consider him to be a suspect."

"That's crazy. Your brother doesn't look like he'd hurt a fly." Liz stood up and walked to a door in the back wall. She opened it to reveal a large office. "Let's talk in here where we'll have more privacy."

I followed her inside. The office was not only big, it was sumptuous. One entire wall was windows. Rain beat down against the glass now, but on a clear day the view of Long Island Sound must have been spectacular. A desk dominated one side of the room. On the other, three leather chairs were grouped around a glass-topped table.

"Is this Rattigan's office?" I headed toward the desk.

"It was." Liz pulled out a chair and sat down. "You won't find anything useful, though. The police have already been through everything. They took Marcus's calendar, his computer, and all his current files."

"Must make it hard to keep the business running." I had a look anyway. Aside from a blotter and pen set, the desktop was empty. The credenza beside it held only a printer and a fax machine.

"At the moment we're just treading water, waiting

until the estate gets settled and we see what happens next."

I wondered if she knew that Rattigan's wife was his main beneficiary. If she didn't, I wasn't going to be the one to tell her.

I left the desk and went over and sat down. Liz crossed her legs and smoothed the creases from her short skirt. Her nails were bitten back to the quick.

"Frank tells me that according to Rattigan's calendar, he had an appointment with my brother at the coffee bar on the evening that he died."

"That's right." Liz nodded. "I took the call myself."

"Except that my brother didn't make that appointment."

The phone buzzed in the other room. I glanced at Liz. She didn't get up.

"Don't worry, someone will get it. It's probably just more reporters anyway. And yes, Frank did set up that meeting. He called around two-thirty. I told him that Marcus was out of the office inspecting a site, but that I expected him to check in and I'd give him the message."

Two-thirty. That probably *was* about the time Frank had called, but he'd been adamant about the fact that he hadn't left any messages.

"Is that the way things usually worked between the two of them?"

Liz reached out and straightened an ashtray on the table. She seemed to be having a hard time sitting still. "What do you mean?"

"I imagine Marcus Rattigan must have been a very busy man. And in the grand scheme of things, I wouldn't think that the deal he had going with my brother was all that important. So I guess what I'm trying to ask is, was Frank in the habit of arranging meetings that way? And was it unusual for Rattigan, busy as he was, to simply acquiesce to such a demand?"

Liz thought briefly before answering. "Now that you mention it, I guess it was a little odd. Usually when the two of them got together, they met here. Marcus wasn't the kind of man who would jump to answer anyone's summons. I'm sure Frank realized that. But I was pretty busy when the call came in. I guess I just didn't think about it at the time."

"It didn't occur to you that it might not be my brother on the phone?"

"No. Like I said, I was busy. I wrote the information down in the book and forgot about it."

Nothing there that would help Frank's chances with the police. It was time to move on to a trickier topic. "I understand you and Marcus Rattigan have known each other for a long time."

"I worked for him for nearly eight years."

"You had a closer relationship, too, didn't you?"

"You've been talking to Gloria," Liz said dryly. "How is the old bat?"

"Coping nicely, from what I could see."

"Why shouldn't she be? She's probably happy he's gone. He dumped her and she never got over it."

"Like you did."

"Well, well." Liz's smile was brittle. "I guess you *have* been doing your homework."

I sat forward in my chair, leaning closer across the space that separated us, as I willed her not to tune me out. "I'm sorry if you think this is an intrusion, but I don't have any choice. Somehow my brother has managed to land himself in the middle of a murder investigation. The police have all but told him he's their chief suspect, and even I can understand why they might see things that way.

"The problem is, my brother didn't kill Marcus Rattigan. If the best way for me to help him is to try and figure out who did, then that's what I'm going to do."

Liz stood up and crossed the room. She stared out the rain-streaked window. "Is that why you came to talk to me? Because you were looking for someone else to blame?"

"I'm looking for the truth," I said quietly.

"So be it." Liz nodded. "The truth is, Marcus and I had an affair. It wasn't any big secret, at least not after Gloria found out. Did you ever meet Marcus?"

"Once."

A phone buzzed again in the outer room. I ignored it; Liz did, too.

"You probably didn't care for him, then. He didn't make the best first impression. And yes, he could be brash and aggressive. He had neither the time nor the patience to deal with people who couldn't see the same visions he did. But that was the public man. Once you got to know him, he could also be sweet and compassionate."

Liz looked at me and shook her head. "I see you don't believe me. It doesn't matter. After all, it's over now. Marcus was a wonderful man. Working here together week after week, month after month, it was just very easy to fall into bed with him."

"And to believe that he was going to divorce his wife and marry you?"

"Yes, I suppose so. At the time, that's what I thought I wanted."

"Then he and Gloria got a divorce and he dropped you, too."

"Oh, my." Liz grimaced. "Gloria really did spin you a story, didn't she? I imagine that's what she wants to believe. I'm sure it makes her feel better.

"The truth is, Marcus and I made a mutual decision to part. It turned out that what was fun and thrilling when we had to sneak around wasn't nearly so exciting when it was all out in the open. Our affair had run its course, and it was time to let it go."

Maybe, I thought. And maybe not. "You didn't find it awkward being here with him afterward?"

"No, why should I? As I said, we both agreed that breaking up was for the best. We were mature adults. There wasn't any reason we couldn't continue to work together."

For the third time since we'd entered the office, the phone buzzed. This time Liz headed for the door. "I'm afraid that's all I can tell you. Please give your brother my best."

I followed her out into the reception area. As I passed a hallway that opened off of it, a door was flung open and a man came striding out. He was tall and blond and looked extremely agitated.

"Liz, what the hell's going on around here? Why isn't anyone answering the phone?"

"I was taking a break," Liz said calmly. She lifted the receiver, greeted the caller, and placed him on hold. "I'm back now, so you can relax."

The man glanced in my direction. "Who's that?"

"Melanie Travis," I said, offering a hand.

He hesitated a moment as if hoping for more information, then took my hand and shook it briefly. "Ben Welch."

"Ben is vice president of Anaconda Properties," said Liz. "He is . . . was . . . Marcus's second in command." She looked at Ben. "Melanie was just leaving. And you have a call on line two."

I watched as he walked back to his office. A second in command might know all sorts of useful things. "Do you suppose Ben would mind—?"

"Probably not, but he doesn't have time. With Marcus gone, he's juggling both their schedules. He doesn't have a spare minute for days."

Earlier she'd told me the firm was treading water. The phone buzzed again. Liz sat down at her desk and reached for the receiver. Clearly my time was up. "Thanks for talking to me," I said and let myself out.

Sam's arrival that evening was heralded by a chorus of barking from Faith. She likes to announce visitors and I've never minded the noise, figuring that a four-legged burglar alarm—which was all I could afford—was a good deal better than none. Usually she quiets right down as soon as she recognizes the guests, but that night she kept on barking. When I looked out my bedroom window, I saw the reason why.

Sam had gotten Tar out of his Blazer, and the puppy was racing in large, looping circles around the front yard. He feinted to the left and then the right, dodging behind the tree and around Davey's bike. Ears flapping, feet scrambling, tail wagging, he was adorable. Faith, standing on her hind legs and looking out the window, could see perfectly well that another dog was having all kinds of fun in her yard while she wasn't having any.

By the time I got downstairs, Davey had opened the front door. Now everyone was in the yard giving the neighbors a show. Predictably my son was shoeless and without a jacket in the crisp October air. Faith was doing her part to add to the excitement by bowling Tar end over end across the grass.

A dumber woman might have gone outside and joined the fray. Instead I stood in the doorway and let them all come to me. The two Poodles went racing past first, heading toward the kitchen and the water bowl.

Davey was next, holding Sam's hand and chattering

about his day. If my son had anything to say about it, they'd have passed right by me and headed straight for the Lego model he was building in the living room. Luckily Sam had other ideas. He let go of Davey's hand and gathered me into a hug.

"That's gross," said Davey. "I hope you're not going to kiss, too."

"We might." Sam looked down at him over my shoulder. "In fact, I'd say it's a real possibility."

Davey made a rude noise.

I frowned at my son, and heir. "If you don't like it, go somewhere else."

"Can't." Resigned, Davey sat down on a step. "If I leave, how will I know when you're done?"

"We'll call you," I said.

Davey shook his head.

There's definitely something inhibiting about having a six year old staring at you. Especially when he's *your* six year old. Sam began to chuckle. His hold around me loosened.

"Later?" I asked with a sigh.

His lips brushed lightly across my cheek, his response was low in my ear. "Count on it."

Dinner was one of my favorites: pot roast and onion gravy, with noodles and carrots on the side. Sam supplied a bottle of red wine. Davey supplied most of the conversation. No chance that this boy was going to grow up to be the strong, silent type.

Under the table, Tar snored softly. Faith lay down, too, but she kept her eyes open in case any choice tidbits should happen to fall her way.

"I forgot," Sam said over coffee. He reached down and dug around in his pocket. "I brought something to show you."

"What is it?" asked Davey. "A toy?"

"Not quite." Sam held out his hand and opened it. There was a small white object in the middle of his palm. Davey and I both leaned closer to look.

"Wow . . ." Davey breathed out softly. "It's a tooth!"

"A baby tooth. One of Tar's. He's been teething for several weeks now. I thought you might like to have it."

Davey was beaming. Obviously I wasn't the only one he'd told about Joey's dental precocity. "You mean it's for me?"

"Yup." Sam tipped his hand and let the tooth slide into Davey's palm. "You can put it under your pillow tonight. Maybe the tooth fairy will give you something for it."

Davey held the tooth up to the light, studying it like a jeweler with a rare gem. "She might not like dog teeth."

"I bet she'll be happy to have it. You can tell Joey all about it the next time you see him."

Sam looked at me over my son's head and winked. It was the tiniest of gestures but it moved something powerful inside me. Warmth flowed through me like a melting tide. My chest constricted. The tips of my fingers tingled.

Until that moment I hadn't been sure. I'd told

myself that Sam and I were good together, that he awakened feelings that had been allowed to lie dormant too long. But I'd never allowed myself to call it love. Now I looked at Sam and knew.

"Are you okay?" he asked.

I swallowed heavily. "Fine."

"Jeez," said Davey. "It's only a puppy tooth. You look strange."

"Thanks." The sarcasm was good. It restored my equilibrium.

Sam and Davey went back to examining their prize. I sat there and looked at the two of them and knew I was the luckiest person in the world.

Some women want flowers or sonnets. Others hold out for pearls. I fell in love over puppy teeth. It figured.

Twelve

Usually when Sam's around, Davey likes to stay up as late as possible. That night he was so excited about the prospect of a visit from the tooth fairy that he rushed right upstairs after dinner. Sam and I followed so that we could make a small ceremony out of placing the tooth beneath the pillow.

Faith came along and watched the proceedings curiously. She sleeps on Davey's bed at night and thinks of herself as his guardian. In her mind it was only fair that we should consult her on any impending changes to her domain.

Davey held out the tooth so that the Poodle could sniff it. When she tried to lick it up off his palm, however, he snatched it away and placed it under the pillow. "That's mine," he said firmly. "The tooth fairy's going to pay me for it."

With a thoughtful expression on his face, he looked past Faith to Tar, who was sitting on the floor beside the bed. It wasn't too hard to figure out what he was thinking. My son, the budding entrepreneur.

"How many teeth do puppies have anyway?"

"Not very many." Yes, I was lying. Mothers have to do that sometimes. "Besides, most of Tar's have already fallen out, haven't they?" I sent Sam a meaningful glance.

"Right," he agreed, then gave my son a playful poke. "Though if you're lucky we might find a few more."

"Great." Davey stifled a yawn. His eyes were already closing.

We turned off the light and tiptoed out.

"Alone at last." Sam's eyebrows waggled. He looked much cuter than Groucho Marx.

Before I had a chance to answer, someone knocked on the front door. We hurried downstairs before the dogs could start to bark. The porch light was on, and Aunt Peg's face loomed in the window. Seeing us both, she smiled and waved.

"I didn't know she was stopping by," said Sam. His arm, which had been cradling my waist, dropped away.

"Neither did I."

"Cheers!" Peg marched inside when I opened the door. "I brought dessert. Is Davey asleep already? He'll just have to have his pie in the morning."

"Pie?" I asked faintly.

"Pecan." She waved a fragrant white box under my nose. "My favorite. Is there water on for tea?"

"There might have been if I'd known you were coming."

Ignoring the jibe, Aunt Peg headed toward the kitchen. "I'll just get it started myself. Plates? Forks? Sam, maybe you could find some napkins?"

"Yes, ma'am."

I glared at him and he grinned right back. Aunt Peg has always been a favorite of his. Then again, he doesn't know her nearly as well as I do.

There was little I could do besides follow along, so I did. "Aunt Peg," I said. "Why are you here?"

"To get an update on my nephew's situation, why else? You know I like to stay on top of things. Has anyone called me?" Her accusing look encompassed us both. "Well, there you have it. I had to come and see for myself."

"Why didn't you just ask Frank?"

"Is he at home?" Peg inquired. "Or have they already carted him off to jail?"

"Frank's in jail?" Sam looked somewhat stunned.

My brother and Sam don't get along very well and, speaking as the woman in the middle, I can only say that it's a man thing. Still, I'm sure he expected that a bombshell like that might have been mentioned earlier.

I opened the cabinet and got out three plates. "No, he's not in jail. Aunt Peg's being melodramatic."

"Not by much," Peg said briskly. "Don't tell me Melanie hasn't told you that her brother is the chief suspect in a murder investigation."

"No." Sam's eyes narrowed slightly. "Actually, she hasn't."

"I was just about to," I said, my second lie of the evening. What was happening to me? I used to be such a truthful person. Thank God, I didn't have a wooden nose.

Yes, I had promised myself that I'd fill Sam in on the details of Marcus Rattigan's murder. But now that the time had come, I wasn't looking forward to the task. The problem was that over the last year and a half I seemed to have gotten involved in an unexpected number of murders, several of which had placed me in serious danger.

Sam's a pretty mellow guy, and he knows I treasure my independence. But after he'd heard about my skirmish with a killer the summer before, something had changed. Maybe it was because our feelings for each other were deepening. Maybe it was because he'd suddenly realized, as I had, just how fragile the line between life and death could be. Sam hadn't ordered me to start minding my own business, but he had made his feelings on the subject pretty clear.

At the time, with the knowledge of what it felt like

to have a gun pointed in my direction very fresh in my mind, I'd even agreed with him. However that was before I knew that the next person to come to me for help would be my brother. A stranger I might have turned away, but Frank was family. I hadn't had any choice.

"We've got time now," Sam said, sounding deceptively reasonable. "Why don't you tell me all about it?"

"Who wants pie?" I asked, falling on Aunt Peg's offering like a lifesaver. I cut three large wedges and slipped them onto plates. "Maybe I have some whipped cream in the refrigerator. Let me just—"

"Mel."

His tone stopped me in my tracks. "Yes?"

"Quit stalling."

Acceding to the inevitable, I walked over to the table and sat down. "Okay, here's the story."

I told them everything. For Sam's sake, I started at the beginning, quickly rehashing the incidents of the burst pipe and broken floor and then proceeding directly to the murder. Sam lives in northern Fairfield County and since most of Anaconda's property deals had taken place in towns along the coast, he didn't know who Marcus Rattigan was.

Aunt Peg stepped in then to offer a brief biography, while I took the chance to make some inroads into my pie. The gooey filling was rich and dark, the pecans just salty enough to offset the sweetness beneath. Even without whipped cream it was terrific.

It was a good thing Sam was a dog person because Aunt Peg's knowledge of Rattigan's life was heavily tipped in that direction. Though Sam had been living in Michigan ten years earlier when Winter was showing, it turned out that he not only remembered her, but had seen her at the Detroit and Chicago International shows.

"She was a gorgeous bitch," he said. "I generally prefer the bigger breeds, but in her case I'd have happily made an exception. She *thought* she was big and her expression just dared you to tell her she wasn't. When she won Best in Show at Chicago, she just about brought the house down."

"She was like that every time she showed," Peg agreed. "The truly great ones generally are."

With Rattigan's dog-show credentials established to everyone's satisfaction, I took over the rest of the tale. Aunt Peg listened as avidly as Sam as I outlined my conversations with Gloria Rattigan, John Monaghan, and Liz Barnum.

"You've been busy," she said with satisfaction, when I was done.

"I'll say." Sam sounded less pleased.

"Gloria had the best motive," said Peg, thinking aloud. "Unless you think Liz Barnum was lying."

"Don't forget about Frank," I said. "Apparently Rattigan was thinking of pulling the plug on the conversion. That would have left Frank out of a job *and* quite a bit of money.

"He also had the means, since he was acting as general contractor for the construction. When a skylight came falling out of the ceiling, that was his responsibility. As for opportunity, according to Rattigan's calendar, Frank had arranged for the two of them to meet that evening at the coffee bar."

I looked around the table. "All I can say is, it's a good thing Rattigan didn't leave Frank anything in his will or I'd have had to drive down to Cos Cob and arrest him myself."

"Now, now," said Peg. "Things aren't quite that bad. You said you were planning to talk to one of Gloria's neighbors."

"Roger Nye. Gloria left a message about him on my machine. He's expecting me tomorrow morning."

"And what about those protesters you mentioned? Surely they could stand some scrutiny."

"I'm going to try and track some of them down on Sunday. Supposedly they all live right in the area. And if I get really lucky, I might even find a neighbor who noticed someone climbing around on the roof."

"There you go." Peg eyed the pie as if debating whether or not to have another piece. "Don't break out the handcuffs for Frank just yet. There are all sorts of possibilities here."

On the other side of the table, Sam was silent. He's wonderful at figuring things out and I hadn't realized until that moment how much I'd wanted, and needed, to hear his input. Beneath the table I slid my foot along the floor until it connected with his.

Methodically chewing a bite of pie, Sam didn't look

up. I slipped off my loafer and ran my toes up the side of his calf. He glanced at me and lifted a brow.

"Well?" I said.

"You don't want to hear what I have to say."

"Yes, I do."

Sam set down his fork and straightened in his seat. The movement shifted his leg away from mine and suddenly I was sure that the distance he'd placed between us wasn't accidental.

"I think your brother ought to be allowed to fight his own battles for once."

Uh oh.

"You baby him, you coddle him, and then you wonder why he never grows up. What was he doing getting involved with a man like Marcus Rattigan in the first place? And you . . ." His gaze shifted to Aunt Peg. "What were you thinking, giving him money? What he really needed was a swift kick in the butt."

"Money was easier," Aunt Peg said with dignity. "I'm too old to go around kicking people." She pushed back her chair and stood. "Perhaps I should leave you two to sort this out."

"No!" Sam and I said together. It seemed likely to be the only thing we agreed upon all evening.

Aunt Peg ignored us both and left.

Sam stood, as well. He gathered up the plates and dumped them in the sink. I boxed the pie and shoved it in the refrigerator. In less than a minute, we'd run out of things to do.

Sam crossed his arms implacably over his chest. "I

know you don't want to hear this, Melanie, but I have to *say* it. I don't want you getting involved in Marcus Rattigan's murder. Let the police do their job. That's why they're there."

Before he'd finished speaking, I was already shaking my head. "The police think Frank is guilty. They're not trying to clear him, they're trying to gather enough evidence to convict him."

"I know Frank needs you," Sam said softly. "But I need you, too. I can't just stand by and watch you put yourself in danger."

"I'll be careful."

"I know you will. But it's not enough."

He reached under the table and scooped up his sleeping puppy. Then he walked out of the kitchen without looking back. I almost didn't follow. When I did, Sam was standing beside the front door.

"You've been lucky so far. What am I going to do when your luck runs out?"

The expression in his eyes was bleak. Bleaker still was the knowledge that there was no answer I could give that would satisfy us both. Sam reached for the knob and opened the door.

"I love you," I said, hoping that the words would work their magic, that they would turn him around and bring him back into my arms.

"I know," said Sam.

He walked out into the night.

I went upstairs, slipped the tooth out from under Davey's pillow, and left a dollar and a dog biscuit in its place. Then I went to bed and stared at the ceiling until my eyes hurt, because it was better than crying myself to sleep.

Saturday morning Davey was up just after dawn. The thought that the tooth fairy might visit had made him sleep fitfully, and when he discovered that Tar's tooth had indeed been exchanged for cash, his shriek of joy was probably loud enough to wake the neighbors. I know it woke me.

Hoping for another hour of sleep, I congratulated Davey on his good fortune and told him to go downstairs and watch TV. My son was not that easily deterred.

He stood in the doorway in his woolly-footed pajamas, a dollar and a dog biscuit clutched in his hand, and said, "Where's Sam?"

"Who?" Not the most intelligent answer I might have come up with, but considering that I was operating on about four hours of sleep, it didn't seem all bad.

"Sam," Davey repeated. "He was here last night. I thought he was staying over."

If I ever needed a reminder that every decision I made, big or small, impacted on two lives not one, Davey was there to point it out.

"He had to go home," I said lamely.

"Why?"

Good question. I sat up and patted the bed beside me. Davey came over and hopped up. Faith did, too.

She was eyeing the biscuit in Davey's hand with proprietary interest.

"You know that you and I don't always agree about everything, right?"

Davey nodded.

"Sometimes that's true for grown-ups, too."

"Did you and Sam have a fight?"

"No, of course not," I said quickly. When I was growing up, a fight had meant screaming and throwing things. "It was more of a disagreement."

Davey's lower lip began to quiver. "Did he go away forever?"

I reached out and pulled him into my arms. "No, Sam didn't go away forever. He'll come back and we'll all be together again. I promise, okay?"

"Daddy went away and he didn't come back for years."

Of course, I thought belatedly. If I hadn't been so tired, I'd have realized where the questions were coming from.

"Sam and Daddy are very different people," I said firmly. "You know that, right?"

"I guess so." He didn't sound entirely convinced.

Faith reached out a front paw and laid it gently on top of Davey's hand. She could see the biscuit and she could smell it, but she was much too polite to snatch. That didn't stop her from pointing out the obvious, however.

"Are you going to give Faith that biscuit?" I asked.

Davey looked at his dog and shook his head. "It was

Tar's tooth, so I guess the tooth fairy left it for him. Faith can have another biscuit. I'm going to save this one for Tar. That way, Sam will have to bring him back real soon."

"Fine by me," I said.

Even six year olds are entitled to a little insurance.

Thirteen

According to an item I'd read in the paper, Marcus Rattigan's funeral was scheduled to be held that morning while I was meeting with Roger Nye. I guessed that meant Rattigan's neighbor wasn't planning on paying his last respects. Hopefully, that boded well for our interview. The way Frank was managing his defense, the more suspects I could come up with, the better.

After breakfast Davey and I got in the Volvo and headed to Belle Haven. My son adores cars: talking about them, watching them, riding in them. Any trip that involves a stint on the highway immediately gains his favor. You don't need to take I-95 to get from Stamford to southern Greenwich, but we did anyway.

By the time we reached Belle Haven, Davey was in a great mood. I'd cautioned him that he was to stay out of trouble and let me do most of the talking, but I knew from past experience that these pep talks I often feel bound to deliver don't necessarily do any good. Nor was I reassured when, as soon as I parked the car in Roger Nye's driveway, Davey jumped out and ran ahead.

The house in front of me wasn't quite as large as Gloria's, but it was still three times the size of anything in my neighborhood. Situated beyond the Rattigan home and slightly down a rise, the red brick colonial sat on several acres of terraced and landscaped lawn. Low brick gateposts topped by a pair of plaster lions guarded the end of the short driveway.

I might have taken a moment to marvel at the excess, but Davey had already climbed the wide steps and rung the doorbell. As I crossed the driveway, I could hear the deep chimes that sounded within. The heavy wooden front door drew open just as I reached it.

Roger Nye was a portly man with ruddy skin and a pair of deep lines etched on either side of his mouth. He smelled faintly of cigar smoke and immediately frowned at the sight of us.

"I've bought wrapping paper to support the elementary school, magazine subscriptions from the middle school, and I know the Girl Scouts are going to be coming by soon with those damn cookies. What are you two selling?"

"Nothing," I said quickly as Davey took a step back and angled himself behind my legs. "My name is Melanie Travis. Gloria Rattigan said you were expecting me?"

"Oh, yeah, right." His frown softened but didn't entirely disappear. "She told me you'd be by. I guess I didn't think you'd bring a kid. Sorry about that." He peered at Davey, then squatted down and held out a hand. "What's your name?"

"Davey Travis." My son looked half afraid that shaking hands might cost him his own, but after a moment the manners I'd drilled into him won out and he allowed his fingers to be briefly touched.

"Hey, come on, I'm not as bad as all that."

"Mr. Nye—"

"Roger. Call me Roger. I've got three kids of my own, but they're mostly all grown up now. I guess I must be losing my touch. Come on inside. Gloria said you wanted to talk about Marcus. Fair warning, you won't hear anything good from me."

"That's okay. I—"

"Wait a minute, I've got an idea." Roger ushered us in and shut the door. He swung around and faced Davey. "Do you like trains?"

"Trains?" Davey screwed up his face like he'd never heard the word before.

"You know, model trains. Lionels. I've got a whole set downstairs. Nobody plays with them much anymore. Maybe you'd like to have a look while your mom and I talk."

"Sure," said Davey.

A door off the hallway led down a flight of carpeted steps. Roger led the way, flipping on light switches as we went. At the bottom of the stairs, we found ourselves in an expansive playroom.

Davey's gaze went immediately to a large platform

that filled nearly a third of the room and held an elaborate display of model trains. Tracks circled the table in several configurations, winding in and out of model towns and tunneling through a snow capped mountain. There were roads and bridges and signal lights galore. The train itself seemed to be at least twenty cars long and had a locomotive that looked fully capable of belching smoke.

"Wow!" he cried. "Cool!"

Roger grinned. "Kids always get a kick out of this. Just let me get it turned on for you." Judging by the look on his face, kids weren't the only ones who got a kick out of Roger's model trains.

While he fiddled with the controls and showed Davey how to operate the switches, I walked over to a sliding glass door on the other end of the room. As the house had been built on a slope, we were still above ground even though we'd come down a flight of stairs. From where I stood I could see Long Island Sound, the water bright blue and peacefully calm in the morning light.

The engine whistled behind me. I turned and saw that Roger had plopped an engineer's cap on Davey's head. My son was enchanted; he worked the controls and the train began to move. Roger left him to it and came to join me.

"He can't break anything, can he?" I asked cautiously.

"No, it's pretty well kid-proof."

The whistle shrieked again. It was followed by the soft patter of footsteps on the stairs and a moment later a small, squarely built dog came trotting into the room. Her coat was mostly light brown with a black saddle and splashes of white on her chest and feet. The hair was long and curly, and looked as though it hadn't been brushed in a while. She had vee-shaped ears that folded over above her head and a muzzle that was gray with age.

"That's Asta," said Roger, patting his leg to call the dog to him. "My wife named her after that terrier in the movies. You know, *The Thin Man*? She's getting on now, doesn't get around as well as she once did, but oh, does Asta loves those trains. Doesn't matter where in the house she's sleeping, when she hears that whistle, she comes and finds me."

"She's a Fox Terrier, then?" I had another look. Accustomed to the sharply chiseled trims I'd seen in the show ring, I hadn't recognized her breed.

"She sure is." Roger sat down and helped the dog up into his lap. Immediately she lay down and snuggled her head on his arm. "That reminds me. I guess I do have one good thing to say about Marcus, after all. He's the one who gave me Asta. She was only a tiny pup at the time, but she grew up into a wonderful pet."

I glanced over to check on Davey, then sat down, too. "I know Mr. Rattigan owned a Fox Terrier but I'd been told that he wasn't a breeder. I didn't realize he ever had any puppies."

Roger nodded. "This goes back awhile. Probably nine or ten years. Back then, he and I were pretty friendly. I know he showed some dogs, because whenever they won I had to hear all about it whether I was interested or not. But I never saw any dogs over at his house. As far as puppies went, this was the only one."

I held out my hand and Asta opened her eyes long enough to see if I was offering any food. Seeing only fingers, she turned her head away. "Do you know where she came from?"

"Some hotshot litter he had. I remember Marcus made a big fuss about it at the time. The dam had done a whole lot of winning, more than any other dog in the country, he said. That was supposed to make the puppies something special. Huh!" Roger snorted softly. "He never even gave us the papers so we could register her with the American Kennel Club."

His stubby fingers stoked the top of the terrier's head and she leaned into the caress. "Didn't matter to Millie and me, though. We didn't have any interest in that dog show nonsense, and with or without papers, Asta was still a great pet."

"You've known Marcus Rattigan a long time then?"

Roger nodded. "Nearly a dozen years, I guess. That's how long ago it was he moved next door. Gloria told me your brother got mixed up in some sort of business deal with him. I must say you have my sympathy."

"I understand you and he had a disagreement . . . ?"

"That would be a polite way of putting it. What we had was a knockdown, drag out fight. I'm just sorry I didn't try and sue the pants off him. Problem was, Marcus was clever. I knew what he did, and he knew it, too, but I didn't have any proof."

"Proof of what?"

"The man was a killer. Some might not have seen it that way, but I did. He killed my trees." Roger's skin mottled with anger at the memory.

"Your trees?"

He rose and set Asta on the ground at his feet. "Do you mind a walk outside? It's a nice enough day. Come on, and I'll show you what I mean."

I glanced over at Davey. He was totally absorbed in the trains. "We're going outside for a few minutes. Are you going to be okay?"

"Sure," my son said blithely. "Go ahead."

I followed Roger and Asta out the sliding glass door. The backyard was large and sloped downhill to the right, trailing off in a patch of woods at the end of the property. To the left, visible above some low foliage, was Gloria Rattigan's house.

"Right here," said Roger. He stopped next to a graceful looking tree whose leaves were painted with vivid autumn colors. There was a wooden bench beneath it and a concrete birdbath off to one side. "Look at this." He scuffed at a pile of fallen leaves with his foot and uncovered a tree stump that had been cut off at ground level. "This too." Roger pushed the leaves around some more and revealed another. "Both of those are Marcus's doing."

I stared at the stumps and decided I really wasn't sure what all the fuss was about. "What exactly did Rattigan do?"

"Just like I told you before. He killed my trees!

Flowering dogwoods they were, three of them planted on the days that each of my three children was born. Jeff was first." Roger pointed to one stump. "His was white. Then came Susan. Hers was pink. After that was Fred, another white. The trees had been here for years before Marcus even moved in. Beautiful. In the spring you never saw anything so pretty."

Wind whipped up the hill and scattered the leaves at our feet. I gathered my jacket more tightly around me. "Why did he want to kill them?"

Roger waved an angry hand toward the house up the rise. "He said they were spoiling his view. Can you believe that? I guess it didn't matter when they were small but after they grew some, he decided they were in his way.

"Marcus came marching over here one day and demanded that I cut the trees way back. He said they were devaluing his property. As if that was my problem. If he'd wanted a house on the Sound he should have bought one. It wasn't up to me to supply him with a view."

I could see his point. "What did you do?"

"Nothing. Not a damn thing. The dogwood trees were on my property and I had every right to have them there. I figured that would be the end of it."

Asta had been sniffing around the yard. Now she came ambling back with an old tennis ball in her mouth. Roger took it from her absently and tossed it down the hill. The terrier ran off in pursuit.

"She'll be stiff tomorrow," he said, gazing after her.

"I should know better than to throw that ball. Hell, I do know better. It's just that she enjoys chasing it so much."

We both watched as Asta lay down with the toy between her front paws and began to chew. "Where was I?" asked Roger. "Oh right, the trees. The following spring all three started doing poorly. I thought maybe they needed some fertilizer so I had a guy from the gardening center come out and take a look. He said the trees were already dying by the time he got here. It was too late for two of them, and he barely managed to save the third."

"What makes you think Rattigan had anything to do with it?"

"Because we found the evidence right down in the roots. Someone had taken some of those tree spikes, you know, the kind people use to help trees grow? He'd emptied out the vitamins and nutrients, filled them up with turpentine and lodged them in the soil under the trees. It was plain as day that's what killed my dogwoods."

"I assume you confronted him?"

"I damn sure did!" Roger's voice rose. "Marcus didn't admit what he'd done, but he sure didn't deny it, either. All he said was, it didn't matter what I thought because I'd never be able to prove a thing.

"Those dogwoods were special to me and Millie. I'd told him that, but he just didn't give a damn. That's the way he was. It's probably wrong of me to say so, but I'm glad he's dead. The world's a much better place without Marcus Rattigan in it."

Trees, even special trees, didn't necessarily seem like a motive to me. Then again, one thing I've learned is that almost everyone will go to great lengths to protect what's important to them. "Have you seen Rattigan lately?"

"Just last month, as a matter of fact. I ran into him in the Town Center. I would have walked right by, but he was the one who stopped me. He asked how the Sound was looking these days. Of course, I didn't answer."

Roger's hand clenched at his side. "Marcus just laughed and said if he'd known at the time that all he was doing was increasing the value of a house that would go to Gloria in the divorce, he wouldn't have gone to so much trouble. He made me so angry I couldn't even see straight. The only thing I wish is that whoever murdered Marcus could have gotten to him sooner."

Asta returned with the tennis ball and we headed back inside. Gloria had characterized her neighbor as a mild-mannered person, but based on what I'd seen that morning, I wasn't ready to agree. There was definitely something about Marcus Rattigan that seemed to bring out the worst in everyone around him.

Inside, Davey was right where we'd left him. When he was younger he used to disappear whenever I wasn't watching. This time he'd been so enthralled he hadn't moved. The train came chugging through the tunnel, rounded a turn, and pulled to a smooth stop in front of the station.

"Time to go," I said.

"Aww Mom . . ."

"Mr. Nye has been wonderful to let you play with his trains, but we can't take up any more of his time." I picked Davey's denim jacket up off a chair and helped him into it.

"Just one last question," I said as Roger escorted us back to the door. "You knew Marcus Rattigan for a long time. Who do you think might have wanted to kill him?"

He didn't even have to stop and think. "That field's probably wide open. If I were you I'd be looking for the last poor bastard Marcus screwed."

Great, I thought. That would be Frank.

Speak of the devil. When we got home, my brother's car was in the driveway. The garage door was open and Frank was in the front yard raking the leaves that had accumulated during the last week. Since he's usually not the type of person to make himself useful, I saw this burst of activity as a potentially bad sign.

Faith was barking at the front window and probably had been since Frank arrived. Davey hopped out of the car and ran to let her out so she could bark at my brother in person. I knew Frank was expecting me to stop and see why he was there. Just to be perverse, I pulled the Volvo past him into the open garage and parked.

When I got back outside, Frank was on the ground.

Davey was sitting on top of him, screeching as he was tickled mercilessly. Faith was bounding circles around the two of them, ears and topknot flapping, leaves sticking to her coat like burrs. My family, I thought fondly. We looked like a traveling circus had come to town.

"What's up?" I asked Frank.

He stopped tickling long enough for Davey to make his escape. That gave Faith the opening she was looking for. She scooted in and ran her long pink tongue down the length of my brother's face.

"Yeech!" Frank leapt to his feet. My brother is not a dog lover.

"She was only giving you a kiss," Davey said reproachfully.

"I'll confine my kissing to the human species, thank you." Frank reached down and picked up the rake. The leaves he'd piled up had been pretty much scattered again by dog and child.

"If you want to keep working, feel free."

"No, I was just killing time until you guys got back." He leaned the rake against the side of the garage and we all went inside. "Got any beer?"

"In the fridge."

Davey ran upstairs with Faith to dig out something he wanted to show Frank, and I followed my brother out to the kitchen. "Did you go to the funeral?"

"Yeah." Head stuck in the refrigerator, my brother didn't elaborate.

For the sake of advancing the conversation, I

reached around him, plucked a can of beer off the door, and handed it to him. "How was it?"

"Pretty dreary. Smaller than I would have expected."

"I guess Rattigan didn't have too many friends."

"Maybe not, but I'd have thought the business community would have managed a better turnout." Frank popped the top on the can and took a long swallow. "The police were there."

"Looking for likely suspects, I'd imagine."

"Looking for me is more like it," Frank complained. "It seems like every time I turn around, there they are."

"That's their job," I said, though I was no more pleased about the situation than he was. "Did you get a lawyer?"

Frank nodded.

"A good one?"

He scowled in my direction. "I'm not a little kid, you know. I am capable of managing some things for myself."

A week ago I might have debated that. Now, with Sam's stinging appraisal of the situation still fresh in my mind, I didn't say a thing. Maybe he was right, maybe I was being too overprotective. But under the circumstances, how could I help it?

Feeling decidedly grumpy about the whole mess, I crossed my arms over my chest. As any psychologist can tell you, it's not a friendly gesture. "Did you come here for a reason?" I asked my brother. "Or are you all out of beer?"

"Of course there's a reason. I have good news."

What a pleasant change. "You've discovered an alibi? The skylight was defective? The police have found a witness?"

"Not quite." Frank's enthusiasm was undimmed by my recital of his current woes. "It turns out I'm going to be able to open the coffee bar, after all. I've found a new partner"

Fourteen

Oh, lordy, I thought. Here we go again. "Who?"

"Gloria Rattigan. She's Marcus's ex-wife. I met her this morning at the funeral."

"I know who she is," I said with some exasperation. "How can you even be thinking of going into business with someone you've known less than a day?"

"Why not? Everyone was talking about the fact that she's going to get nearly the whole estate. I figured she hadn't had time to make any plans yet, so I pulled her aside and made her a little proposition."

Unfortunate choice of wording, that. I leaned back and tried to assess my brother's looks objectively. Not drop dead handsome certainly, but he did have a nice smile, a full head of hair, and an air of youthful vitality. Were there enough muscles under those clothes to satisfy an older woman on the prowl? Judging by Gloria Rattigan's response, perhaps.

"Frank, Gloria's looking for a new husband."

"So? All the better. That means she'll stay out of my

way and let me do my job."

Even for Frank, this was a degree of density beyond which I had come to expect. I thought again about what Sam had said and didn't say a thing.

"We've already made our first joint decision and changed the name. Gloria didn't like The Java Joint. We're going with The Coffee Klatch. Cute, huh?"

Only to the seriously desperate. Like my brother.

"The police still have the building cordoned off," I pointed out. "You're not going to be able to get back to work until they solve the murder."

"Or you do." Frank finished his beer and rinsed the can in the sink. "I want to get things moving again. Hurry up, okay?"

He wasn't kidding. Only my brother could throw out an outrageous statement like that and not be kidding.

Times like this make me wish I'd been an only child. "I'm doing the best I can—"

"I know that." He crossed the room and tousled my hair. Frank started doing that the year he grew taller than me, and I've always hated it. "You're a brick, Mel. The best detective I could have hired for free. Hey, where's the kid? I thought he wanted to show me something."

Lucky for him, he left the room. Otherwise I might have told him what I really thought.

When Frank and Davey reappeared, I was making lunch. My brother had already eaten but he still thinks of himself as a growing boy, so putting away another sandwich wasn't a hardship. I sounded him out on his plans for the rest of the day and when it turned out he didn't have any, Davey and I invited him to join us. Babysitting Frank isn't my favorite thing to do but it is one way to keep him out of trouble.

The Stamford Nature Center was celebrating Octoberfest, and the three of us spent the afternoon enjoying the festival. We ordered Chinese food for dinner, then wasted half an hour arguing over movie choices. I was hoping for Jane Austen. Frank wanted Arnold Schwarzenegger. Davey required a non-violent plot. In the end we compromised on a Robin Williams comedy and laughed ourselves silly.

My brother can be decent company when he puts his mind to it. He listened when Davey talked to him and shared his popcorn without a quibble. I even saw him feed Faith a piece of Moo Shu pork from the tips of his chopsticks. It might not have been the evening I'd hoped to spend with Sam, but it was good enough to keep me from crawling to the phone and calling him first.

Sunday morning Davey and I feasted on a big breakfast, then worked off the calories playing Frisbee with Faith at the Greenwich beach. In the afternoon I dropped him off for a play date at the Brickmans', then put Faith in the car and drove over to the coffee bar.

A trail of bright yellow crime scene tape crisscrossed the door and fluttered from the railing. Dry leaves blew across the steps; a shipment of wood sat forgotten on the porch. Though it had been empty less than a week, the store already had an air of desertion about it.

I got out of the car and walked around the building. A bright blue tarp covered the hole in the roof where the skylight had been, but no repairs had been made. There were woods in three directions but now with most of the branches nearly bare, I was able to see several houses in addition to the one across the street.

Since the neighborhood was zoned for two acres minimum, the chance that any of the residents had noticed something amiss had to be slim. Still, it couldn't hurt to canvas the area. At the very least, I might get to talk to some of the protesters who'd been nailing up posters and filing complaints at town hall.

Faith likes an adventure as much as the next dog and she danced at the end of the leash as we crossed the road and made our way to the nearest house. Though most of the curtains on the front of the house were drawn, there was a minivan parked in the driveway. I rang the bell and didn't have to wait long for a response.

Immediately the chimes were followed by the sound of excited yapping from inside the house. Judging by the high pitch, the dog wasn't large. Nails skidded across the floor and there was an audible thump as the defender of the home crashed into the other side of the door. A moment later the barking resumed, this time accompanied by the sound of the nails scratching on wood.

Faith dipped her head from side to side and cocked an ear inquiringly. I reached down and cupped my hand gently around her muzzle warning her not to bark in case she'd been tempted to reply. She wagged her tail and continued to stare downward in fascination, seeking the source of the noise.

After a minute we heard a voice from within. "Kissy, get out of the way! Get out of the way, I tell you. How do you expect me to open the door if you won't move?"

A lock drew back. The knob turned. The door had barely begun to open before a tiny orange missile launched itself furiously onto the steps.

Kissy, presumably. She was five pounds of apricot hair and sharp teeth. There were pink bows in each of her ears, and her long toenails were painted with a matching shade of polish.

I winced slightly, the reaction not entirely due to the fact that Kissy had fastened her teeth on my ankle. Anyone with Standard Poodles spends lots of time battling the stereotypical notion that all Poodles are small, loud, and useless. Here before me was the rare Poodle that fit the insult. Kissy was the dog that was giving us all a bad name.

Her owner was a large woman, not in height, but in heft. Her fleshy features were broad and flat, and her short brown hair had been permed to frizz around her face. "Cut it out! Don't do that! You're going to hurt somebody!" she cried, leaning down to scoop the little dog up in her arms. "Sorry, Kissy gets a little hyper."

"That's all right. I'm used to—"

The woman's gaze moved past me and fastened on Faith. "Good God Almighty. What is that?"

"A Standard Poodle. Your dog's larger cousin." Luckily, Faith didn't understand enough of what I'd said to realize how badly I'd insulted her.

"That's no Poodle." The woman leaned down for a closer look. Secure in her mother's arms, Kissy felt brave enough to curl a lip at Faith disdainfully. "What'd you do to its hair?"

Considering that her dog had painted toenails and bows in its ears, I could hardly see that she was in a position to talk.

In the interest of goodwill, however, I refrained from pointing that out. "The trim is required for the dog show ring. The bands and wraps are there to keep the longer hair out of her way."

"A show dog, huh? Kissy could have been a show dog. That's what her breeder told me. She's got AKC papers and everything."

It's a common misconception that any dog that's AKC registered is qualified to be a show dog. Registration papers guarantee that the dog in question is purebred; they say nothing about the dog being a quality representative of its breed. Kissy was undoubtedly beautiful in her owner's eyes, but with her rounded back skull, roached back, and splayed feet, I doubted there was a dog show judge in the country that would have been pleased to see her walk into his ring.

"Say hello, Kissy." The woman held the little Poodle out, dangling her darling in front of Faith's nose and making *num-num* noises that I supposed meant to approximate a greeting.

She was lucky Faith had a good temperament. Another dog might have taken a chunk out of Kissy's face. Frankly, I was tempted myself.

"A giant size Poodle. That just about beats all." The woman drew Kissy back and looked at me expectantly. "Something I can help you with?"

"Yes, there is. I'm trying to gather some information about the building conversion that's going on across the street."

The woman glanced in the direction of Frank's store. "What about it?"

"Are you aware that a man was killed there last week?"

"Hard not to be. The police have been by asking questions and we had a couple of reporters, too." Her expression brightened. "You a reporter?"

"No, I'm related to the man who's been in charge of most of the work. He told me that some of the neighbors had formed a protest group to try and shut the project down."

The woman's eyes shifted back and forth. "I wouldn't know anything about that."

"Then you don't mind the fact that a coffeehouse is going in across the street?"

"I didn't say that. This is a nice neighborhood. Lots of kids around here. We don't need any more traffic, or strangers driving around at all hours of the night. It just isn't right."

She hugged Kissy to her chest with one hand, then reached out and braced the other on the door. I pressed on quickly before she could decide she'd said enough. "Speaking of traffic, did you happen to notice any cars parked at the coffee bar last Monday night? Or see anyone climbing around on the roof?"

The woman glared. "Now how would I notice something like that? It's not as if I have nothing better to do than stare out the window. I'm a busy person, you know."

"I'm sure you are. It's just that this is your neighborhood and you look like the type of woman who'd stay on top of what was going on."

"You got that right. I hate to say it, but I didn't see a thing. First time I knew something was wrong was when the police cars and ambulance came flying up here Tuesday morning. Good thing the buses had already been by. You wouldn't want kids seeing something like that on their way to school."

"Something like what?" I asked curiously, wondering what the neighborhood scuttlebutt had had to say about the scene.

"Like a dead body! I heard there was blood everywhere and he had a big piece of glass stuck right through his heart." She shivered effusively and Kissy rocked back and forth with the motion. Clearly the details of this story had grown with each retelling. "Are you saying you know the people who were mixed up in that?"

"Just one of them. And he only got mixed up in it by accident." That was sort of true—if you considered general idiocy to be an accident of birth.

"I guess it must have been pretty exciting."

"Not really. Look, it's important that I find some of the people who were part of the protest group. I understand that you weren't involved . . ." The amount of sincerity injected into that statement would have choked a less accomplished fibber. ". . . but maybe you know someone who was. Seeing as it's your neighborhood and all."

"I don't know."

Of course she did. She just wasn't sure she wanted to say.

I reached out to let Kissy sniff my fingers. The Toy Poodle waited until they came within range, then lunged and snapped with surprising speed. Lucky for me, her aim wasn't as sharp as her teeth.

So much for buttering up the woman's dog.

"I'm going to be walking around talking to most of the neighbors anyway," I mentioned persuasively. "I wouldn't have to say where I'd gotten my information."

"I guess you might want to check with Mike and Dottie Daniels. They're in the yellow house on the corner. I don't know anything for sure, but I imagine they might have had something to do with a few protests in their day." The woman snickered as though she'd said something funny.

176

"Thanks. And if you happen to remember anything else about last Monday—"

"I won't." She backed inside and pushed the door shut.

"Goodbye to you, too," I muttered.

Faith jumped up, placed her front paws on my chest, and gave me a doggy smile. I reached around and ruffled my hands through her hair. No doubt she was just as pleased to be removed from Kissy's presence as I was.

I went back and forth across the street, trying three more houses on my way to the Danielses'. People were home at each but I gathered no new information. Nobody had noticed anything unusual at the coffeehouse on Monday. Two people admitted to seeing the petition that had circulated the neighborhood. One had signed it, but both claimed not to know any of the protesters personally.

By the time I reached the yellow house on the corner, my enthusiasm was flagging. Frank had been sure that the protesters, though angry, were basically harmless and I was inclined to agree with him. Circulating petitions and making posters didn't sound like the sort of group activity that was likely to escalate into murder.

Before I was even halfway up the driveway to the Daniels house, I could hear music. Vintage rock and roll, with a thumping beat and great guitar work. By the time I reached the front door, the band was recognizable as the Rolling Stones. Inside, the music

177

must have been deafening.

I rang the bell, but of course nobody came; they couldn't hear me. Faith and I waited on the step until the song ended. In the lull before the next song started, I picked up the knocker and pounded on the door. With luck, the occupants of the house would realize that the sound wasn't a continuation of the beat.

The music began again. This time the melody was so seductive that I was swaying in time when the door opened. Quickly I straightened and tried to look dignified. I needn't have bothered.

The tall, skinny man who faced me was dancing in place himself. Older than me by at least a dozen years, he had a close cropped beard and the kind of lean features that had probably labeled him as a tortured, artistic soul in the sixties. His thin dark hair was tied at the base of his neck with a leather thong, and his clothes, jeans and a T-shirt, looked as though he might have slept in them.

"Hello," he said, grinning. "I thought I heard something. Hey, great dog!"

"Thanks. I was wondering—"

"Hang on a minute, okay?" He turned away and yelled, "Dottie, turn that down; would you? I can't hear a thing!"

While we waited for the music to be lowered, Mike Daniels waved me inside. Most people are justifiably hesitant about inviting a strange dog into their houses, but my host didn't seem to mind. Faith padded along behind as we headed into the living room.

Plump, overstuffed chairs were grouped around a coffee table that appeared to be homemade. A sideboard held a collection of colorful candles. The big screen TV had a football game on, and everywhere I looked there was clutter, piles of newspapers, stacks of magazines. There was a faint, sweetish odor in the air. It took me a moment to identify it as marijuana.

Abruptly the volume dropped. After a moment my head stopped pounding. Even Faith looked relieved. "Mike Daniels," he said, still smiling. "And you are?"

"Melanie Travis. I've been talking to some of your neighbors about the building conversion that's going on down the street."

"I know. Mrs. Mayhew called." He saw my blank look and added, "The woman in the house across from the store? She warned me you were on your way. Probably warned the whole block, in fact. We don't call her the 'Voice of America' for nothing."

"Oh." That didn't sound promising.

"Have a seat. Just push something on the floor and make yourself comfortable. Dottie'll be along in a minute."

I'd barely sat down when Dottie appeared. She was just as tall and skinny as her husband and her clothing was virtually identical. The two of them looked more like twins than husband and wife. She was carrying a glass of iced tea which she set down on the table.

"Let's see the dog," Dottie said. "Mrs. Mayhew said it looked like a circus clown. She was exaggerating, right?" Her gaze dropped to Faith. "Whoa, not by much. Does it bite? How come it has those puffs of hair all over like that?"

I took a moment to explain that Faith's trim was a modern descendant of a traditional German hunting clip. Standard Poodles were originally bred to retrieve birds in the cold waters of German lakes. Hunters had favored dogs with long, thick coats until they discovered that when the coats filled up with water, they became too heavy to swim with and dragged the Poodles down.

At that point they'd conceived the idea of clipping off all the hair that wasn't strictly necessary for the dog's well-being. The long mane coat on the front of the Poodle was meant to protect the heart and lungs. The rosettes over the hips covered the kidneys. The puffs of hair at the bottom of each leg kept the joints warm so that they wouldn't stiffen up in the cold water, and the pompon on the end of the tail served as a flag, marking the Poodle's spot when he dove underwater after a bird.

"Stranger than fiction," Dottie said when I was done. By now, she was sitting on the floor with Faith draped shamelessly across her lap. In a minute they'd be sharing the tea. "Is that the truth?"

"I believe so. My Aunt Peg's the one who told it to me, and she knows everything about Poodles."

"And here I thought folks did that just to make the poor dogs look stupid."

"Don't mind her," said Mike. "I know you came to talk about the murder. Mrs. Mayhew said you have a friend who's involved?"

Mike Daniels listened with interest as I outlined what I knew. "I'm hoping to find someone who might have seen anything that went on over there Monday evening," I said at the end. "Failing that, I'd like to know who was leading the group of protesters who were trying to shut the project down. Mrs. Mayhew seemed to think you might be able to help."

I know I'd told her I'd keep her name out of it, but that was before she broadcast a warning about me all over the neighborhood. No wonder everyone else had been so reticent. I was just about at the end of the street. Mike and Dottie Daniels were my last chance.

Mike stood up and wandered over to the window. "When the leaves are out, you can't really see the store from here. If some kind of funny business was going on, we wouldn't have known about it."

"I understand you're part of the protest group, though."

"We sure are," Dottie spoke up. "This is a quiet, residential neighborhood. The last thing we need is some big business moving in and setting up shop."

I'd hardly have classified Frank's coffee bar as big business, but the issue wasn't worth debating. "So you signed the petition, and maybe nailed up a few posters?"

"No law against that," said Dottie. Faith was now licking her arm. "We were just exercising our right to free speech."

"You were the ones who spearheaded the movement?"

Across the room Mike shook his head. "I wouldn't mind taking credit, but to tell the truth we hadn't even thought of trying to stop the thing until we got a flyer in our mailbox. Turned out that a man who lives around the other block was more upset by this than anyone. He's the one who organized the protests."

"Could you give me his name?"

Dottie nodded. "Sure. Like I said, we're all well within our rights here. No reason he's got to hide. He's a guy by the name of John Monaghan."

Fifteen

"John Monaghan?" I said, surprised. "I know him."

"Well, there you go," said Mike. "You should have tried talking to him first."

I had. He'd admitted knowing some of the pro-testers, but he'd certainly never mentioned that he was the one who'd organized them into a group. Not only that, but he'd characterized Marcus Rattigan as an old and valued friend. So why had he been trying to undermine Rattigan's newest project?

"I guess I should have," I said slowly. "You're sure it was John Monaghan who started the protest?"

"Hard to make a mistake about a thing like that. He got everyone together over at his house for a meeting about what to do next. John was the one who planned our whole offense."

On the big screen TV, the Jets were mounting an offense of their own. I watched as the quarterback was sacked by a player the size of a Buick and wondered how far the protesters had been willing to go in their quest to preserve their neighborhood.

"There have been a couple of suspicious accidents at the store over the last few weeks," I said. "A water pipe burst and a section of floor caved in. Is that the kind of thing your group had in mind?"

"No way," Mike said quickly, but Dottie grinned. "Power to the people," she said.

"Meaning?"

"A little passive resistance never hurt anybody."

"This resistance was hardly passive. And a man was hospitalized as a result of it."

"We don't know anything about that," said Mike. "Dottie was just kidding around. If someone got hurt down there, we're sorry to hear it."

Interesting, I thought. Someone had gotten murdered down there, too, but he hadn't mentioned being sorry about that.

I snapped my fingers and Faith got to her feet, shook out her hair, and came to my side. "Thanks for your time," I said, rising. "You've been a big help."

"No problem," said Mike. "Now that Marcus Rattigan is gone, does that mean the building project will be dropped?"

"I really don't know."

"We'll find out." Dottie braced a hand on the floor and climbed to her feet. "And then maybe we'll go back to work. To tell the truth, having the chance to make signs and petitions again after all these years was kind of exciting. There's nothing like a good protest to keep you young."

On our way back to the car, I took off Faith's leash and collar and let her run. On a Sunday afternoon, the neighborhood was so quiet that not a single car passed us during the ten minute walk. The opening of a coffee bar would certainly change that. I could understand why the neighbors would be loathe to give up even a measure of their peace and solitude.

From where I'd parked in the store lot, John Monaghan's house was barely a five minute drive. I called ahead from the car phone, and though he sounded surprised to hear from me, he said he could spare a few minutes to talk. When I arrived he was out front, raking the gravel in his driveway, and obviously waiting for me.

John lifted a hand in greeting as I stopped the car and got out. "Lawn service is supposed to take care of this, but they never seem to get it just right," he said, setting his rake aside. "Is that your Standard? Hop her out. Let's have a look."

Faith was only too pleased to come bounding out of the car and be admired. "That's a pretty bitch. You say you got her from your aunt?"

"Margaret Turnbull," I confirmed, nodding. "Cedar Crest Standard Poodles. She lives in Greenwich."

"The name sounds familiar. I'm sure we must have been at plenty of shows together. Poodles are pretty much out of my sphere, though. I'm much more

184

familiar with the terrier people."

That made sense. At the shows people with a common interest tended to hang out together. They see each other at the ring during judging and group together in the grooming area so that they can chat before and after, too.

"Aunt Peg's a member of the Belle Haven Kennel Club. Maybe that's where you heard of her."

"Maybe," said John. "I haven't joined an all breed club myself. All I see is too much infighting among the members and not enough useful stuff getting accomplished."

Since Belle Haven not only ran a dog show but also sponsored eye and tattoo clinics, donated money to genetic research in dogs, and made monthly visits to local nursing homes, I was sure Aunt Peg would have disputed that characterization. My only exposure to the club had taken place around the time that one of the members had been murdered, however, so I wasn't about to leap to Belle Haven's defense.

"I've been talking to some people in the neighborhood about the group that was protesting the coffee bar conversion," I said. "Last time we spoke, you said you probably knew most of the participants."

"That's right."

"However you neglected to mention that you were the person who had organized the protest group. Instead, you told me you and Marcus Rattigan were friends."

"We were."

"And yet you passed put flyers and petitions aimed at getting his latest building project shut down? I'm afraid that doesn't make sense to me."

"I can see how it might not," John admitted.

I waited for him to elaborate, watching as Faith spied a squirrel and chased it across the lawn and up a tree. Sitting back on her haunches, she looked up and followed its progress through the branches. A minute later when the squirrel disappeared into its hole, John was still silent.

"You should know that I will be giving this information to the police," I said finally.

"I'd rather you didn't do that."

"Then you'd better explain to me what's going on." I could see by his expression that John didn't like my tone.

"It's really not your concern."

"It *is* my concern. The fact that my brother's a suspect means that I'm involved, too. And if indeed you were Rattigan's friend, I would think you'd be just as eager as I am to see his murderer brought to justice."

John reached in the pocket of his baggy khakis and pulled out a pipe. He took a few minutes to tamp down the tobacco and locate a lighter, then lit the flame and drew down deeply. A curl of smoke eddied up into the air.

"What I am about to tell you doesn't present Marcus in the best light. Now that he's gone, perhaps it's unfair of me to reveal such things about his business dealings. On the other hand, maybe it doesn't matter as much as it once might have."

"Go on."

"As I'm sure you know, Marcus was an entrepreneur. At any given time he usually had a number of projects at various stages of completion, all of them considerably larger than the conversion he contracted to do with your brother."

I nodded. "I wondered about that. From what I'd read about Marcus Rattigan, this coffee bar idea of Frank's seemed much too small for him to have bothered with."

"Under normal circumstances it would have been. But if you've read about Marcus in the newspapers, then you also probably know that some of his projects have had an alienating effect on certain communities."

Some? I thought. Make that nearly all. "Like the high density apartment complex he built in Wilton? And the low-income housing he tried to get state approval to force into New Canaan?"

"Precisely. Marcus was rather driven when it came to his work. He built his buildings to make a profit and that was pretty much all that mattered. Let's just say that if along the way, certain legalities had to be manipulated to suit his needs, he wasn't above getting his hands dirty."

For all his apparent reticence, so far John hadn't told me anything I didn't already know. Uncertain where he was heading, I said, "Frank told me that everything about the coffee bar conversion was on the up and up. But I know he'd gotten that idea from Rattigan. Are you trying to tell me that the permits weren't in order?"

"No." Smoke puffed from the side of John's mouth as he spoke. "The coffee bar wasn't the problem. If anything, it was a diversion. Marcus was concerned about another tract of land he'd just purchased up in north Stamford, along the New York border. Forty acres that had recently become available from a single estate. Some of it runs along the reservoir, and all of it is pristine, untouched."

"And Marcus wanted to develop that land?"

"Of course. That's what he did. Unfortunately, there's an environmental group that's convinced the land should be maintained just as it is. They feel it should be turned into a park, or perhaps a nature preserve."

Faith, who'd been exploring a row of rhododendron bushes along the front of the house, came trotting back to see what I was up to. I reached down and scratched beneath her chin. "Then, why didn't they buy the estate when it became available?"

"They didn't have the money. A tract like that costs millions. Marcus had the cash and he made the deal. He was all set to start building new homes over the summer. Then the environmentalists got involved and the next thing he knew there was an injunction preventing him from going forward until the case could be heard in court. All of which was costing Marcus a good deal of unnecessary money and aggravation."

"What does all this have to do with Frank?"

"With your brother, very little. With the coffee bar conversion, a great deal. At least that's how Marcus explained it to me when he asked me to help out."

"Help out?" My hand stilled. Faith leaned in closer and pressed against my leg. "By forming a protest group?"

"Odd as it may seem, yes. Marcus asked me to stir up some ill will among the neighbors. He was hoping for as big a flap as possible. The coffee bar meant nothing to him. Oh, I imagine it could have made a profit but the amount of money generated would have been negligible compared to the other deal.

"The only reason Marcus ever signed on in the first place is because when your brother approached him, he saw an opportunity to ease his way past the environmentalists. Two projects in the same town. Both being protested by groups who were concerned about the quality of life in their neighborhoods. Eventually Anaconda Properties would win approval for the development they really wanted by ceding graciously on the other."

"Wait a minute!" Thoughts racing, I digested what he'd said. "You mean that Rattigan never had any intention of opening the coffee bar? That he was planning on abandoning the project as soon as he got the go ahead on the other tract of land?"

"That's right. The conversion served no other purpose for him. He'd have let it go without a backward glance."

I felt a sinking feeling in the pit of my stomach. Much as I didn't want to believe it, I knew that John was telling me the truth. It all explained so much.

Now I knew how a person as powerful as Marcus Rattigan could have gotten involved with someone like Frank. I understood why Rattigan hadn't assigned one of his own construction crews to do the work; and why he hadn't protested when Frank, the neophyte, had declared that he would act as general contractor. No wonder he hadn't wanted to put any more money into the place. Sometime soon he'd been planning to turn his back and walk away, leaving my brother to deal with the consequences.

Suddenly I wasn't as eager to get this information to the authorities as I'd been earlier. I wondered how much of this Frank had known. I wondered how much he'd suspected. No doubt the police would be curious about that, too.

This was just great, I thought with annoyance. Every time I turned up new information, my brother's motive grew faster than a litter of Great Dane puppies. Much more of this, and I was going to be tempted to switch sides.

"I appreciate your candor," I said to John. "You've been very helpful."

"I don't know about that." His lips, gripped around the stem of his pipe, still managed a frown. "Marcus was no saint, I'll grant you that. But he still didn't deserve the end he came to."

Easy for him to say. He didn't have a brother

who'd gone into business with the man.

On the way home I stopped at the supermarket and bought ingredients for a simple dinner, then swung by and picked up Davey. It was already Sunday evening; the weekend was almost over and I felt as though I'd worked straight through.

The light was blinking on the answering machine when I walked into the kitchen and the tape took only a second to rewind. Aunt Peg's message was short and pointed: "Well?"

I put the food away, let the dog outside, and got my son settled on the couch with a Richard Scary book. Then I sat down and dialed.

"Well, what?" I asked when Peg picked up.

"For starters, did you and Sam manage to sort things out the other night?"

"Yes and no. Mostly no."

"Then work on it!" Aunt Peg's never been one for pulling her punches. "After all the time and trouble I took getting you two together, I'm not going to stand around and watch you muck things up."

"What makes you think *I'm* the one mucking things up?"

Peg's silence spoke eloquent volumes.

"Sam wants me to stop looking into Marcus Rattigan's murder. He thinks I should stop getting involved in other people's problems, period."

"He's worried about you," said Aunt Peg. "That's sweet."

"He all but issued me an ultimatum. I don't find that sweet at all."

"You did come within a hair's breath of getting yourself killed last summer."

"I never should have told you that."

"Actually," Peg pointed out, "you never should have told Sam. I rather enjoyed the story myself."

Of course she had. A Poodle had come to my rescue. "I am who I am," I said stubbornly. "Sam's either going to have to deal with that, or . . ."

"Or what?"

I didn't have an answer for that. At least not one that I wanted to think about right then. Instead I changed the subject and told Aunt Peg about the people I'd spoken to earlier.

"Marcus Rattigan actually asked John Monaghan to picket his own building site?" she said. "How very odd."

"Except that, unfortunately, when you factor in John's explanation it all makes sense. In Rattigan's view, Frank must have looked like a nice plump pigeon, ripe for the plucking."

"What an awful man he must have been," Aunt Peg said thoughtfully. "I'm glad I never knew him better. I wonder how he ever got involved in the dog show game."

"Probably through John Monaghan. I would imagine it was the usual sponsor scenario. John, the breeder, found himself with a truly great dog and lacking the funds to give her the career she deserved.

Rattigan had the money and the need for ego gratification. But there was something funny about their arrangement."

"What's that?"

"I meant to ask John about this, but I was so surprised by everything else he told me that I totally forgot. Maybe you can explain it to me. When I went to see John last week, we talked about Winter for quite a while. He confirmed what you said, by the way. She only ever produced a single litter of puppies."

"That's not unusual with bitches that have had extensive specials careers," said Peg. "For some reason they often seem to have reproductive problems. There are a number of theories why that is, but nobody knows for sure."

"In this case they did. She developed acute metritis after delivering the litter and had to be spayed. But that wasn't what was odd. John told me that there were three male puppies in the litter and that he'd kept them all."

"Coming from a bitch as fabulous as Winter, that makes perfect sense."

"Yes, but here's what doesn't. Yesterday when I went to see Roger Nye, he had a Wire Fox Terrier, too. Her name was Asta, she was nine years old, and he'd gotten her from Marcus Rattigan. Rattigan told Roger at the time that Asta's dam was the top dog in the country."

"Winter?"

"It had to have been. So what I'd like to know is,

was John lying when he told me he'd kept all the puppies from that litter? Or was Rattigan lying when he gave the puppy to his neighbor?"

"Judging by what we know about him," said Peg, "I'd have to guess that the liar was Rattigan."

"That's my impression, too, but why would he have bothered? The Nyes didn't care about showing, and Roger said Rattigan had never even given them the registration papers. All they wanted was a pet. Also, Roger said that the Rattigans had never had any dogs, Fox Terriers or otherwise, at their house. The only exception was when Marcus showed up with this puppy."

"Which makes her even more likely to be Winter's puppy, since she was the only Fox Terrier Rattigan owned." There was silence on the line as Aunt Peg thought for a minute. "All right, let's turn things around. Say for the sake of argument that John was the one who'd stretched the truth. Maybe Winter has grown to such mythic proportions in his mind that he didn't want to admit she'd produced a less than perfect puppy."

"No, that can't be it. I asked John about the puppies and he admitted quite readily that none was as good as the dam. He seemed to think that was to be expected."

"Of course it was," Aunt Peg said firmly. "Dogs like Winter don't come along very often, you know. But there's something else that's troubling me about that story."

"What?"

"No matter whose puppy Asta was, I find it highly surprising that John would allow Marcus to take her and give her away. That's highly unusual. No reputable breeder would ever allow a puppy to be placed without exerting a great deal of control over the type of home it went to. And if Asta was Winter's daughter, John would have been crazy to keep only dogs and let her go."

"So what does it all mean?"

"Darned if I know," said Peg. I hate it when she does that. "Let me give it some thought. Maybe I'll come up with something. In the meantime how's that brother of yours holding up?"

"Better than one might have expected, all things considered. He's met Gloria Rattigan and the two of them are making plans to proceed with the conversion."

"Good for him." Aunt Peg sounded pleased. "That boy may turn out to be an upstanding member of the community yet."

Sure, I thought. If he didn't end up behind bars first.

Sixteen

Monday morning, it was almost a relief to go back to school. At least there, I knew where to go and what to do. And when I asked questions, people gave me answers that made sense.

If you didn't count Spencer Holbrook, that is.

"What do you mean Albany isn't the capital of

Albania?" he demanded as we sat with his latest geography assignment on the table between us. His shirt was grass stained, his tie loosened, and his hair stood straight up in spiky tufts. He'd mentioned something about a wild soccer game during recess, mostly, I suspected, to distract me from the deficiencies of his recent schoolwork.

I waved toward the map on the wall. "Go look it up." I'd have sent him to his geography book but it didn't seem to be among the supplies he'd lugged to our session in his backpack.

"I don't need to look it up. You're the teacher, teach me."

I stiffened my shoulders and lifted my brow. "Is that the way you talk to your other teachers?"

We both knew it wasn't. Otherwise, he would have been marked in my book as a discipline problem. Spencer wasn't a bad kid, he was just a little confused about who was in charge.

"Sorry," he mumbled.

"Did you say something? I'm afraid I didn't hear you."

"I'm sorry. It was a stupid mistake and I shouldn't have gotten it wrong. I'll go look it up."

He crossed the room and stood in front of the world map. Considering that he was searching for Albania in Africa, I figured we were going to be there awhile.

Since I was working on a staggered schedule, Kate and Lucia showed up halfway through Spencer's allotted time period. I sat him on one side of the room to make corrections and turned my attention to the new arrivals.

"How was your horse show?" I asked Lucia.

"It was awesome." The teenager flipped her hair behind her shoulders. "I won every class but one. Mark was champion by a mile. Nobody else even came close."

"Good for you. Did you rewrite those sections I marked in your book report?"

"Uh . . ." Her expression went blank. "Not exactly. I didn't really have time."

"You had time to spend two days riding your horse."

"That's different. That's real life. My dad said he's going to come in and talk to Mr. Hanover about that. You know, like maybe with all these horse shows I'm competing in I could get some credits for life experience?"

It took effort not to laugh. Life experience? Give me a break. What this kid needed was more school experience. Unfortunately, I could just imagine our headmaster, who prided himself on being progressive, falling for such an idea.

"How about you?" I asked Kate. "Homework all finished?"

She nodded shyly and presented the book report. It had been typed up on a computer and was covered in clear plastic.

"This looks great. You must have worked really hard on it."

"I did."

"No shows this weekend for you?"

"No, John didn't like the judges. He's going to Queensboro and Bronx County this weekend, though."

"Are you going, too?"

"I hope so." Kate smiled. "The dog shows are the best part"

"Maybe I'll see you there. I have my Poodle entered on Saturday."

Lucia sniffed her disdain. She was the type of girl who was only happy when the conversation centered around her. Now that it had moved on, she got out her report and carried it over to the table.

With Kate's work already done, I figured she could spare a few minutes. "How long have you known John?" I asked.

Kate thought back. "Probably five years or so. Since I was a little kid. Why?"

"I'm curious about a litter of puppies he once had, but they were born before you met him."

"Winter's puppies?"

"Good guess." I grinned. "How'd you know?"

"Easy. John still talks about her all the time, like she was some sort of movie star or something. Winter was pretty old by the time I came around. She always looked like just another dog to me, not that I would have dared to tell John that."

"Does he ever say anything about the litter she had?"

"Like what?"

I kept my tone casual. "When I spoke to John, he told me she only had male puppies. Then I met another man who said there was a bitch, too. I was just wondering who was right."

"I don't know." Kate shrugged. "If you want, I can ask him."

"Don't make a big deal of it," I said quickly. "I'm sure it's nothing."

"No problem. Like I said, John loves talking about her. I'm sure he'll be glad to tell me."

We left it at that, and I put Kate to work. That afternoon when I got home, I took Faith for a quick jog, then went out to the garage to dig through the last month's newspapers. That's one good thing about recycling. As long as what you're looking for is reasonably current, the paper is probably still hanging around waiting to go to the dump.

Since Marcus Rattigan seemed to be a continuing source of interest to the local reporters, it didn't take long to find a reference to his tract of land in north Stamford. There was mention of a pending court case that had been brought by local residents who'd banded together in a group they called Preserve Our Wilderness, or POW. Though the idea of calling any part of suburban Stamford wilderness seemed like hyperbole to me, I had to admit the acronym was catchy. The spokesperson for the group was a woman named Audrey DiMatteo.

I went inside, found her number in the phone book, and gave her a call.

"Forget it," Audrey said when I'd explained who I was. "I don't want to talk about Marcus Rattigan, or land development, or even saving the spotted owl. I've gone through enough grief over this whole mess to last me the rest of my life."

"I know exactly how you feel," I said truthfully. "I assume you're still hoping to block Anaconda's plans to subdivide the property and build on it?"

"Of course."

"In that case I have some information that may be of use to you."

"What is it?"

"I'd rather talk in person." That way, I'd have a fighting chance of getting some of my own questions answered.

There was a long sigh. "Meet me at the old Waldheim estate, then. Do you know where it is?"

"I can find it." I grabbed a pen and scribbled furiously as she barked out directions. "Give me twenty minutes."

I spent the first ten of that waiting for Davey's bus. When it finally appeared, I hustled him into the Volvo, passed him an apple and a wedge of cheese to eat on the way, and sped up Long Ridge toward the New York border.

The entrance to the Waldheim estate was marked by a crumbling wrought iron gate and a sign that warned trespassers to keep out. The long driveway was rutted and overgrown. It led us to a hulking, turn-of-the-century mansion that had clearly seen better days.

Several windows were broken, shutters swung loosely, and one corner of the porte cochere had collapsed, blocking the approach to the door.

A bright red Ford sedan sat, idling, just beyond the house and I pulled up beside it. Audrey turned off her car and got out as I parked. She was a tiny woman, probably in her mid-fifties, with short gray hair and a direct gaze. Her handshake, when we introduced ourselves, was brisk and firm.

"I worried about whether it was wise to come and meet you alone," she said. "But since you brought your child along, I guess you must be on the up and up."

"That's Davey." As he scooted past me and ran toward the house, I wondered if I should have had similar concerns about her. "Do you meet many people who aren't what they seem to be?"

"Remarkably, since I got involved with POW, yes. I've been deluged by lawyers, fanatics, fund raisers, and environmental commandos, not to mention the press. Publicity's good for our cause, I just wish there weren't so many people trying to jump on the bandwagon with us."

Her gaze followed Davey's progress. "Don't let him go too close to the house. That place is really a ruin. It'll be a miracle if it stays up long enough for someone to tear it down."

I relayed her warning and Davey changed course. In a setting like that, there was plenty to keep him busy. Of one accord Audrey and I began to walk.

"This is a beautiful piece of property."

"It's gorgeous. Can you blame us for wanting to preserve it? There are so few undeveloped tracts of land left in Stamford and almost none this size. If we allow this land to be broken up into cookie cutter housing lots, its unspoiled beauty will be lost forever."

I must be getting cynical. To my ear, her rhetoric had all the spontaneity of a sound bite.

"How long had POW been battling with Marcus Rattigan?"

"About six months, I guess. He purchased the land in the spring and filed his plans almost immediately thereafter. Before he came along, we'd all held out hope that someone with tons of money would scoop up this place and restore it to its former glory. I guess we were pretty naive."

"What were your chances of preventing him from going ahead with his development?"

"Fair." Audrey frowned. "All right, not great. But we had a shot. Once we found out what he had in mind, we knew we couldn't allow him to proceed without a fight."

"Legally, he was within his rights to build on the land, wasn't he?" That's what the newspaper had said, but I wanted to be sure.

"As things stand now, yes. That's why we initiated our suit. We're also hoping to sway public opinion by taking our campaign to the media. With enough support from concerned citizens, the town of Stamford could have bought the land from him and turned it into a park or nature preserve."

It didn't sound too likely to me. Like most small cities, Stamford ran on a tight budget. Any extra funds went for education or increased police and fire protection. The land we were standing on was worth millions. Raising that kind of money under any circumstances wouldn't have been easy.

"Feeling as strongly as you do about this land, I guess you weren't displeased when you heard that Marcus Rattigan had been murdered."

"Not entirely." She smiled thinly. "No."

"You said a moment ago that some of the people in your group were fanatics—"

"No," Audrey corrected me. "I said that we'd been approached by some outsiders whom I would have characterized that way. Environmental junkies, I started calling them. People who hear about a cause like ours and immediately want to get involved. We thanked them for their offer of help and sent them on their way."

She paused to gaze at the magnificent scenery that surrounded us. "Are you asking me if I think there are any murderers in my group?"

I made my answer as blunt as her question. "Yes."

"It hardly seems likely. Until this came up, we were just any normal group of people—housewives, businessmen, doctors, teachers. We all care about what happens here, but the idea that one of us might resort to murder because of it seems ludicrous. Besides, the fact that Rattigan himself is gone won't necessarily halt the process."

Audrey stopped walking and turned to face me. "I came here today because you told me you had some information that might help my cause. What is it?"

"Are you aware that Marcus Rattigan was also involved in the conversion of another building in Stamford just before he died?"

"That general store/coffee bar thing? The place where he was found?"

"Yes. There was a neighborhood group objecting to what he was doing there, as well."

"That's hardly surprising."

"Not on the surface. But what is surprising was that Rattigan himself was behind the protests. He had asked an old friend of his to step in and stir up trouble."

"How do you know that?"

"It's not important," I said, unwilling to betray John Monaghan's confidence. "Apparently Rattigan was hoping to trade one building project for the other. By giving up the coffee bar conversion that he didn't really care about, he thought he could gain enough goodwill downtown to ensure that his plans here were approved without a hitch."

"That's very interesting," said Audrey. "Considering that we've been pleading our case in the court of public opinion, you're quite right, we might be able to get some use out of that." She turned and started walking toward her car.

"One last thing." I hurried after her. "Before Rattigan was killed in the coffee bar, there'd been several suspicious accidents on the site. A member of the construction crew had been injured. I don't suppose you'd know anything about that?"

Audrey's expression grew tight. "Despite everything I've said, you still seem to think that POW is some sort of militant group. Why is that?"

"A murder's been committed. Isn't that reason enough to be suspicious of anyone who might have been involved?"

"Trust me, the only land that interested us was right here. We didn't care about what went on with Rattigan's other projects. Actually, the fact that he had other things in the works gave us an advantage. It divided his attention."

Audrey started walking again and this time I let her go. Somehow I suspected that the members of POW were a good deal more savvy than she wanted to let on. And if they'd been looking to distract Rattigan's attention, staging a couple of accidents at Frank's place might have seemed like a good way to start.

When Davey and I got home, there weren't any messages waiting for us on the machine. On the plus side, that meant there were no new crises in Frank's life, and Aunt Peg wasn't clamoring for information. Unfortunately, it also meant that another day had gone by without a call from Sam. That made three and counting, in case you're not keeping track.

I know I could have called him and I'd certainly thought about it. Once that initial burst of righteous anger had cooled, I'd seen what had been so perfectly obvious to Aunt Peg. The only reason that Sam was butting into my life was because he cared about me.

I've been single for six years, long enough to know that finding a good man is about as easy as teaching a Jack Russell Terrier not to chew. So I wasn't about to give up this relationship without a fight. The problem was, right then, with my energies being channeled in so many directions, I just didn't have enough to spare.

Sam and I could figure out what to do about this problem, I was sure of it. But at the moment my brother had to come first.

Lunchtime at Howard Academy is a decorous affair. The students sit at round tables set with linen napkins and china plates. A hot meal is served family style; and a teacher is assigned to each table, supposedly to ensure that the conversation is of a sufficiently high intellectual level.

Sitting with the students is a rotating duty. Teachers usually have one week off after having served two. Practically speaking, however, most teachers avail themselves of the hot lunch. It didn't take me long to figure out why. The food at Howard Academy is far superior to anything I could pack in a brown bag.

The meal is followed by recess, which—for some reason—has always been monitored by male teachers only. It doesn't seem fair to me, but it's nice to have sex discrimination working in my favor for a change. For those who choose not to eat with the students, the midday break between classes runs nearly ninety minutes.

On Tuesday, I used the time to zip over to Belle Haven and visit Gloria Rattigan. I'd called that morning and she'd sounded perfectly pleased to hear from me. Lunchtime would be no problem, she'd insisted. Perhaps she could throw together a shrimp salad for us to eat in the breakfast room?

Either this woman was very lonely, or else she was more besotted with my brother than I would ever have thought possible.

Gloria met me at the door dressed in a chic black pant-suit. I wondered if its color was meant to indicate that she was in mourning. If so, the look would have been more convincing without the jaunty red carnation she'd placed in her lapel.

"Come right in," she said. "Estella has lunch almost ready."

"Estella?"

Gloria lowered her voice. "One of the perks of my new inheritance. You have no idea what a relief it is to go back to living in the manner to which I'd become accustomed."

The breakfast room was off the kitchen. It was small but sunny, with a tile floor, trellis covered wallpaper, and floor to ceiling windows on two sides. A glass topped table in the center of the room had been set for two and as soon as we were seated, lunch was served.

"Wine?" asked Gloria. "I have a marvelous Pinot Grigio chilling. Estella?"

"I'd better not," I said as the maid filled Gloria's glass. "I still have to teach this afternoon."

"You're a teacher. I hadn't realized that. It must be wonderful to have a calling." She laughed lightly. "I'm afraid the only thing I was ever called to do was be a wife. Your brother's darling."

I swallowed suddenly and choked on a piece of shrimp. "Drink some water, dear." Gloria handed me a glass. "Your face is turning red."

It took me a moment to get my breath back. As soon as I could, I sputtered, "Surely you don't . . . that is, you and my brother aren't . . ."

"A couple?" Gloria looked vaguely shocked. "Of course not. Frank is darling, but he's a little young, don't you think? Not that I rule out younger men, mind you, just that I prefer ones who've already risen to a certain level of accomplishment. As it happens, I already have Marcus's replacement in mind."

"You don't waste any time, do you?"

"At my age, I should hope not! Estella, pour me another glass of wine, please."

The bottle was sitting on the table between us. I could have easily poured it myself. Estella walked in from the kitchen and refilled Gloria's glass.

"You said you had more questions for me. Detective Petrie has been back, too. I asked if he was close to making an arrest and he said they were still keeping their options open. If you ask me, that doesn't sound terribly promising."

"I don't know," I said. "I haven't been in touch with

the police. The only information I have about their investigation, I've gotten through Frank."

"Isn't he a dear? He and I are going into business together, did he tell you?"

I nodded. "He's very excited about the prospect. He told me you'd chosen a new name for the coffee-house."

"The Coffee Klatch?" Gloria waved a hand dismissively. "I only came up with that off the top of my head. Afterward, I realized we should go with something younger, hipper. You know. These days I find I'm just brimming with ideas. So here's what I was thinking."

She paused for effect. "Ready? We'll call it, Bean There, Done That. Isn't that just delicious?"

Seventeen

Luckily I was saved from answering when the phone rang and Gloria cocked her head and listened while Estella took a message. I didn't know which was funnier: the thought of my brother operating a coffee bar named Bean There, Done That, or the notion of Gloria Rattigan trying to be hip.

I waited until her attention had turned back to me, then said, "I went to see your neighbor, Roger Nye."

"Good old Roger. What did you think? Could he have murdered Marcus? You know what they say. It's always the quiet ones who have hidden depths." Gloria's eyes sparkled. Thanks to Rattigan's murder, she'd not only become rich, she'd also landed a ring-side seat at the best show in town.

"He was very angry at your ex-husband. Roger said the only good thing Marcus had ever done for him was give him a puppy."

"A puppy?" Gloria sounded surprised.

"Yes, Asta. A Wire Fox Terrier. I gather she came from a litter Marcus bred out of a top winning show dog. Do you remember her?"

"No, not in particular. We never had any dogs here. Marcus knew I wouldn't tolerate it. But of course I was well aware when he went through his show dog phase. Marcus was like that, you know. He went through phases.

"All sorts of things came and went, and each one interested him tremendously for a short while. There was his dog phase, his antique car phase, his golf phase. The trouble was, Marcus got bored easily. But even after he got tired of his toys, he could never bear for anyone else to have them. His golf clubs are still sitting in the basement, and his last two cars are moldering in a warehouse somewhere."

"From what I was told, he seems to have given this puppy away."

"I wouldn't know anything about that." Gloria gave a delicate shrug. "I'm afraid I never paid any attention to those silly show dogs. I was perfectly pleased when Marcus's interest moved on."

I finished the last bit of shrimp salad and set down my fork. The only way I'd have gotten the plate any cleaner was if I lifted it up and licked it. Across from me Gloria was picking at her food. Watching her chew each small bite methodically, I got the distinct impression she was counting the calories every time she swallowed.

"Last time I was here, you told me you had a spy in Rattigan's company. Were you keeping tabs on his business or his social life?"

"Both." Gloria smiled complacently. "That was one thing I figured out early on. Take all the information you can get. You never know when something useful might turn up."

"Does your spy still work at Anaconda?"

"I should say so. These days he just about runs the place."

I thought back to my visit the week before: the harried, fair haired man who'd come striding out of his office and been introduced as Rattigan's second in command.

"Ben Welch?"

"You know him?"

"We met once, very briefly." Interesting that Gloria had managed to co-opt Anaconda's vice-president. I wondered if Rattigan had ever realized that he had a stoolie in his ranks, especially one that highly placed. "He seemed to be a very busy man."

"I should hope so. I'm planning to leave him in charge of the operation, and these days there's a lot to do."

"His lack of loyalty doesn't bother you."

Gloria's expression hardened. "Ben was loyal to *me*, that's what's important. Besides, he and I understand each other. Let's just say we have more than a working relationship."

No wonder she'd found a replacement for Rattigan so quickly; she'd already been grooming a successor. Gloria had painted herself as the victim in their divorce, but from where I sat it looked as though she'd planned all along on having her revenge.

"Before Marcus died, did you know he hadn't changed his will?"

"Of course not." Gloria laid her knife and fork neatly along the side of her plate, then waved to Estella to come and clear.

"Did Ben Welch know?"

Gloria didn't answer. Her gaze slid discreetly to the maid, then back. I paused, waiting while Estella gathered the plates and left the room. Gloria used the time to reach for a small leather case beside her place setting, shake out a cigarette and light up.

"It occurs to me that both you and Ben have benefited a great deal from your ex-husband's death," I said.

"So what? I lived with Marcus for fourteen years. The way I see it, I did my time. I deserve everything I got."

"And Ben?"

Gloria smiled as she pulled in a lungful of smoke. "I guess he just got lucky."

Maybe, I thought. Maybe not. I'm not a big believer in luck, good or bad. I don't buy lottery tickets and I don't avoid black cats. For the most part, I think people make their own luck.

So how much of his current good fortune had Ben Welch stumbled into, and how much might he have manipulated to his own ends? I already knew he'd been willing to betray his boss. Had that been the sum of his treachery, or just the beginning?

Back at school I practiced reading with a second grader and worked on a topographical map of South America with a little girl from fourth. It wasn't the kind of work that kept my mind constantly engaged. I had plenty of time to mull over my one short meeting with Ben Welch and decide that I needed another.

I slipped out twice during the afternoon to call Anaconda Properties, reaching Liz both times. Ben wasn't there, she told me the first time. Would I care to leave a message? It was a good thing I hadn't, because she hung up the phone almost before I had a chance to respond.

On the second try I asked to make an appointment with Ben. Liz was ever so sorry she couldn't help me. Due to the demands of his current schedule, Mr. Welch wasn't seeing anyone unless it was absolutely urgent. Click.

Feeling annoyed and increasingly frustrated, I waited until school got out and then did what any upstanding citizen would do. I drove down to the Stamford Police Station and asked to speak to Detective Petrie.

Actually, bearing in mind that I was a mother first and an upstanding citizen second, I also called Alice Brickman and asked her to nab Davey when the bus came by. To my delight, she offered to get my spare key out of the garage and take Faith for a walk, too. The combination cleared my way for a guilt free encounter with Stamford's finest.

The Stamford Police Station is located on Bedford Street, around the corner from the courthouse. The U-shaped brick building always looks busy, and parking space out front is minimal. Only the truly foolhardy would think of flaunting regulations in the police lot, and I ended up driving several blocks before finding an empty spot. As a concession to my destination, I didn't even jaywalk on the way back.

The reception area inside the wide doors was bustling. An officer hunched over a tall counter in the middle of the room and took a statement from a worried looking girl whose ex-boyfriend was calling her at all hours of the night. Youth Court was on the right, and the line for information on the left.

The woman behind the glass barrier took my name and asked me to wait. Benches lined one wall, and I perched on the edge of one. I'd barely sat down when Detective Petrie came to get me. We rode the elevator up to his office on the second floor.

The room he led me to was small and exceedingly neat. The desktop was uncluttered, the two chairs neatly aligned. A window behind the desk looked out over the street. Petrie's coat hung from a hook on the back of the door. He pushed it out of the way as he closed the door and waved me to a seat.

The detective walked around behind the desk and sat down opposite me. There was an air of calm deliberation in everything he did, and I could see how potential suspects might have found him unnerving. Detective Petrie didn't move quickly, but he gave the impression that he always got where he wanted to go.

"What can I do for you?" he asked, folding his hands on top of the desk.

"I came to talk to you about your investigation into Marcus Rattigan's murder. I've uncovered a few things that I thought might be useful to you."

"How's that?"

"Pardon me?"

Detective Petrie leaned back in his chair. He did not look pleased. "I was just wondering how it was that you might have come up with some knowledge about the case. Unless you mean that your brother told you something that he might not have passed along to us."

"No, that's not it." I cleared my throat nervously. "I'm sure Frank told you everything."

Petrie's only response to that was a noncommittal grunt.

"It's just that my brother's been concerned about your viewing him as a suspect."

"Considering the extent of his involvement in the circumstances surrounding Mr. Rattigan's murder, we would be foolish *not* to think of him as a suspect."

"Yes, of course. But I thought you might want to

consider some other possibilities. I imagine you know that Rattigan's ex-wife, Gloria, inherited nearly his entire estate?"

Petrie nodded.

"Are you aware that she is romantically involved with Rattigan's vice-president, Ben Welch, who spied on Rattigan for her before the divorce? And that now that her ex-husband is gone, Gloria's planning to appoint Ben to run the company?"

I'd been hoping my information would surprise and amaze him. Unfortunately, judging by the expression on the detective's face, I hadn't succeeded in eliciting either emotion. Instead of asking for more facts, Petrie asked, "How do you know all this?"

"Gloria told me."

"Why?"

"Because I asked her."

"Is she a friend of yours?"

"No. But there's more." Somehow this was not going the way I'd hoped. I rushed on before he could ask any more questions. "At the time that he died, two of Rattigan's projects were being protested by different groups that were hoping to shut them down. There were the neighbors who didn't want the coffee bar conversion to take place, and also Preserve Our Wilderness—"

"The old Waldheim estate," said the detective. Now he looked almost bored. "We're aware of all that."

"Then you've spoken to John Monaghan?"

"We've spoken to everyone we feel we need to. Mr.

Monaghan's concern for the quality of life in his neighborhood seems quite understandable."

"Did he tell you that he and Marcus Rattigan were old friends? That they used to own a dog together?"

Not one for large gestures, this time Petrie lifted a brow. "One dog? For the both of them?"

"A show dog. Champion Wirerock Winter Fantasy. Monaghan was the breeder and Rattigan paid the bills so that she could have an extensive show career."

Petrie pulled out a pad of paper and made a note. "And this was a source of contention between them?"

"No. As far as I know, they got along fine and the dog did a lot of winning."

He laid down his pen. "So what's the problem?"

I tried to figure out how I could phrase what I wanted to say without dragging my brother into it. "Don't you think it's odd that Monaghan would organize a protest against a building owned by an old friend?"

"Perhaps a little. But no more so than that two friends could be Democrat and Republican, or black and white. Some friendships thrive on their differences."

I sat back and sighed. This wasn't getting me anywhere. "I guess you know that Rattigan and his secretary had an affair."

"We've interviewed Ms. Barnum several times. She said the relationship ended almost a year ago. We saw no reason not to believe her."

"Okay, I give up." As we'd talked I'd managed to

ball up my jacket in my lap. I shook it out and got ready to put it on. "Do you have *any* other suspects besides my brother?"

"I'm afraid I can't comment on that." Detective Petrie's voice was firm, but his eyes were sympathetic. "The investigation is still ongoing at this point. The best thing your brother can do is make sure he's told us everything he knows."

"I'll tell him." It hadn't escaped my notice, as I was sure it wasn't meant to, that this was the second time Petrie had implied that Frank might be holding something back.

The detective stood and extended a hand. "You do that."

When I reached the Brickmans' house, I could hear the noise coming from within as soon as I got out of the car. Of course it helped that the front door was standing open. I walked up and stuck my head inside. "Hello? Everyone alive in here?"

"Come on in," yelled Alice, her voice barely discernible above the din. Music from a CD warred with the Mario Brothers' theme and was punctuated by the shrieks of three children at play.

As I walked through the door, the two boys came flying into the hall and went up the stairs. A moment later, Joey's two-and-a-half-year-old sister, Carly, appeared, her chubby legs pumping hard as she ran after them. Seeing me, she slid to a stop.

"We're playing tag," she announced, touching my

arm, then jumping back. "You're it!"

Alice came walking in from the kitchen. "Ms. Travis doesn't want to play, honey. I think you'd better try and catch one of the boys." She looked up at me. "Shut that door, would you? Our oil bills are through the roof. Joey just can't seem to get it through his head that summer's actually over."

Alice was several years older than me, an age gap that would have seemed insurmountable in high school. Now, with all we had in common, it made no difference at all. She had beautiful strawberry blond hair, which she usually wore pulled back out of the way, and lightly freckled fair skin. Today she looked paler than usual.

I pushed the door closed and heard it latch. "You okay?"

"I'm just tired. You know how it is with kids. You start at dawn and it never lets up."

"Why didn't you tell me?" My tone was half accusing.

Alice and I had met in a neighborhood play group shortly after our sons were born, and quickly become friends. Over the years we'd covered for each other more times than I could count. I used her, and she used me. The reason the system worked so well was because we were scrupulously honest with each other when something wasn't convenient.

"It's no big deal," said Alice. "Come on in the kitchen and have a cup of coffee with me. That'll revive me."

"How's Joe?" I asked as I followed her to the back of the house. Like the rest of the homes on the street, the Brickmans' house was a Cape with a pretty basic floor plan. When Joe had started making some serious money at his law firm in Greenwich, they'd built an addition on the back that added a large family room to the first floor and another bedroom upstairs.

Much as I considered Alice one of my best friends, I hardly knew her husband at all. He worked long hours at his job and wasn't into socializing with Alice's friends when he got home.

"The same as always," said Alice. She set up the coffeemaker and turned it on. "Joe never changes, or if he does, he's not around enough for anyone to notice."

Ouch.

"Anything I can do?" I asked.

"Yeah, sit down and drink coffee with me and talk about something else."

That sounded easy enough. I took a seat at a built-in booth that had been added the same time as the family room, pushed Carly's crayons and coloring books out of the way, and told her about Marcus Rattigan's murder and my brother's involvement in the whole mess.

While I was talking, Alice put two mugs of steaming coffee and a carton of milk down on the table and joined me. By the time I'd finished, she'd brightened. "You know, that's what I like about you, Melanie. No matter how bad my life seems, you've always got something worse going on."

"Gee, thanks."

"No, really. You have a real talent for putting my problems into perspective. What's up with you and Sam these days?"

"A week ago I thought he was about to propose."

"That's great! Congratulations."

"Then he changed his mind."

"That's not allowed." Alice was outraged on my behalf. "If you want, I'll call him and tell him so."

I shook my head. "Even if he changed his mind back, I'm not sure what I'd say. We had a bit of a disagreement."

"Your first?"

"Pretty much so."

"So work things out."

Like Aunt Peg, Alice was a big fan of Sam's. Actually, so were all the women I knew. And while the physical aspect certainly played a part, I knew there was more to it than that. Sam was smart and kind and fun to be around. He loved children and animals. He wasn't perfect but he came closer than any other man I'd known.

"I've been waiting for him to call me," I said glumly. "I've been an idiot, haven't I?"

"Yup."

"How about you?" I countered. "Are you going to work things out with Joe?"

"Of course I am. Do I look stupid to you?" There was a thunderous noise on the stairs as the three kids came running down into the kitchen. "Can you imagine me trying to find someone else willing to be saddled with those two?"

"Sure," I said, grinning.

"You're either an optimist or a liar."

"Put me down as an optimist," I said. "It sounds better."

"Hey, Mom!" cried Davey.

"Hey what?"

"What's for dinner?"

The eternal question. "Wait and see," I said. That's the answer I use when I have no idea but I'm hoping to find something interesting in the freezer. I got up and carried my mug over to the sink. "Is Joe coming home for dinner?"

"He said he would." Alice shrugged. "Men."

I glanced at the boys. "Think ours will grow up to be any different?"

Joey had a light saber he was swinging around the room with abandon. Davey ducked just in time as the toy passed over his head and narrowly missed sweeping the milk carton off the table.

"Maybe." Alice sighed. "If they live that long."

Eighteen

The next day at school, I ducked out again during lunch. Yankee pot roast was on the menu, and its delicious aroma had been wafting through the halls all morning. For the sake of my stomach and my job, I hoped this kind of truant behavior didn't get to be a habit.

As I saw it, the only way I stood a chance of seeing Ben Welch was if I presented myself at Anaconda Properties and refused to take no for an answer. Liz Barnum could bar my access forever by phone. In person I might be able to make a more persuasive case.

Liz was sitting at her desk and talking on the telephone when I arrived. She stared balefully in my direction and took her time about ending the call. By the time she hung up, I was leaning my hip against her desk and eavesdropping shamelessly. Too bad she wasn't talking about anything interesting.

"I'd like to see Ben Welch," I said as soon as she put the receiver down.

"He isn't available."

"That's what you told me yesterday."

Liz smiled condescendingly. "That's because he wasn't available then, either. If you'd care to leave a message . . . ?"

She would write it down and drop it into the wastebasket as soon as I left, I thought. "Why are you protecting him?"

"I'm not. I'm simply telling you the truth. Ben isn't available. He isn't even here."

So much for my grand plan to storm his office if she wouldn't let me by.

"It seems like he's been out of the office a lot lately." Acting on a hunch, I added, "I guess he's been with Gloria."

Liz's smile froze. "I doubt that."

"I don't. I gather they've been spending quite a lot of time together."

"They have business to discuss—"

"I'm sure they do. But that's not all that keeps Ben busy when he's with Gloria."

Her fingers had been tapping an irritated rhythm on the desktop. Now her hand stilled. "Do you know what you're talking about, or are you just trying to annoy me?"

"I know enough."

She glanced down the hallway, then she pushed back her chair and stood. "Let's go into Marcus's office. I'd rather talk privately."

Once there, Liz shut the door carefully behind us. "I don't think much of innuendo, so let's get straight to facts. I know you've been asking a lot of questions. What exactly have you found out?"

"Not so fast," I said. "Before I tell you anything, we're going to make a deal. I'm damn sick and tired of running around in circles. I'm neglecting my job, my boyfriend's mad at me, and I've barely had a chance to walk my own dog. I'll tell you what I know but only if you agree to do the same for me."

Liz thought for a moment, then nodded grudgingly. "I guess that's fair enough."

I stuck out my hand. She looked surprised but didn't hesitate, and we shook on the matter.

"Did you ever wonder how Gloria found out about your affair with Marcus?" I asked.

"No, not really. I just assumed he'd slipped up somewhere. Maybe I was hoping that subconsciously he'd wanted to be found out."

"So that Gloria would have a reason to divorce him?" Liz nodded.

"She wouldn't have, you know. Gloria's the type of woman who wants desperately to be married. If she had to overlook a few transgressions on the part of her husband, I'm sure she could have managed it. Anyway, Rattigan didn't get careless. Gloria told me herself that she had a spy in the company."

"A spy?" Liz snorted. "How very dramatic. It sounds just like something Gloria would think of."

"Apparently she wasn't the first to come up with the idea. She claims that Rattigan had their servants keeping tabs on her, and that she was only retaliating."

The phone began to ring in the reception area. Liz seemed oblivious. "What does any of this have to do with Ben?"

"He's the one she chose to do her dirty work."

"No." Her tone was emphatic. "Ben wouldn't have done something like that."

"How do you know?"

"Because . . . because . . ." Liz's hands flailed ineffectually.

She seemed to be taking things personally, which made me think that my hunch had been right. Gloria wasn't the only one who'd been looking for a successor after she lost Marcus, and Ben Welch had been even busier than I originally suspected.

"Marcus was the one who gave Ben his start in business," said Liz. "The two of them weren't just co-workers, they were friends. I can't believe he would have hurt Marcus that way."

"According to Gloria, she offered extra incentives. Their relationship doesn't end with business."

"Gloria's a liar!"

"She's not lying about this. Now that Rattigan's gone, she's planning to keep the company and let Ben run it."

Liz struggled to regain her composure. "She hasn't made any announcement to that effect."

"No, but Ben knows."

"He doesn't know anything of the sort. If he did, he would have told me."

"Are you sure? Obviously he hasn't told you everything. No matter how close your relationship is." I gazed out the window and let the thought dangle.

"I know what you're thinking," Liz snapped. "You're thinking I went straight from Rattigan's bed to Ben's, but it wasn't like that. Believe me, it wasn't like that at all."

She began to walk around the room, letting her fingers glide softly over familiar objects. "Ben was the one who courted me. He knew what had happened with Marcus, of course. He offered me consolation, and a shoulder to cry on. It all started very innocently. We had lunch together a couple of times a week. From there, our feelings for each other just grew."

"So that's why you didn't leave the company after

Marcus ended your affair?"

"Partly, I suppose. But mostly because I have a damn good job here. Salary, benefits, and a lot of responsibility. I'd have had a hard time matching that anywhere else."

Last time she'd insisted that ending their relationship had been a mutual decision. This time, I noticed, she hadn't corrected me. This lying thing was getting to be an epidemic. Not that I was immune certainly, but didn't anyone tell the truth anymore?

"Tell me about the day Rattigan died," I said.

Liz stopped wandering. She squared her shoulders and faced me. I was glad to see that anger seemed to be shoring up the chinks I'd made in her facade. "What about it?"

"Why did Rattigan go to the coffee bar that evening?"

"I don't know."

"You told the police that he had an appointment with Frank."

"I'm well aware of that," Liz said stiffly.

"I imagine you're also aware that the police have been treating my brother as their chief suspect, at least partly as a result of what you told them."

"Frank *did* call here that day. All I did was embellish a bit. At the time I thought I had a good reason."

"Which was?"

She grimaced slightly. "Ben didn't have an alibi for the time Marcus was killed. He'd taken some work home from the office and spent the whole night by himself in his apartment going over some plans."

"Did he ask you to cover for him?"

"No, it was nothing like that. It just occurred to me that naturally the police would be looking into Ben's whereabouts. I thought that it wouldn't hurt to shift some of the blame in another direction."

"You thought it *wouldn't hurt?*" Lord, was I steamed. If I were a cartoon character, there would have been smoke coming out of my ears. "What made you choose my brother as your scapegoat?"

"That part was obvious." Aware of my annoyance, Liz was treading lightly now. "Frank is such a sweetheart. I thought anyone would be able to tell that he couldn't have done it. Besides, it's not like he had anything to gain from Marcus's death."

Little did she know, I thought. It was beginning to look as though half the town of Stamford had had something to gain from Rattigan's murder.

Liz walked toward the door. "Listen, when you see Frank, tell him I'm sorry, okay? I never thought the whole thing would cause this much trouble for him. Honest."

"I'll tell him," I said tightly. The phone was ringing again and a glance at my watch confirmed that I had barely twenty minutes to get back to school before my next class. "Are you going to tell Detective Petrie about this, or am I?"

"I will," Liz said. "Don't worry, I'll call him as soon as you leave. Actually, it'll be a relief. I've been kind of worried about lying to the police. As for Ben, that snake, he can take his chances."

We walked out of the office together. Whoever had been calling had given up. For once, the phone was silent.

"Speaking of Ben," I said. "Do you think he knew about Rattigan's will? That he'd never gotten around to changing it after the divorce?"

"I doubt it. I can't imagine it's the kind of thing they'd have ever discussed."

"Did Marcus keep a copy of his will here in the office?"

"Sure. I remember the last time he updated it about five years ago. The damn document went back and forth to the lawyer's office a dozen times before everyone was satisfied. Then Marcus had four copies made up. One stayed with the lawyer, one went into his safe-deposit box, one he took home, and the other was put with all his legal papers here."

"Do you mind if I have a look at it?"

"It's confidential," said Liz.

"I won't tell, if you won't."

She thought for a moment, then shrugged. She opened a drawer in her desk and took out a small key. I followed her to a cubicle down the hall. The tiny room had a whole wall of file cabinets, but only one was locked. She took the key, fitted it to the lock, and slid the drawer open.

Liz thumbed through the folders from front to back, then frowned and started over. "It isn't here."

"Could it have gotten misfiled?"

The look Liz gave me could have charred stone. "Maybe the police have it?"

"No, they don't. I kept a record of everything they took, and I know I would have remembered." She shut the drawer and relocked it.

"What about Ben? Does he have a key to these files?"

"Of course he does. Ben has access to everything. Marcus trusted him implicitly."

We were both silent then, and I knew we were thinking the same thing. That trust could have cost Marcus Rattigan his life.

I made it back to Howard Academy with only moments to spare. As I flew across the parking lot and in the back door, I could hear the bell ringing. Shedding my coat as I ran, I rounded a corner and didn't see Russell Hanover until I'd nearly plowed right into him.

"Well, hello!" He reached out with both hands, grasping my shoulders to steady me. "Running late, are we?" His deep voice placed heavy emphasis on the word running.

"Just a bit." I raked back my hair and tried out a smile.

"We've missed you at lunch the last two days. You do understand we feel quite strongly about our teachers taking the opportunity to interact with their students outside of class?"

"Yes, of course. It's an excellent idea." And would

be even better if we weren't expected to monitor their table manners at the same time.

"There's nothing amiss, is there?"

"No, I just had some business to take care of." Somehow I couldn't see trying to explain to Russell Hanover that my brother was a suspect in a murder investigation. He'd probably be shocked to his well-bred, New England core. "It won't happen again."

"Quite right," Russell agreed, continuing down the hall.

The rest of the afternoon sped by. My students were prompt, well prepared, and eager to learn. One boy proudly displayed a written report we'd worked on together that had earned him a B, the highest grade he'd ever achieved. I hugged him briefly, then let him do a victory dance around the room while I ran the title page of the report through the copier. I hung it, grade prominently displayed, on the bulletin board behind my desk.

It's good to have a day like that every so often to remind me why I became a teacher in the first place.

Promptly at 3:15 P.M., I arrived at Hunting Ridge to pick up the boys. With Halloween a week away, they were arguing over who had the better costume planned. The year before, Davey had been a fireman in a big yellow slicker and red rubber boots. This year he was aiming for a more macho look.

"Batman's no big deal," Joey scoffed at my son's costume. "I'm going to be Dracula. I'll have a cape and fangs that drip blood."

"I'll have a cape, too," Davey defended his choice. "And a cowl and my very own Batmobile."

That got Joey's attention. "You don't drive."

"No, but I have a model. My mom said I could carry it."

"I'm sure you're both going to look great," I said. "What are the other kids going to be?"

The discussion of costumes, and the parade that would take place at their school on that day, carried us the rest of the way home. As I turned onto our road, I glanced automatically toward the house. There was a car parked in the driveway. Not Frank's black sports car, thank God, this was a blue Ford Blazer.

Sam's car.

"Hey!" Davey cried from the backseat. "Sam's here!" Joey sat up and craned his neck to look.

"I hope he brought Tar!"

As the car rolled to a stop, Davey was already unfastening his seat belt. He and Joey spilled out of the car and hit the ground running. Sam opened his door and got out. He had indeed brought Tar with him and the puppy joined the boys in the yard.

For a moment I hung back, feeling uncertain. Then I realized Sam was doing the same thing.

He was wearing faded corduroy pants, with a wheat colored roll-neck sweater and a denim jacket thrown on top. The wind had ruffled through his blond hair and when he looked in my direction, I noticed the squint lines that fanned out around his eyes. He was everything I'd hoped for, and more than I'd ever expected to find.

I resisted the impulse to throw myself into his arms and opted for the mature approach instead. After all, there were children present. "I was going to call you."

"I was going to call you, too," Sam said. "Then I realized I couldn't say what I needed to say over the phone. So here I am. I'm sorry. I was stupid."

"Yeah, you were. So was I."

"So what are we going to do about it?"

"Kiss and make up?" I suggested.

"I was hoping you'd say that." Two long strides and I was in his arms. "God, you smell good," he murmured.

"Hey, Sam." Joey tugged on Sam's jacket.

He had to give a second yank before Sam paid any attention. Let's just say I had him distracted. When Sam finally glanced down, Joey waved a hand toward the street. "Isn't that your puppy?"

While we'd been occupied, Tar had spotted a pair of neighborhood dogs running loose at the end of the block and decided to join them. Now he was galloping down the sidewalk with Davey racing in pursuit. Though he was only four months old, the puppy's legs were long and he was covering a surprising amount of ground.

"Damn!" Sam thrust me away. He put his fingers to his lips and whistled shrilly.

Tar's stride never even wavered. Davey's did, though. He turned to look back at us, tripped over a seam in the sidewalk, and went down in a heap.

I was already running, but Sam passed me as though

I were standing still. He reached Davey first, paused briefly, then raced on to scoop up his puppy, who was now cavorting in the street with his newfound friends. Luckily, there were no cars coming.

When I reached Davey, he'd already pushed himself up into a sitting position. His palms were scraped, and there was a new hole in the knee of his jeans.

"Cool!" he said, hopefully inspecting the opening for signs of blood. There wasn't any. He reexamined his palms and held them up so I could see. "Do you think I'll get a scar?"

I started to shake my head, but Sam came up behind me with Tar cradled happily in his arms, and poked me before I could respond. "Could be," he said. "Those are some awesome scratches."

Awesome? Once I cleaned the sand off we'd be lucky to even see them.

Sam held out a hand and pulled Davey to his feet. "Thanks for trying to catch him for me."

"Sure. I didn't want him to get run over or anything."

"Good thought," Sam agreed seriously.

They headed down the sidewalk together, leaving me to follow along behind. When we got back to the house, Joey was sitting on the steps. Faith was barking and throwing herself against the front door, a breach of manners meant to illustrate her displeasure at missing out on the fun.

Joey turned to Davey. "So are we going to play, or what?"

My son looked back and forth between Sam and his friend, clearly torn.

"You're going to play," I said. "Sam's going to be here awhile, right?"

He nodded.

"The two of you can hang out later after Joey goes home."

We went inside; me to console Faith with a belly rub and several extra biscuits, the boys racing upstairs to check out Davey's Batmobile model, and Tar to drink half a bowl of water, then flop over on his side on the kitchen floor.

I opened the back door and let Faith into the fenced yard, and turned around to find Sam pulling something out of the mail I'd thrown on the counter. "Look what came." He held up a flat, white, cardboard envelope.

"What is it?"

"Your win picture from the dog show."

"Great!" I snatched it from him and ripped open the flap.

"It might not be great," he said, peering over my shoulder. "Lots of them aren't. It's hard to photograph a black dog indoors and get the lighting just right."

Slowly I withdrew the picture from the inner sleeve. Faith looked good, her silhouette outlined by the blue skirt I'd worn specifically to contrast with her inky coat. Her head and tail were up, and her gaze was fixed alertly on the squeaky toy the photographer had thrown, just out of range, a moment before he snapped the photo. The judge was holding out the ribbons Faith had won and smiling proudly.

Then I saw myself, wearing a goofy grin and looking stunned to be there. "Oh." My shoulders slumped.

"What's the matter?" Sam took the picture. "I think it's good."

"I look like I'm in shock."

"As I recall, you were. Don't worry, nobody looks at the person. The dog's what matters in these pictures and Faith looks terrific."

Maybe there was a compliment in there. If so, I couldn't find it.

Dinner was hot dogs. As I told Sam, people who want gourmet meals shouldn't drop in unexpectedly. He ate three hot dogs and two helpings of baked beans and insisted they were the best he'd ever had. I doubted that, but I was in much too good a mood to argue.

After dinner Davey asked Sam to bring Tar up to his bedroom. Curious, Faith and I went along, too. Davey opened the top drawer in his desk and took out a dog biscuit.

"I've been saving this," he said. "The tooth fairy brought it and I was going to give it to Tar since it was his tooth. But when I got up the next morning, you were gone.

Sam and I exchanged a glance over my son's head.

"I'm back now."

"Are you going to stay?" Davey's tone was strident.

Another time I might have corrected him. Now I was too busy waiting to hear what Sam would answer.

"Yes," he promised. "I'm going to stay."

Nineteen

I should have known a mood like that would be too good to last. The next morning when I got to school, I found out just how short-lived it could be. I had Kate and Lucia for third period and when the two of them entered the classroom, Kate was skipping in place and ginning broadly.

"What's up?" I asked.

"I hope she tells you," said Lucia. "She won't say a word to me."

"That's because it has nothing to do with you." Kate put her books down and turned to me. "I did what you told me to."

I thought back quickly. "You reread those short stories Miss Scott assigned?" Could redoing an English assignment be the cause for this much excitement?

"No!" Kate squealed, then quickly lowered her voice. "I found out about Winter's puppies!"

With everything else that had been going on recently, I'd forgotten all about that. "You talked to John?"

Kate nodded. "I just casually brought it up the other day after school. John was showing me how to strip a terrier. The dog he was working on was one of Winter's great-grandchildren, so it was easy to get the conversation started."

Lucia was still listening in. "What do you mean he stripped it? He cut off all its hair?"

"No. Well, kind of. But not really." Kate frowned and gave up.

I'd never seen the grooming procedure done, but I knew enough to offer a layman's explanation. "Wire Fox Terriers are supposed to have a very harsh outer coat. If you clipped them or scissored the hair like you do with Poodles, it would ruin the texture. So instead the coat is hand plucked, with the groomer pulling out very small amounts of hair each time. The process is called stripping."

"Big deal," said Lucia.

"You asked," Kate pointed out.

"I thought it was going to be something interesting."

"It is interesting."

If I didn't intercede now, they'd spend the next fifteen minutes arguing. "Lucia, do you have your book report ready for me to look at?"

"Almost."

I pointed toward the table. "Why don't you work on it while Kate and I finish this up?"

"How come I have to work and she doesn't?"

"How come her book report is done and yours isn't?"

No dummy, Lucia quickly saw the wisdom in not trying to answer that question. She took her backpack over to the table and sat down.

So that we wouldn't disturb her, Kate and I crossed

the room to stand by the windows. "So what did John say?" I asked.

"It was really weird. I figured he'd tell me that he'd sold one of the puppies, or that I was mixed up, or that ten years later, who cared anyway? But he didn't. He got this really strange look on his face and he said it was none of my business. Then he told me he thought I should go home."

Uh oh. "And did you?"

"Well, yeah, sure. I mean, what choice did I have? It's his kennel. Usually John likes having me around because he says that I'm a big help, but if he wants me to leave . . ."

"I'm really sorry, Kate. I never meant to cause trouble for you."

"Don't worry. Everything turned out okay. Maybe even better than okay, because I got the information you wanted. It was really cool!"

Kate looked smug. I hoped that wasn't a bad sign. I flipped the latch and opened the window to let in some fresh air. "What do you mean?"

"Yesterday when I got home from school, John had left a message with my mom. He had to go into the city for the day so he wanted me to check on the dogs in the afternoon. You know, make sure everyone had fresh water and pick up the runs?"

I knew how that went. I'd been pressed into service a few times at Aunt Peg's myself.

"So, of course, I went over and everything was fine."

"How did you get into the kennel? Do you have a key?"

"No," said Kate. "That's the cool part. John keeps a spare key to the kennel hidden in his garage. I've used it plenty of times before, so I knew just where to look. He keeps an extra key to the house in the same place."

She stood there and smiled, waiting for me to make the connection. It didn't take long.

"You didn't!" I cried, horrified.

"Why not? Like I said, John was acting really strange, and all I could think was, maybe he had something to hide. So I went in and looked."

Oh, lordy. I winced slightly, half afraid that lightning was about to strike me dead for corrupting the youth of America.

"It was great!" Kate giggled. "Sneaking around, opening up drawers, and trying not to leave any fingerprints. I felt like Nancy Drew."

"You're not Nancy Drew," I said sternly. "And you shouldn't have done that."

"Why not? John asked me to look after the dogs. For all I know, he might have left one in the house."

"You're justifying."

"And you're curious." Kate grinned. "You want to know what I found out, don't you?"

"Of course I want to know. I just don't want you to think that I approve of your methods. Good God, what would Mr. Hanover say?"

"About what?" asked Lucia, tuning back into the

conversation from her seat on the other side of the room.

"Nothing!" Kate and I said in emphatic unison.

She was still smiling. I didn't know whether to kiss the girl or yell at her some more. Then again, the yelling didn't seem to be having much effect.

"Okay," I said in a lower tone. "What did you find out?"

"For one thing, John is about the most organized man in the whole world. He keeps all his papers in a cabinet in his library and everything was labeled so I could see just where to look. He had two whole drawers just for his dog stuff. One was filled with a stack of notebooks that said Dog Ownership and Breeding Records on the front."

"I've seen those," I said. "My Aunt Peg breeds Standard Poodles and she has the same ones. The American Kennel Club hands them out. The AKC is very particular about how records are maintained because they need to know that pedigrees are correct and that dogs that are supposed to be purebred, actually are."

Kate nodded. "John had everything filled out and up to date. He even had the book covers labeled by year so all I had to do was flip back through until I found the one that had Winter's litter in it."

That was all. If you didn't count entering the house illegally, that is. I held my tongue and let her continue.

"There's a separate page in the back for each litter," said Kate. "And then an individual listing for each puppy down below. On the page for Winter's litter, the names of three puppies were written in, and John had checked off the column saying he'd kept each one."

"Then Roger Nye was wrong," I mused aloud.

"Who's he?"

"A man I met who thought he had one of Winter's puppies. He'd gotten her from Marcus Rattigan, Winter's co-owner."

"The man who was murdered in your brother's building."

I looked at her sharply. "How do you know that?"

"I read about it in the paper."

"The papers mentioned Frank's name, but none of the articles identified him as my brother. How did you know about that?"

"Jeez." Kate sighed loudly. "It's not like you're the only one who can figure things out, you know."

Apparently not. The realization came with a bit of a jolt. It wouldn't hurt to keep an eye on this girl.

"You didn't let me finish," she said.

"There's more?"

"Lots more. And it gets even stranger."

"I'm all done." Lucia pushed back her chair and stood up. "Do you want to look at my book report now?"

"In one minute, okay?"

Lucia cocked her hip and propped her hand on it. She was being ignored, and there was only so long she'd stand for that. "What do you want me to do in the meantime?"

"Write a short descriptive piece," I said off the top

of my head. "Use lots of adjectives and similes."

"What do you want me to describe?"

"Anything you want."

"Okay." She sat back down. "I'll do Mark."

A detailed description of her horse. That was just what the world needed.

"Quick," I said to Kate, feeling like a co-conspirator. "Tell me the rest."

"Remember I said that there were two drawers with kennel records? The other one was filled with big manila envelopes, one for each dog. Mostly they held things like pedigrees, registration slips, health records. But Winter's had some other things. There were a couple of Best in Show pictures and a certificate from when she won the Quaker Oats award. And there was something else, too—an unused blue slip with her name listed as dam."

Blue slips are the forms that the American Kennel Club returns to a breeder after a litter is registered. The breeder reports how many puppies of each sex have been born and the AKC sends a blue slip for each one. These slips are then given to the puppies' new owners, who fill them out and send them in to complete the individual registration process.

"When Winter's litter was born, John must have originally told the AKC there were four puppies, so they sent him four slips," I said, thinking aloud. "Then later, for some reason, he decided to only register three of them."

"Pretty weird, huh?" said Kate.

"Really weird," I agreed.

I wondered what the hell it meant.

After school I picked up Davey and Faith and we went to see Aunt Peg. I wish I could say that the visit was my idea, prompted by familial loyalty and a sense of devotion to aging relatives; but the truth of the matter was Aunt Peg had left a message on my answering machine telling me to get my butt over to her house that afternoon, or else. When we arrived, Frank was there. His car was in the driveway and I parked beside it.

"It's about time," said Peg, opening the door and releasing the tidal wave of black Standard Poodles. Faith was swept down the steps with them and the group raced around the yard, all flying legs and ears.

"I just got home from school."

"That explains earlier today. What about Monday, Tuesday, and Wednesday?"

"I was busy."

"As if that's an excuse." She looked down at Davey. "Who's this fine young man?"

"It's me, Aunt Peg." My son giggled. "Davey!"

"You're not Davey. You're much too tall."

"No, really!" Davey shrieked. "It's me."

Aunt Peg pretended to consider. "Have you been growing? Soon you'll be as big as I am."

My son's eyes opened wide. "Nobody's as big as you—"

I jabbed him in the shoulder, but I wasn't quick enough.

"What?" asked Davey, looking injured. "Nobody *is*."

"Hey, gang." Frank appeared in the hallway. "Why didn't you tell me the meeting was taking place outside?"

"What meeting?" I asked as Aunt Peg called the dogs and ushered everybody in. Davey and the Poodles ran on ahead to the kitchen.

"Frank brought me a cake from the St. Moritz bakery," she said. Sweets always distract her. Maybe she was hoping I wouldn't notice the change in subject. "Wasn't that nice of him?"

"That depends. What did he want in return?"

"Mel." Frank groaned. "Don't be like that."

"Like what?"

"Like a big sister—"

"Quit squabbling," Peg said sternly. "We have bigger things to worry about than the fact you two don't like each other."

That brought me up short. "Who said we don't like each other?" I demanded, glaring at my brother.

"Not me." He held out his hands innocently. "Who just called me a user?"

"That would be me," I informed him. "The usee."

"Very funny," said Frank. "Nobody asked you to get involved."

The enormity of that lie left me gasping. Even Aunt Peg looked a bit nonplused.

"That's quite enough from both of you," she said. "I asked you here because I thought it was high time we got together and hashed things out.

"Now you have two choices. Either we're going into the kitchen to have a piece of cake and discuss this problem calmly and rationally, or you can stand here and continue to argue in which case I'll probably feel compelled to knock your two heads together. As Davey so recently pointed out, I'm big enough to do it. Which will it be?"

Well, that let us know where we stood.

"Cake for me," said Frank, grinning devilishly. He hooked his arm through mine. "How about you, sis? It's mocha."

Luckily, we're not the kind of siblings that hold grudges. Tempers fade as quickly as they tend to flare. Besides, Frank knew darn well that mocha cake was my favorite.

"Cake, it is," I agreed.

With cake and milk on a tray in front of him, Davey was happy to be banished to the family room. We adults sat at the kitchen table. With a thick wedge of St. Moritz's wonderful mocha cake in front of me, I brought Frank and Aunt Peg up to date about what was going on.

"I can't believe it," said Frank. "Marcus was really planning to cut out and leave me holding the bag?"

"It looks that way. And I doubt if Ben Welch is any more trustworthy. Or Gloria Rattigan, for that matter. If I were you, I'd watch my step with those two."

"I sure don't see them as a couple." Frank was skeptical. "She's got to be ten years older than he is. If you ask me, Ben and Liz make more sense."

"They did for a little while. At least until Liz found out what Ben was up to." I smiled innocently. "From what I've been able to find out about Ben, he's looking for two things in a woman: money and power. And thanks to Rattigan's murder, Gloria now has both."

"Do you think she wanted them badly enough to commit murder?" said Aunt Peg.

"You could ask the same about Ben." I glanced at my brother. "By the way, Liz has admitted she lied when she told the police you'd left a message. Rattigan didn't have an appointment to meet you at the coffee bar that evening."

"So why was he there?" asked Frank.

"When we figure that out, we'll probably know who killed him." I cut off a large bite of cake and slipped it into my mouth. "Here's something else that's strange," I said to Peg. "Dog stuff."

Frank rolled his eyes.

"Remember Asta, Roger Nye's Fox Terrier? The one he said he got from Rattigan? In all likelihood, she was one of Winter's offspring. There *were* four puppies in that litter, although for some reason, John Monaghan decided to register only three."

"I wonder why." Peg frowned. "You saw the bitch. She didn't have any visible deformity, did she?"

"No, I thought she was cute. And Roger was obviously besotted with her."

"So thanks to Marcus Rattigan, she got a good

home. But what reason could John have had for not keeping her? Did you ask him?"

"A friend of his asked him for me. John got angry and refused to discuss it.

"Maybe you should try asking Gloria Rattigan. She might know something."

"I *did* ask her. The only thing she knows is that she doesn't like dogs and won't allow them in her house."

"Oh." Peg's tone was disparaging. Clearly Gloria had just dropped another notch in her estimation.

"So what?" Frank said impatiently. "Dogs in the house. Dogs out of the house. Who cares? It doesn't matter a fig as far as Marcus's murder is concerned. Let's all try and focus for a minute, okay?

"My life is in chaos. I can't even go back into the coffee bar because the police have wrapped the whole place up in yellow tape. How can the two of you possibly think this is a good time to sit around and talk about dogs?"

"We're predictable that way," said Aunt Peg, her voice deceptively mild. "What would you have us talk about?"

With a show of great patience, as if he were addressing second graders, my brother said, "You have to look for a motive."

"Motive?" she repeated. "Like anger? Or money? Or maybe potential humiliation?"

"All of those."

Peg and I looked at each other. Frank had never been included before when we'd sat down and discussed a murder. Now we both knew why.

"We've already found the person who has those motives," I told my brother. "That part was easy."

"Easy?" Frank yelped. "Who is it?"

I shook my head and told him. "You."

Idiot.

Twenty

Later that night after Davey was asleep, I gave Roger Nye a call.

I've poked around in murder investigations before, and I've found that what works for me is to start by asking lots of questions and then look for the bits and pieces of information that don't fit in. I think of the process as a giant jigsaw puzzle. Some of the pieces fall into place naturally. Others have to be twisted and turned to make them work.

Then there are those few that simply refuse to be part of my big picture in any logical way. As far as I could figure out, everything I knew about Champion Wirerock Winter Fantasy and her only litter of puppies fit into that category. There was definitely a discrepancy between what John Monaghan professed publicly about his bitch and what had to be true.

Not knowing why was like having an itch I couldn't scratch. John wasn't talking. Gloria didn't have the information I needed. It was too late for Rattigan to be any use at all. That left me with Roger Nye. I hoped he had something interesting to say because I was fast running out of options.

He picked up the phone on the fourth ring, and sounded impatient before I even said a word. It took me a minute to convince him that I was neither offering free credit nor soliciting funds for charity, but when I reminded him about Davey playing with the trains and asked after Asta, he grew less wary.

"I just have a few questions," I said quickly. "I hope that's okay."

"We still talking about Marcus Rattigan?"

"Kind of. More about Asta actually."

"Asta?" He lowered his voice to a croon. "Good girl. You're a good girl. Can you believe that?" he asked me. "She looked up when I said her name. What's my dog got to do with anything?"

"I'm not actually sure. You said that Marcus Rattigan gave her to you when she was a puppy?"

"That's right. She was just a tiny thing, all hair and eyes. I wasn't sure I wanted a puppy, but Millie fell for her like a ton of bricks, so that was that."

"I was wondering whether you know how Rattigan came to have her in the first place. And why he wanted to give her away?"

"After all this time, who remembers a thing like that? Why don't you check with Gloria? She might know."

Damn. Another dead end. "I did ask Gloria. She didn't know anything about Asta. She told me they'd never had any dogs in the house because she wouldn't allow it."

"That sounds about right," said Roger. "Not that I want to say anything against Gloria. She's a fine woman, and God only knows how she put up with a man like Marcus all those years, but she is particular about that house."

"You said that your wife was the one who was really taken with the puppy. Is there a possibility she might remember?"

Roger took so long to reply that I knew I'd said something wrong.

"Millie passed away two years ago," he said finally.

"I'm sorry."

"I'm sorry, too." Roger sighed. "Finding Millie was the best thing that ever happened to me. We had nearly thirty years together, so I guess I was pretty lucky. I still think about her every day. Do you know how I remember her best?"

I'd intruded on his memories; the least I could do was let him talk about it. "How?"

"She used to carry her needlepoint outside and sit under the dogwoods to work on it. Warm weather, cool weather, she never seemed to mind. Spring was her favorite, though, when the dogwoods were in bloom and everything smelled so nice. Millie said just being there made her feel closer to the kids when they were so far away. After she was gone . . ."

Roger's voice broke. He cleared his throat and, after a moment, started again. "After she was gone, when spring came around again, I thought I might try sitting out there myself. See if she was right, see if it made me feel closer to her."

Roger paused again. I heard him blow his nose. "When I went out there, that's when I realized that the trees were dying. I'll tell you, that just hit me like a ton of bricks. I'd have given anything to bring them back. But I couldn't save them any more than I could save my Millie. Losing them was like losing her all over again."

"I'm very sorry," I said once more.

"Now maybe you understand. Marcus Rattigan was a terrible man. I'm glad he's dead and I hope he rots in hell."

I hung up the phone and went upstairs to check on Davey. The moon outside threw a shaft of light across his bedroom and I could see that he was sleeping peacefully, one arm curled around Faith, who was lying by his side. Their two heads shared the pillow. Faith thumped her tail up and down in greeting but didn't stir otherwise.

I hadn't planted any trees when my son was born. At the time I was struggling to come to grips with the deaths of my parents, killed together in a car wreck several months earlier. Davey's birth had helped me to deal with the sense of loss; he had filled in the empty places in my heart and made me feel whole again.

Would I kill to defend him? I was quite certain I would. Could someone, fueled by anger and grief, commit murder over the loss of a loved one's memories? I hoped I'd never have to find out.

• • •

Occasionally when I sleep on a problem, the answer presents itself in the morning. It isn't a foolproof system, unfortunately; but when it works it's a veritable epiphany. I went to bed that night thinking I'd never find out why John had lied about Winter's litter and when I woke up Friday morning, I realized that I'd been looking at things all wrong.

I'd asked Gloria about the puppy because she'd been living with Rattigan at the time. Why on earth was I assuming that the wife would know? Men don't talk to their wives. My own marriage had been living proof of that. Men talk to their secretaries and their mistresses.

Applying that theory, the answer should have been obvious. The person I needed to see was Liz Barnum.

After my run-in with the headmaster on Wednesday, I didn't dare sneak out of class for so much as a phone call. And due to the early dismissal, the lunch period was shortened, as well. After school I was supposed to be bathing Faith in anticipation of Saturday's dog show. Washing and blowing dry a Standard Poodle coat—and doing the job right—takes three or four hours. I'd planned to get started before Davey came home so that I could finish by dinnertime.

I knew all that, but it didn't seem to matter. Promptly at two o'clock, I found myself racing out to the parking lot, hopping in the Volvo, and speeding to downtown Stamford. When my son's in the car I try to set a good example. When he isn't, I'm not above cranking up the radio and breaking a few rules.

When I got to the offices of Anaconda Properties, the door was standing open and Liz wasn't behind her desk. Though I could hear the hum of various machines working in other parts of the office suite, the reception area was empty. As I was debating what to do next, the door to the ladies' room down the hall swung open and Liz came hurrying out.

She was rubbing her lips together to smooth her lipstick and as she strode past me, I caught a whiff of smoke that clung to her clothing and hair. She yanked open the top drawer to her desk, palmed a pack of cigarettes inside, then slammed it shut.

"Bathroom break," Liz said as she sat down.

"I didn't know you smoked."

"I don't." She stared up at me defiantly. "The whole building's smoke free."

"Even the ladies' room?"

"Damn. Does it smell that much?"

"Enough," I said. "New habit?"

"Old habit." She grimaced. "I gave it up years ago."

"What made you start again?"

"Stress. Smoking's a great pacifier. Don't ever let anyone tell you it isn't."

Three chrome-and-canvas chairs were grouped around a glass topped table. I pulled one over beside the desk and sat down. "Stress over Rattigan's murder?"

Liz shrugged. "I was handling that. Hell, I thought I was handling everything. Then Ben told me it wouldn't be a bad idea to update my resume."

"He's firing you?"

"Of course not. At least not in so many words." Liz reached up self-consciously and smoothed back her long hair. "He just said he wanted me to be prepared. You know, in case."

"In case Gloria decided to exercise her rights as chief stockholder?"

"Something like that."

"You went to bat for Ben," I mentioned. "It'd be nice of him to do the same for you."

"Yes, well, as I've discovered lately, Ben Welch isn't exactly the *nicest* man I've ever known. Maybe I should thank you for that."

Her tone was brittle and there were spots of color in her cheeks. I decided not to hold my breath while I waited for gratitude.

"How long have you worked for Anaconda?" I asked.

"Since the very beginning, almost. Marcus decided to form his own company fourteen years ago. I was one of the first people he hired." Liz's eyes narrowed. "And if they think they can just dump me now without a fight, they can think again."

"Is there a chance you might remember something that happened about ten years ago?"

"Probably," said Liz. "There wasn't much that went on around here that I didn't know about."

Big talk. I wondered if she was trying to convince me, or herself. Or whether she really was stockpiling a list of grievances to fight back with.

"Back in those days, Rattigan was involved with a number of show dogs. Were you aware of that?"

"Are you kidding? When Marcus got interested in something, he threw himself into it whole hog. For a while he had pictures and ribbons hanging on the walls in his office. We even had some of those glossy dog magazines sitting out here on the table." Liz chuckled, remembering. "I'll tell you, some of the clients really looked twice at those."

"Did you ever see any of the dogs?"

"You mean like real? In person?" She shook her head, and my shoulders slumped. "They didn't stay with Marcus. Most of them had handlers or co-owners that they lived with. I don't think Marcus even saw the dogs himself unless he went to a dog show."

"I was wondering about one dog in particular." No point in stopping now. Liz was my last shot. "She was a Wire Fox Terrier named Champion Wirerock Winter Fantasy. Her call name was Winter, and she did a huge amount of winning one year."

"Sure," said Liz. "I remember her. For a while it seemed like Marcus hardly talked about anything else. He said she was the top show dog in the United States and she had to fly all over the country to go to dog shows. I remember him saying it was a real shame she couldn't qualify for frequent flyer miles."

"After Winter retired from showing, she had a litter of puppies," I said. "She was living with her co-owner then, but somehow Marcus ended up with one of the puppies."

"Yeah, I know. He brought it with him to the office." I straightened in my chair. "You just told me you never saw any of the dogs."

"I thought you meant the show dogs. You know, the ones all done up in those fancy hairdos? This one was just a baby, no more than eight weeks old. She was adorable.

"Marcus came in one morning carrying her in his pocket. He put her down on the ground and the first thing she did was pee. Marcus started swearing, but I thought it was pretty funny. It was a good thing that little baby held it as long as she did."

"Did he tell you what he was doing with the puppy?"

"He said he had to find a home for it. He couldn't take it back to his house because Gloria would have had a fit. The puppy was really cute, though, so he figured it wouldn't be too hard to find someone who'd take it. I was tempted myself, but my building doesn't allow dogs.

"I put down a couple sheets of newspaper and went out and bought some biscuits. I think she stayed here one or two nights before Marcus said he found someone who wanted her."

"That was his neighbor, Roger Nye. He still has her. But what I'm curious about is how Marcus came to have that puppy in the first place. Why didn't she stay with Winter's co-owner like the rest of the litter did?"

"Wait a minute." Liz screwed up her face as she

thought. Creases fanned out from her eyes and mouth. One look in the mirror, and she'd never make that face again. "I remember Marcus saying something about that at the time. It didn't make any sense to me. There was some particular word he used. Give me a sec. It'll come to me."

A word? John Monaghan hadn't kept the puppy because of a word? There was nothing to do but wait it out.

After a minute Liz smiled triumphantly. "The other guy, the co-owner? Marcus said he wanted to cull the litter."

"Cull it? You're kidding."

Liz gave me a scornful look.

"Sorry. It's just that that's such a drastic move. Some breeders do cull litters, of course, but usually only when there's a serious genetic problem. Occasionally you find people who'll do it when there aren't enough homes for the puppies they produce. But that wouldn't have been a problem with Winter's litter. So why would John have wanted to get rid of her?"

I stopped as a sudden thought struck me. "What if he didn't want to? What if Rattigan stole that puppy? Maybe there was a dispute over the terms of their co-ownership contract."

"That's crazy," said Liz. "Marcus wouldn't have done something like that."

Sure he would have, I thought, if he'd figured there was something to be gained by it. Everything I'd learned about Marcus Rattigan pointed to a man who didn't hesitate to put his own concerns above everyone else's.

"I'm telling you," Liz said firmly, "Marcus saved the puppy from being put to sleep. She was sweet and adorable, but the other guy didn't want her. I asked Marcus how anyone could kill a baby like that, and he said that was just the way some breeders are. If a puppy wasn't perfect, they didn't want anything to do with it. It was lucky for that puppy that Marcus was there, and that he was just too kind and caring to let such a terrible thing happen."

Kind and caring. Liz Barnum had to be the only person in the world who'd apply those particular words to Marcus Rattigan. Now that he was gone, I guessed she'd forgotten how he'd dumped her after his divorce. Or maybe, faced with the prospect of Gloria as her new boss, Liz's memory of Marcus had taken on a rose-colored hue.

I'd learned all I could from her; it was time to move on. "Is Ben here today?"

Liz didn't even hesitate. She waved a hand toward the hallway and said, "Third door on your right. I know he's busy, so I won't bother to announce you."

Right. Liz might say she wasn't leaving Anaconda, but an attitude like that told me she already had one foot out the door.

"Thanks," I said.

"Don't mention it."

The door to Ben Welch's office was closed. I knocked, then opened it without waiting for a response. Ben was hunched over a messy pile of papers on his desk. His face was twisted into a grimace, and a pair of wire-rimmed glasses rode low on his nose. He was flipping pages with one hand; the other massaged his temples. He looked like a man who was working on a major headache.

"Liz, I thought I told you—" He looked up and stopped.

"Hi, I'm Melanie Travis. I crossed the room quickly before he could tell me not to. "We met last week."

"Yes, of course." Despite his words, Ben looked as though he hadn't a clue who I was. Nor did he care.

"Where's Liz?"

"I don't know. She wasn't at her desk when I came in." It wasn't really a lie, I told myself. More in the nature of damage control. "Do you have a minute?"

"Not really—"

"It's about Marcus Rattigan's murder."

"You're a reporter, then." Ben sat back in his chair and frowned.

I couldn't see any point in beating around the bush. Judging by his demeanor, Ben wasn't going to allow me much time. "No, I'm what you might call an interested bystander. Marcus Rattigan kept a copy of his will in this office. Were you aware of its contents before he was murdered?"

Ben's expression tightened. "I have no intention of answering that question."

"Did you know that Gloria was Rattigan's chief beneficiary and that after they divorced, he never got around to updating the document?"

"That was none of my business." Ben got up and came around from behind the desk. "And it certainly isn't any of yours."

He grasped my arm in a determined grip. Out-muscled and outweighed, I turned and went along meekly as he marched me toward the door. We were close enough that I could smell his aftershave, Geoffrey Beene's Grey Flannel. Too bad, I'd always liked the scent before.

"What did Gloria promise you in return for acting as her spy?" I asked in the few seconds I had left. "Did she tell you that someday you'd be running the company?"

I'd hoped to shake him up, but Ben's composure didn't waver. "Gloria wasn't in any position to make promises regarding this company," he said firmly. "And I wasn't in need of her backing. As to Marcus's will, whatever decisions he made regarding the disposition of Anaconda Properties were entirely his own."

That wasn't an answer, it was corporate doublespeak for butt out. Before I could tell him so, Ben propelled me the last few inches into the hallway and shut the door between us.

As I strode down the hallway and let myself out, Liz was nowhere to be seen. The phone on her desk was ringing stridently. It didn't sound as though anyone cared enough to pick up. I hoped the missed call was an important one.

Twenty-one

Thanks to the early dismissal, I still had time when I got home to change into my running clothes and take Faith for a quick jog around the neighborhood before Davey's bus arrived. I passed the Brickmans' house on my way home. Alice, who'd been standing in the doorway watching for the bus, came out to say hello.

She looked at Faith and shook her head. "If that dog grows any more hair, you're going to need a lawn-mower to get through it. Isn't she cold with her butt all shaved down like that?"

"I don't think so."

The winter before, Faith had been in the puppy trim, which meant she had a blanket of dense hair all over her body. This would be the first time we'd faced the cold weather in the continental trim. So far, Faith didn't seem to mind. As we talked about her, she jumped up on her hind feet and twirled in an exuberant circle.

"Besides, the hair grows pretty fast so there's usually some cover back there. The reason she looks so naked is that I'm showing her tomorrow so I just clipped her yesterday. Now I have to go in and give her a bath."

"Yikes," said Alice, considering the possibility. "In the tub?"

"In the tub," I confirmed.

"Better you than me. How long does it take?"

"The bath isn't so bad. For the blow dry, probably three hours."

"You're nuts," said Alice.

I didn't debate it. The heady addiction to the shows and the competition is hard to explain to someone who's never experienced it.

"Why don't I take Davey when he gets off the bus?" said Alice. "At least, then, he'll be out of your hair. Three hours?" She glanced down at her watch. "He'd better stay for dinner, too. It's only meatloaf. There's always room for one more."

I could have hugged her. Having done this job before, I knew it went a whole lot faster when I didn't have to juggle Davey's needs at the same time. Instead I settled for offering to reciprocate the next time she got stuck. These things always seem to even out in the end.

Blowing a show coat dry is manual labor, plain and simple. It's one of those jobs that requires lots of patience and minimal talent. So as I worked I had plenty of time to think.

I pondered Marcus Rattigan's relationships with his ex-wife, his co-breeder, his neighbor, and his secretary. I wondered how much of an impact localized protest groups had ever had upon his business and whether he was accustomed to taking his vice-president into his confidence. All in all, I had lots of great questions and no great answers to go with them.

As a teacher, I found the situation doubly frustrating. I'm used to being the person standing in the front of the room who knows what's going on. Not this time. If solving Rattigan's murder had been a class assignment, I'd have been sitting in the back row with my head down, hoping desperately not to get called on.

I finished Faith by seven and called down the block to see how Davey was doing. Alice said the kids were fine, and the happy shrieks I heard in the background were proof enough for me. When she told me to grab some dinner and come by to get him whenever I was ready, I didn't argue.

Instead I made another phone call. So far, I'd taken John Monaghan's word that he'd organized the neighborhood protest group at Rattigan's behest. Now I wondered if that was wise. Everything I'd learned thus far said he'd lied about Winter's litter. And if one topic was open to prevarication, why not another?

Audrey DiMatteo picked up on the fifth ring. When I gave my name, she remembered me immediately.

"You're the lady with all the questions. The one who was so interested in Marcus Rattigan."

"Right. Tonight I'm interested in someone else."

"So what?" Her tone wasn't encouraging.

"So I'm hoping you might be able to help me."

"What are you offering in return?"

She'd responded well to bribery the first time, but unfortunately, I didn't have another tidbit handy. "How about a chance to help bring a murderer to justice?"

Audrey laughed at that. "Who do you think you are? Wonder Woman?"

I wish.

"Look," I said. "The guy that was in business with Rattigan on the coffee bar conversion is my brother. Right now he's the number one suspect for a murder he didn't commit. All I'm trying to do is offer the police some other options."

"You didn't mention anything about that before."

"I didn't think it was important."

"Maybe I would have."

Audrey was silent for a moment. I wondered if she was trying to figure out a way to use that information for leverage. If so, she was welcome to it. First I had to keep my brother out of jail, then I'd worry about his future business prospects.

"I only have one question. It's really simple."

"All right," Audrey said grudgingly.

"When you were protesting the development of the Waldheim property, did you ever think of coordinating your efforts with the other group, the one that was working against the coffee bar conversion?"

"Monaghan's people?" Her answer was quick and decisive. "No."

"Why not?"

"Like I told you before, POW is just a group of concerned citizens who want to do our part for the environment. Those other people are way beyond where we wanted to go. Our members are not looking to resurrect the sixties and we're sure not into destroying any property."

I took a deep breath before continuing. "And they were?"

"What do you think? You told me yourself there'd been some accidents on the site. A man broke his leg, didn't he? And that doesn't even count what happened to Rattigan."

"Yes, but how do you know that Monaghan's group was behind that stuff?"

"If you mean do I have proof, the answer is no. But I heard things, and John Monaghan showed up at one of our meetings. Hey, it's hard enough for a group like ours to get credibility, we sure weren't looking to take on any fanatics. Monaghan said he had some ideas that might be helpful for us, you know, that would step up the action. I told the guy to take a hike."

"Why didn't you tell me this before?"

"Why didn't you ask?"

Good question.

"Do the police know this?" I asked.

"How the hell should I know?"

"Well, did you tell them or not?"

"I might have. I don't really remember. At the time I was a whole lot more concerned about how Rattigan's death was going to affect us."

"And?"

Audrey snorted. "As far as we can tell, the reins of power passed from a money grubbing developer to his money grubbing ex-wife. Life's a bitch sometimes."

"Tell me about it."

I hung up the phone, fixed Faith's food, and ate a salami and cheese sandwich while she picked at her gourmet kibble. If Detective Petrie didn't know what Audrey had told me, he definitely needed to talk to her. I doubted he'd be happy to hear from me again, but that was his tough luck.

I could call on him in the morning, I thought, but that would make me late for the show. I glanced down at Faith. Freshly bathed, clipped, and brushed out, she looked gorgeous. Better still, she looked like a winner.

Petrie could wait, I decided. I'd get in touch with him tomorrow afternoon, when I got back from the show.

I gulped as a sudden, unnerving thought hit me. Did this mean I was turning into a dog person?

The Flushing Meadows Dog Show is held in Queens at an outdoor park that sits in the shadow of Shea Stadium. In late October, that means you're taking a chance, weather-wise. Best case, there'll be plenty of sun and cool autumn temperatures; worst case, you'll wish you'd never gotten out of bed that morning. The year before this had been Faith's first show and the weather had been beautiful. This time around, we weren't so lucky.

It wasn't raining, but that was about the best you could say. The thermometer hovered around fifty, and a stiff wind blew through the park, toppling portable chairs and causing the tents to rattle and flap. Not the kind of day I'd have chosen to spend standing outside under a tent, grooming a dog.

I'd already pulled socks on over my stockings and wasted ten minutes rummaging in the back of the closet for Davey's parka from the year before. Predictably, when I found it, the sleeves were too short and the hem barely reached his waist. I zipped him into it anyway, and told him he looked fine. Better warm than fashionable.

As I pulled up beside the green and white striped grooming tent to unload, the canvas roof dipped and billowed above us. I was dressed in a turtleneck, wool sweater, and corduroy skirt; but even so, I felt the chill as soon as I got out of the car.

Several of the professional handlers had tied plastic windbreaks to the tent poles, which served as partial walls around their grooming areas. Other exhibitors huddled over steaming cups of coffee, their chilled fingers wrapped around the hot mugs. Next week the indoor circuit started. For now, we all had to suffer through.

As usual, Aunt Peg had beaten me there. I found her setup and unloaded my grooming table, crate, and tack box into the area she'd saved. Usually at dog shows, the exhibitors' tent is filled to capacity. Today, there was plenty of room.

Not that I imagined for one minute that any exhibitor had stayed home because of the inclement weather. Dog show people are a hardy bunch. Once an entry is made and a good judge anticipated, they've been known to brave blizzards and hurricanes with equal aplomb. More likely, the empty tent meant that most exhibitors were showing and leaving, rather than turning the event into an all day affair as they might have done in nicer weather.

"Good lord," said Aunt Peg, when I got back from parking my car. "You look like Nanook of the North. Don't tell me you're wearing kneesocks. Are you sure you wouldn't like a muffler to wrap around your head?"

I hopped Faith up onto her table, which I'd lined up beside Hope's. "At least I'm almost warm. You must be freezing."

The unwritten rules of dog show etiquette dictate that exhibitors dress for the ring as they would for any other important social occasion. For the women, this means skirts or dresses; for the men, jackets and ties. Aunt Peg was wearing a high necked corduroy dress in a shade of green that had obviously been chosen to complement her dog rather than her skin tone. Her only concession to the weather was the down vest she'd buttoned on over it.

"I feel fine. Heaven knows what everyone is complaining about." She stopped brushing Hope and helped clear a spot on top of her crate where we could get Davey settled. "Are you cold?" she asked her nephew.

"Not me, I'm Batman. I have superpowers." Davey unzipped his jacket to show her that he was wearing the jersey from his Halloween costume underneath.

"You don't say. I thought Superman was the one with the powers."

Standing behind my son, I quickly shook my head. The costume was already made. As far as I was concerned, it was much too late for any discussion. "Batman has a cool car. Don't forget about that."

"The Batmobile!" Davey cried, pulling his model out of the bag of toys we'd brought. "Can I get down and drive it around?"

"I guess so. Just don't go too far and don't get in anyone's way."

Supplying his own sound effects, Davey zoomed away down the aisle.

Aunt Peg watched him for a moment, then reached over and flicked her fingers through the shorter hair on Faith's chest. Though it had been straight the night before when I'd finished blowing her dry, now it was beginning to kink and curl.

"You rushed through her bath, didn't you? You're never going to get the job done right until you learn to take your time."

"As soon as I have more time, I'll use it. Besides, in this wind, I doubt if the judge will even be able to see the difference. Guess who I saw yesterday?"

"In the afternoon, you mean? When you should have been home working on your dog?" Once Aunt Peg has a complaint in hand, she hates to let go until she's sure her point is made.

Instead of answering, I opened my grooming bag and pulled out slicker and pin brushes, a comb, and a spray bottle filled with water that I hooked on the edge of the table. Faith, who knew what was coming, turned a tight circle once around the rubber matted tabletop and lay down.

Poodle coats are brushed on each side, layer by layer, from the middle of the back to the bottom of the stomach. The hair is always brushed upward, not down; and the left side, which will face the judge when the dog is in the ring, is always done last. It takes a good amount of time to brush out a Standard Poodle, so instead of arguing, I simply got down to work.

"All right," Peg said finally. "Who?"

"Liz Barnum."

"Marcus's secretary?" Her fingers flew through Hope's hair as she talked. Peg's eyes were on the show coat, but I had her attention. "What did she have to say?"

"That the reason Rattigan gave the only bitch puppy from Winter's litter to his next door neighbor was that John Monaghan wanted to cull the litter and was planning to put her to sleep."

"No!"

"That's what she told me."

"She must have been mistaken."

"Or misinformed. Her memory seems pretty good, but who knows what Rattigan told her at the time? What if John and Marcus had a disagreement over the terms of their co-ownership contract? Maybe Marcus thought he was owed this puppy after all the money he'd spent. What if he stole her from John to even things up?"

Aunt Peg was willing to consider the idea, but she didn't look convinced. "If he wanted the puppy enough to steal her, why would he turn around and give her away? Besides, I thought John told you he and Marcus were old friends."

"He did." I finished the first side of Faith's mane coat and ran the slicker through her bracelets. Then I tapped her back and she stood up and turned over.

"That hardly sounds like the kind of behavior that would be conducive to continuing a friendship."

"I'm not sure the friendship did continue. Listen to what else I found out." I blew on my fingers to warm them, then parted Faith's hair and began to brush as I told her about my phone conversation with Audrey DiMatteo.

There's very little that can distract Aunt Peg when she's working on a dog, so when she laid down her brush to listen, I knew she was perturbed. "We're talking about the possibility of a stolen puppy. Do you honestly believe anyone would commit murder over that?"

Since it wasn't as though I had a lot of other theories, I was beginning to grow attached to this one. "Someone might," I said defensively. "Maybe a really dedicated breeder."

"I *am* a dedicated breeder. And I'll tell you right now there isn't a puppy in the world that's that important. If you ask me, the ex-wife did it. Anyone who won't even allow a dog into her house is definitely someone who can't be trusted."

Good old Aunt Peg. At least she's consistent.

"You don't think John did it because he's a dog person."

"I'll admit that biases me in his direction. But that's beside the point. What you're telling me doesn't make sense. The theft took place a decade ago. If it made John angry enough to kill, presumably he'd have done something at the time."

I'd wondered about that myself. "I never said I had all the answers."

"No, but you certainly implied you had some of them." Aunt Peg hates it when any relative of hers comes up short. "Why don't you go talk to John after the judging and straighten this whole mess out? He's here today, you know. His new dog won the breed from the classes this morning."

"How'd you find that out?" Generally, Aunt Peg didn't follow the action in the Fox Terrier ring.

"You had a visitor earlier, a girl named Kate. It seems she'd seen us together at the Rockland show. When she saw me setting up, she came by to ask if you were here yet."

Peg waved down the tent. "She said they were set up down at the other end and that they'd be here all day because Summer had to stay for the group. So there'll be plenty of time to look him up later, after the Poodle judging. And this time, try to get your facts straight, will you?"

"Yes, Mom."

Aunt Peg sent me a baleful look. "If you were my

child, you'd know better than to go barking up the wrong tree." Presumably I'd also be taller and better groomed. I picked up my brush and went back to work.

Twenty-Two

When Aunt Peg and I are at a dog show together, she usually allows extra time in her schedule to help me get Faith ready. Preparing a Poodle for the show ring is a long and painstaking process. There are dozens of small steps to be completed, and each one is dependent on myriad tiny details. Slip up even slightly anywhere along the line, and the finished product will suffer.

After a year of showing, I've reached the point where my grooming skills are just about adequate. I'm better than a beginner but nowhere near the level of skill that the professional handlers achieve. I have to compete against the pros, however, and that's why Aunt Peg's masterful assistance is a godsend.

Since she is Faith's breeder, the Poodle's appearance and achievements reflect directly upon the Cedar Crest line. Knowing this, I had perhaps been guilty of taking Aunt Peg's help for granted, or at least assuming that it would always be there. That morning, however, I was in for a rude awakening.

After I finished brushing Faith, it was time to put in her topknot. The ponytails she wears on her head at home are loose and floppy. Their purpose is to keep the long hair out of her way and allow it to grow without tangling.

In the show ring, however, the topknots the Poodles wear are tight and precise. The rounded bubble of hair above the eyes complements the dog's expression while the mass of loose hair above and around it provides a softening frame for the face. I parted the thick strands of hair with a knitting needle and put in the front elastic just behind Faith's eyes.

On my first try, my bubble was loose and uneven. On the second it tilted to one side. Muttering under my breath, I cut out the rubber band with a small pair of scissors and called for Aunt Peg's help.

"You can do it," she said. "Try again."

"I've tried twice already. At this rate, I'll never get her sprayed up."

"Sure you will," Peg said blithely. She had Hope's topknot already in, and the bitch was standing on the table while Peg scissored the trim. "It's time you began doing things for yourself."

I spritzed Faith's topknot hair with water, gathered it up, and started over. "Two weeks ago, you couldn't wait to push me out of the way and fix Faith's lines."

"Quite right. And then you took my nice trim into the ring and beat me with it."

We were both silent for a moment, pondering the implications of *that.*

"What do you know?" Aunt Peg said finally. "I always thought I was a good sport and now it turns out I'm a sore loser."

Looking suitably annoyed, she set down her scissors, strode over to my table and in less than a minute had a perfect bubble arranged above Faith's eyes. "I hope you were paying attention," she said. "I'm not going to keep this up forever."

"I wouldn't dream of asking you to." I sprayed up Faith's mane coat myself and did all my own scissoring. When I was finished, she didn't have the highly polished look of her sister, but I was glad to see that she was still a very presentable Poodle.

The ring where the non-sporting breeds were being judged was at the far end of the other tent. As our scheduled time approached, I left Peg to keep an eye on Davey and the Poodles and went to get our armbands from the steward. The judging was running a few minutes late and there was a line to pick up numbers.

As I waited, a trio of Bulldogs circled the ring. Obviously enjoying the cool weather, the heavyset dogs were unusually animated. The judge, who was bundled up just as warmly as I was, watched them with a smile on her face.

"Hey, Ms. Travis!" I jumped slightly at the sound of an excited squeal. Kate Russo came skipping up beside me. "I thought I'd find you here. Are you showing today? Where's your Poodle?"

"She's back at the grooming tent. I just came over to get the armbands."

"I met that lady you're with, Mrs. Turnbull, right?" I nodded.

"Did she tell you that Summer won this morning? He beat the specials and everything! John's really psyched. He says this is just the beginning. Summer might even be a better dog than his grandmother."

"That's great." I peered around the person in front of me as the line inched forward. Bulldogs were wrapping things up in the ring. If I didn't get the armbands soon, Aunt Peg and I were going to be late. "Please congratulate John for me. I'll come by later and watch him in the group."

"There's something else." Kate stepped closer and lowered her voice. "You know how you wanted me to ask questions?"

"One question," I corrected, frowning. Though she'd gotten the information I needed, I still felt guilty about Kate's burst of extra initiative. "I hope you haven't been bothering John again."

"Of course not." She managed a wounded look. "I just figured it wouldn't hurt to keep my ears open. You know, keep tabs on how things are going?"

"Kate," I said sternly. "You weren't supposed to go overboard. I never asked you to spy on anyone."

"I'm not spying, I'm paying attention. There's a difference. Did you know that John is looking for a backer for Summer?"

"He mentioned it briefly. I don't believe he'd found anyone yet when we spoke about it."

"Well, he has now—"

"Breed?" asked the steward as the person in front of me took his armbands and stepped away.

"Standard Poodles. I need two." I looked in the steward's book and pointed out Faith's and Hope's entries. Once again, they were entered in two different classes: Hope in Bred-by-Exhibitor and Faith in 12—18 Months. The steward checked them off, then fished through the pile of numbers on the table, looking for the ones I needed.

"It's some guy with a lot of money," said Kate.

I reached around her and plucked two rubber bands out of the bag. "They always are."

"John said the man was here today to look at Summer and if he liked what he saw, they'd go ahead and make out a contract. So I got this idea—"

"Next?" The steward slapped the two armbands into my hand. Pushed from behind, I wasted no time in stepping out of line.

"Can we talk about this later?" I said to Kate. "I've got to get back and get my dog."

"Well sure, but—"

Behind me, the steward began calling the first Standard Poodle class into the ring. Dogs were judged first, followed by bitches, but the entry wasn't large and I knew Faith's class would be called within minutes.

"Gotta go," I said and ran.

When I got back to the setup, Aunt Peg was pacing beside the tables. "You took long enough. Are you sure they haven't started yet?"

"They just did. Puppy Dogs are in. We'd better hurry."

Faith stood up, wagging her tail. I kissed her on the nose, stuffed some dried liver in my pocket to use for bait, and hopped her off the table. "Where's Davey?"

"Right here," said my son, poking his head out of Faith's crate. "Aunt Peg told me to stay somewhere where I wouldn't get lost."

"Good thinking. We're going up to the ring now. Can you carry my hair spray and extra comb?"

"Sure." Davey held out his hands. Having a job to do made him feel important. "Aunt Peg called you a slowpoke."

"Aunt Peg didn't have to wait in line to pick up numbers. Come on, everybody ready? Off we go."

By the time we got back to the Poodle ring, Winners Dog was being judged. There was only one Puppy Bitch; then it was Faith's turn. I tried to remember everything Sam had coached me to do two weeks earlier, but we were the only entry in the class and our time in the ring passed so quickly it was all a blur. Aunt Peg was also alone in her class and there were no Open Bitches. That left only Hope, Faith, and the winner of the Puppy Class to compete for Winners Bitch.

The judge took her time with the decision. Aunt Peg, clearly in no mood to be beaten again by her upstart niece, used every handling trick she knew to showcase her bitch to advantage. I wasn't surprised when Hope was awarded Winners Bitch, but I was disappointed. Having tasted the thrill of victory once, I'd been hoping I could turn winning into a habit.

Peg left the ring with the all important purple ribbon, and Faith was awarded Reserve Winners over the puppy. The first time she'd won Reserve, I'd been ecstatic. Now I'd been around long enough to realize all it really meant was that I wasn't getting any points. I stuck the striped ribbon in my pocket and joined Davey outside the ring as Peg and Hope went back in to compete for Best of Variety.

While the judge sorted through her entry, I looked around hoping to spot Kate. It was a shame I'd had to run out on her earlier when she'd wanted to talk. She'd said something about John Monaghan choosing a sponsor for his new dog. Frankly, the subject didn't interest me much. But it had interested Kate for some reason.

Too late I was realizing the magnitude of the mistake I'd made in asking her to talk to John about his puppies. Kate was obviously a mystery buff, and somehow she'd gotten the idea that she should do some investigating of her own. I was going to have to talk to her about that hare-brained idea before she managed to parlay her small involvement into big trouble for both of us.

Now that I was free, however, Kate was nowhere to be seen. In the ring the judge awarded Best of Variety to one of the specials and gave Hope Best of Winners. Aunt Peg collected her ribbon and exited the ring. She declined to have her picture taken for winning only a single point and we headed back to the other tent.

"Can I have your armband?" asked Davey, trotting alongside.

"I don't see why not." I slipped the cardboard number down off my arm. "Do you want to wear it?"

Davey nodded and looked at Aunt Peg. "Can I have yours, too?"

"Are you going to wear them both?" she asked.

"Sure. One on each arm. Then everyone will think I'm showing two dogs."

Armbands are worn one at a time in the ring, and only on the left arm where the judge can see them easily for identification purposes, but I couldn't see any point in bursting Davey's bubble. We stopped and I banded both numbers on over his jacket. "Now you look very official."

Davey grinned proudly. "Can I hold Faith's leash?"

I hesitated before handing it over. "You have to be really careful. You're sure you won't let go?"

Though Davey walks Faith all the time at home, dog shows are an entirely different proposition. With all the noise and activity, not to mention the thousand other dogs in attendance, even the best behaved pets tend to forget their manners and training.

Faith was very obedient and I'd have trusted her in almost any situation. But I'd also seen dogs that had gotten loose accidentally on the show grounds. Surrounded by so much confusion, many panicked and responded by running blindly. I wasn't about to let that happen to Faith.

"I can do it," said Davey. "Honest."

I reached down and wrapped the lead carefully around his left hand. When Faith jumped forward, Davey went flying after her, but we made it back to the setup without mishap.

Peg and I spent the next half hour taking our Poodles apart. The tight topknots they'd worn in the ring had to be taken down and replaced with more comfortable looser ones. Ear hair needed to be wrapped and banded. I finished by spraying Faith's neck hair with a conditioner that would cut the hair spray so it would be easier to get out later.

By the time the Poodles were back in their crates, lunchtime had come and gone. All the food at the concession stand looked limp and overcooked. While I was contemplating a platter of soggy sandwiches, Aunt Peg bypassed the lunch offerings entirely and went straight to dessert. She filled a tray with two Danish pastries and three large cookies. Immediately Davey fell in line behind her.

I could have wasted my time lecturing them both about fat content and empty calories but when Peg offered me the third cookie, I ended up defecting to the other side instead. I could always make up for it later by serving lots of steamed vegetables for dinner.

Yeah, right.

The groups had already started by the time we finished eating. The grooming tent is a great place to hear all the latest gossip, and throughout the day there'd been plenty of talk about John Monaghan's new Wire Fox Terrier, Summer. Like me, Aunt Peg was curious to see him. When a voice over the loudspeaker called all terriers to the group ring, we quickly cleaned up and hurried over to watch.

The terrier group is the largest of the seven groups recognized by the American Kennel Club. The breeds contained within it are diverse with respect to size and coat and color, but all were originally bred to hunt small game. The group takes it name from the Latin word *terra,* meaning earth, and most terriers are great diggers. They are also lively and intelligent, and the terrier group is one of my favorites to watch.

The dogs filed into the ring and lined up in size order, which placed the Airedale and the Kerry Blue at the head of the line and the Australian Terrier and Dandie Dinmont toward the end. John and Summer were midway down the length of the ring. As soon as they found their spot, John knelt on the ground behind the compact dog and stacked him.

I sidled closer to Aunt Peg so we could talk without being overheard. "What do you think?"

"Give me a chance! I haven't even seen him move yet."

Dogs are judged on both their conformation and their movement, as each is an indicator of their suitability to do the job for which the breed was developed. But that wasn't the only reason Aunt Peg wanted to reserve judgment until she'd seen Summer move.

Like Poodles, Wire Fox Terriers have coats that require a great deal of upkeep and preparation for the ring. And, as is true with any coated breed, a skillful groomer can arrange the hair to create the illusion of correct conformation where it doesn't exist. The judge in the ring has the opportunity to feel the dog with his hands, but spectators must rely on a visual assessment. Watching a dog in action is often the only way from ringside to ferret out structural problems that artful grooming has hidden from view.

The judge lifted her hands and the exhibitors stood. The entire line of dogs circled the ring once, stopping back where they'd begun as the first dog in line was brought to the middle of the expanse for his individual examination.

"Well?" I asked.

"Very nice." Peg likes to take a cautious approach when offering opinions. "Looks young. Is he?"

I opened the catalogue and had a look. "Sixteen months."

"He'll be better at two."

"But will he be as good as Winter?"

"Winter's a season," Davey said firmly. "Not a dog. Summer's a season, too."

I squatted down beside him and pointed at the Wire. "See that dog there? His name is Summer. He was named after the season."

"Actually," Peg corrected, "unless I miss my guess, he was named after his grandmother. The name's certainly close enough that anyone in the know would instantly make the connection. I'm sure that's what John had in mind."

I stood back up and let my gaze drift down the line. Two dogs behind Summer was another terrier breed of similar size and shape. To my untrained eye, the major difference between them was their color. While Summer's coat was predominately white with a black saddle and some smaller patches of tan, the other terrier had no white at all. He was a rich reddish tan all over and also sported the same black saddle.

"You're frowning," said Aunt Peg. "What's the matter?"

"That dog in the middle of the line." I pointed to the one I was talking about. "What breed is it?"

"Welsh Terrier."

"He looks a lot like the Fox Terrier, doesn't he?"

"I suppose," Peg allowed. "Although I'm sure the breeders of each would be happy to tell you all about the differences between the two breeds."

"The funny thing is . . ."

"What?"

"He looks like Asta."

She turned and stared. "Who does?"

"That Welsh Terrier. I mean, Asta was all woolly and ungroomed. She certainly wasn't trimmed the way these dogs are. And you know perfectly well that the subtle distinctions go right over my head, but color-wise—"

"Colorwise?" Aunt Peg repeated. "Asta didn't have any white on her?"

"She had some. There was a big white patch on her chest, and some on her legs."

"There you go, then." She turned her gaze back to the group.

"But seeing the two breeds together, it's hard not to realize how similar they are."

"Of course there are similarities between a Wire and a Welsh. Anyone can see that."

Yes, but there was something more. Some tiny bit of knowledge I knew I had but couldn't quite come up with. Someone else had mentioned Welsh Terriers to me recently. Who was it?

As I watched the judge go over the Soft Coated Wheaten, I remembered. "John Monaghan used to dabble in Welsh Terriers years ago."

"Lots of dog people have more than one breed," Aunt Peg said distractedly.

She wasn't really listening to me, but I didn't mind. What I was thinking seemed too outlandish to voice out loud anyway. What if Asta's father had been a Welsh Terrier? That would certainly explain why John hadn't wanted her.

I stared off into the distance, letting the idea simmer. It had obvious flaws, among them the fact that John had kept and registered the other puppies from the litter. Those three dogs had provided the basis for everything he'd shown since, including Summer. So there couldn't possibly have been a Welsh Terrier mixed up in that pedigree.

Or could there?

Twenty-three

On sunny summer days, dog shows draw lots of spectators. But in late October, with the weather raw and blustery, just about everyone who isn't entered can think of something better to do. By the time the Terrier group went into the ring, the few members of the paying public who'd chosen to brave the elements had probably long since gone home. That meant the people now lining the ring to watch the judging were mostly judges and exhibitors—in other words, a knowledgeable and opinionated group.

Tuning in to the conversations around us, I found we weren't the only ones who were interested in John's new Wire Fox Terrier. When Summer's turn came and the dog was placed on the table to be examined, the ringside abruptly fell silent. Its collective attention focused; the air of anticipation was palpable.

The judge moved her hands quickly over the dog, then waved him to the ground. She was using a down and back pattern to assess movement, and John took Summer the full length of the ring. As soon as the Wire began to move, there was a small scattering of applause. Most of the spectators held back, however, reserving judgment until they'd seen enough to decide for themselves whether or not this would be another great one.

The judge had one last look, then sent the pair to the end of the line. Most handlers would have let their dogs relax at this point as the judge turned her attention elsewhere; but John had a different agenda. Playing to the ringside, he used bait and a squeaky toy to keep Summer stacked and alert. A Border Terrier was on the table, but the majority of the spectators was still riveted on the Wire.

Ten minutes later the judge made her cut, pulling eight terriers, including Summer, out into the middle of the ring. This time when the Wire Fox Terrier was moved, the applause that accompanied him was louder and more enthusiastic. Judges aren't supposed to be influenced by audience opinion, but that's never stopped spectators from trying.

The judge motioned the Bedlington Terrier into the top spot, then placed Summer second, followed by a Skye Terrier and a Cairn. She sent them around one last time, pointing to each with a flourish to indicate her final decision.

"Too bad," I said. "I thought Summer was going to get it."

"His turn will come," said Peg. "That Bedlington's a good one and it's done quite a bit of winning. Summer hasn't even finished his championship yet. Winning Group two from the classes is quite a coup. His owner should be very pleased."

I turned to check on Davey. The person standing next to us had brought a Newfoundland up to ringside. Davey and the big black dog were curled up together on a blanket on the ground. Considering the chill in the air, both looked amazingly content.

"Ice cream," said Davey, looking up from his cozy perch.

"What?"

"I want ice cream."

Just the thought was enough to make me shiver. "No way. It's too cold."

"Too cold for what?" asked Aunt Peg.

"Ice cream."

"Says who?"

"Says her." Davey stood up and pointed. Just in case there was any doubt.

"You've got to be kidding," I said to my son.

"Why would he be kidding?" asked Peg. "I wouldn't mind having some myself. Do you think the food concession brought any?"

"Why don't you two go see?" I suggested. The judge had handed out the rosettes for the terrier group, and the hounds were coming in to take their place. "I wanted to talk to John anyway. How about if I meet you back at the crates later?"

Hand in hand, the sweet tooth twins marched off in search of ice cream. I turned and headed the other way.

The wind was whipping harder now, blowing dark clouds up from the south. The show ground was emptying rapidly. Under the handlers' tent only a smattering of setups remained. Even the pros were packing up and going home. I decided to see if I could grab John before he left, and worry about talking to Kate on Monday.

Cutting across the open space in the middle of the tent, I saw John and Summer down at the far end. In the next aisle over, the man who'd handled the Cairn had his van backed up to the tent and his crates loaded. As I approached, he was folding up his grooming tables and shoving them in the back of his van.

John saw me coming and waved. He slipped Summer off the tabletop and put the dog inside a wooden crate, which had been stacked on top of another. There was a tackbox beside the crates, and John tossed the big red ribbon inside, followed by the Fox Terrier's lead.

"Congratulations," I said. "Summer looked great in the ring."

"I thought so," John agreed. He continued packing up. "He got his second major today. I wouldn't have minded beating that Bedlington, though."

"Next time." I leaned back against the edge of the grooming table. "I was wondering if you'd mind clarifying a few things for me."

"Depends what they are. I imagine I've said just about all I need to on the topic of Marcus Rattigan."

"Fine. Let's talk about dogs."

John shrugged, his shoulders moving slightly beneath his bulky coat. He was folding towels and gathering equipment and didn't bother to look up, but I figured I could take that as acquiescence.

"Ten years ago you owned the top winning dog in the country. Breeding Winter and showing her to that point was a real achievement. When you retired her,

I'm sure you were hoping her career as a brood bitch would be every bit as illustrious. Her first litter had four puppies—"

"Three," John corrected. He straightened and stared at me. "I told you there were three puppies in that litter."

"Yes, you did. But after I talked to some other people, I began to wonder if you were telling the truth. Gloria Rattigan's neighbor has a bitch he got nine years ago from Marcus. At the time he was told she was Winter's daughter."

"That's impossible."

"I don't think so. I know you applied for four blue slips from the AKC when the litter was born. There was another puppy, a bitch, that was never registered."

"Who told you that?" John demanded.

I ignored the question and kept on talking. We were in a public place. There was nothing he could do but listen. Maybe if I made him mad enough I'd finally begin to get some answers.

"There's something else. That story you told about Marcus asking you to protest his building project. I couldn't really buy that. Once people began to get injured on the premises, Rattigan had to have known he'd be opening himself up to the prospect of massive lawsuits. So I began to wonder what you were really up to. And everything always came back to that single litter of puppies. Winter's litter."

John was deliberately ignoring me now. He had his back to me and was bending over to fish through the tackbox. I heard the metallic rattle of a choke chain as he rearranged his collars and straightened his leads.

A van door slammed shut behind me. There was a loud belch, followed by a burst of exhaust, as the Cairn handler's truck came to life and lumbered away.

"I figure there are two possible scenarios," I said. "One, you and Rattigan had a disagreement, maybe over the terms of your lease contract. Whatever it was made him angry enough to steal a puppy from Winter's litter."

"You don't have any idea what you're talking about," John snapped. "Why don't you just go away and leave me alone?"

"Then there's another possibility." I didn't really believe this one. I only thought that if I could get John talking, eventually he might let the truth slip out. "I saw Winter's daughter last week. Her name is Asta and she lives in Greenwich. Today when I was watching the terrier group, I couldn't help but realize how much she looked like another dog in the ring, the Welsh Terrier that was standing two places back."

Abruptly John stood. His face was flushed, his stance rigid. Inside the crate Summer began to whine softly. The terrier reached out with a front paw and threaded his toes through the metal grill. John didn't spare him a glance.

"You're not a breeder," he said. "What do you know about anything?"

"I know enough."

The words held more bravado than I felt but I'd come too far to back down now. I glared at John and he was the one who lowered his gaze first. Then all at once his features seemed to crumble. For a moment I almost thought he might cry.

"Marcus wasn't a breeder, either. That was the problem. I couldn't make him understand that we had to get rid of the puppy. I should have smothered her then and there. It was my mistake to let Marcus have a say. After all he'd done for Winter, I thought I owed him that much. I should have just taken care of things myself."

"Rattigan wouldn't let you do that, would he?"

John snorted loudly. "Bastard was too softhearted. Probably the only time in his life *that* was true. He said there was no need to kill the poor thing. I'll admit she was cute. Marcus said he'd find her a home. Little mutt. I thought it'd be okay to let him take her."

Little *mutt?*

"Tell me about Asta's sire," I said, quickly regrouping. "What went wrong?"

"You know that much, I'm sure you can guess the rest. We had a mismate. It's not as uncommon as you might think. But with a bitch of Winter's caliber it was a disaster, especially when we found out later that was the only litter she'd ever have.

"I'd spent years planning how I was going to breed that bitch when the time came. She was so good, I could have taken her any number of ways. Finally I picked just the right dog. He was an excellent Wire—

not as good as she was—but then, none of them were.

"We got three good breedings from the dog, and on Winter's sixteenth day in season, I brought her back home and put her back in the kennel. I was so excited, I was ready to set up the whelping box then and there."

John shook his head and let out a windy sigh. Two days later one of my Welshes got to her. Damn dog was two pens down. Close enough to smell her, I guess, but not to reach. At least that's what I thought. Son of a bitch must have climbed up and over the chainlink like a rat. By the time I saw them, they were tied good."

"What did you do?"

"Do? There wasn't a damn thing I could do. By then, the damage was done. I could only hope the breeding didn't take. Good God, it was her eighteenth day! When I found out she was in whelp, you better believe I prayed that all the puppies she was carrying had been sired by the first dog."

"You mean . . . ?" I let my voice trail away.

It hadn't occurred to me earlier but now, suddenly, I remembered a case I'd read about where fraternal twins had been sired by different fathers. If it could happen in humans, why not dogs? When I was watching the group judging, I'd had all the pieces, I just hadn't managed to put them together.

"It's possible for a litter to have two different sires, isn't it?"

"It's not only possible, it's perfectly plausible. The

bitch produces a number of eggs and if they mature at different times, I guess it just depends on who's in the vicinity on the day."

Behind John another exhibitor pulled a car up beside the tent and began to load. I lowered my voice so we wouldn't be overheard. "Did Rattigan know what had happened?"

"He knew. We were friends back then. We co-owned the bitch, I felt I had to tell him. I assured him that the first three breedings had probably knocked her up good, and he didn't seem too worried.

"As soon as the puppies were born, though, I knew we had a problem. The girl stuck out like a sore thumb.

Still, she was the only bitch so I had to give her every chance. That's why I sent away for four blue slips, just in case.

"When did you decide that you couldn't register her?"

"Had to be around seven, eight weeks. I guess I'd really known all along, but that was when I gave up hope. It wasn't just the bitch's color, her head was all wrong, too. The boys' heads were long and narrow; hers was short and wide. It didn't take a genius to see that she'd been sired by the Welsh."

Judging by the way the exhibitor in the next setup was throwing things into his car, he hadn't had a very good day. Two tricolor Basenjis stood side by side on his backseat and watched the proceedings through the rear window.

"So you had to give up Winter's only girl," I said. "It was bad, but it wasn't the end of the world. You still had the three boy puppies."

"I told you you didn't understand." John scowled at my ignorance. "You've never registered a litter of puppies, have you?"

"No."

"According to AKC rules as soon as Winter got herself bred to two different dogs on the same heat, the entire litter was ineligible for registration. It says so right on the form. It wasn't just a matter of picking out the bastard puppies. I was supposed to dump the whole lot of them."

Oh my God, I thought. That was the key, the piece of the puzzle I'd been missing. What Marcus and John had done, and the secret they'd shared, had tainted the entire Wirerock line. John had once said that everything he'd bred in the last decade had come down from Winter. Every puppy he'd sold, every dog he'd shown. Including his new superdog, Summer.

"Twenty-five years in dogs and I'd never broken a rule before," John said unhappily. "Oh, maybe I'd bent one or two, but nothing like this. But I didn't have any choice. I couldn't let Winter's genetic potential die with her. Legal or not, I *had* to register the litter."

"I can see that," I said truthfully. In John's position I wasn't sure I wouldn't have done the same thing. "Once the puppy was out of sight, there wouldn't have been any way for someone to ever guess that there had been a problem."

"Right. And nobody ever did. Why should they? The other three dogs were fine. Oh, not as good as their dam, maybe, but that's not unusual. Lots of old time breeders will tell you that quality often skips a generation.

"I finished all three of Winter's sons. That was easy, they were good dogs. All three have been used at stud plenty, too. No harm in that, either, their pedigrees were perfectly correct."

"So what went wrong?"

"What?" John blinked his eyes and looked at me. He was so engrossed in his story, that for a moment I think he'd almost forgotten I was there.

"Ten years passed and everyone was happy. Then something must have gone wrong. What was it?"

"What was it?" John repeated. "It was Marcus Rattigan sticking his big fat nose back in where it didn't belong."

"I thought the dogs were just a passing phase for him, that he'd lost interest and moved on." I stopped abruptly, remembering what Gloria had said.

Even after Rattigan grew bored, he never gave up anything that he thought of as his. He'd kept his golf clubs and his antique cars. And maybe after all the money he'd spent on Winter's career, he'd felt entitled to keep an interest in her progeny.

"Marcus had a short attention span," said John. "When he was into something, his intensity was fierce. When that interest dried up, it was like switching off a light. But according to the terms of our contract, he was supposed to get two puppies back from the first litter. So I let him take the bitch. I even offered him one of the dogs. It's not as though I needed all three."

John smiled slyly. He was the dog man, not Rattigan. To the untrained eye, a litter of eight-week-old puppies all look remarkably alike. I'd have been willing to bet that the dog he'd offered Marcus was the least of the three. Not that he'd have told Rattigan that.

"He turned you down?"

"He sure did. That year we spent campaigning Winter was pretty intense. By the time it was over, Marcus was ready for a break. Ready to move on. He told me he didn't have any use for the puppy, that I should keep him with his blessing."

John lifted his hands innocently. "I only did what he told me to do. That doesn't make it my fault when he comes back later and says he's changed his mind."

"You mean recently?" I asked, wondering if another piece of the puzzle had just fallen into place. "Rattigan decided he wanted a puppy after all?"

"Wanted, hell!" John spat out. "He said he deserved a puppy. That after all he'd done for me, I owed it to him. And if you knew Marcus, you knew that only the best would do. He didn't want just any puppy."

With a sinking feeling of inevitability, I knew what he was going to say. "He wanted Summer."

"Of course he wanted Summer. I told him to go to hell. He had his chance. He had everything with

Winter—the fame, the glory. Strutting around the show grounds like he owned the place, like he owned the dog, when all along he was just some poor schmuck who was fortunate enough to get his name on a lease.

"Do you know that Marcus's name was the only one listed on Winter when she was shown? He made that a condition of the contract. Whenever he ran an ad touting all she'd won, he listed himself as owner, but never said a word about me, the breeder, the person who'd done all the work. If he could have figured out a way to delete my name in the catalogue listing, I'm sure he'd have done that, too."

I could understand why he was upset. Like any breeder who'd been lucky enough to produce a really good one, he'd felt justifiably proud of his dog. Sponsors aren't easy to find, however; and even though he'd agreed to Rattigan's conditions to finance Winter's career, it must have been hard to watch the dog go on to glory without him.

"Summer is my dog!" John said angrily. "My shot!"

I glanced around to see if anyone was listening. The Basenji man was gone; he must have finished loading while we'd been talking. The few other setups left at that end of the tent were empty, and I could guess why. Best in Show was being judged. Anyone who'd stayed this long wasn't going to miss the show's grand finale. Across the field, I could see the remaining exhibitors gathered around a far ring.

The judging was bound to finish soon. Then

everyone would come trooping back to pack up for the day. In the meantime I hoped I could keep John talking.

"What did Rattigan do when you turned him down?"

John's face tightened into a snarl. "He told me that wasn't an option. Like he thought I'd just cave in and give him what he wanted. I told him to take a hike. At first he did, but he came back. Said if I was going to keep him out of dogs, then he'd do the same for me."

"How?"

"Marcus was going to turn me in to the AKC. Tell them about Winter's breedings and let them take it from there. He would have ruined me and destroyed my whole life's work. He was going to fix it so I could never show dogs again.

"I tried to reason with him, but he didn't give a damn. That was the worst part. Tit for tat, he said. If I didn't give him what he wanted, he'd get his revenge. That's when I knew there was only one way I could fix things. Marcus Rattigan had to die."

Twenty-four

I should have said something quickly, but I didn't, and the words hung in the silent air between us. Their echo was loud and utterly damning.

"He was going to ruin me," John repeated. He was still angry, and he wanted to make sure that I understood. "I didn't have any choice."

I glanced toward the Best in Show ring. The judging was usually pretty quick—fifteen or twenty minutes, tops. How much more time did I have to kill?

Bad question, under the circumstances.

"How did you do it?" I asked.

John folded a towel and threw it on a stack beside the crates. "It wasn't hard. I'd already been over to the coffee bar a couple of times so I knew my way around. With all the equipment the crew left hanging around, it was easy to climb up on the roof, saw through the frame of the skylight, and then loosen a few bolts. Once Marcus was standing where I wanted, one good shove was all it took."

"How did you get him to come to the coffee bar? You didn't call him at his office."

"Of course not. Do I look dumb to you? I had his cell phone number."

Modern technology. Where would we be without it?

"Didn't Rattigan think it was odd that you wanted to meet him after hours?"

"Who knows what he thought?" John said, smirking. "The only thing that mattered was that he agreed readily enough. All I had to do was dangle Summer under his nose and he came running."

John reached around behind him and got something out of the tackbox. I heard the faint sound of applause coming from the ring. Had the judge made his choice, or were the spectators just having their say? There was no way to tell. When I looked back at John, he was staring at me with an odd expression on his face.

"So you told Rattigan you'd give him Summer," I said, eager to distract him.

"I sure did. Marcus thought he'd won again. He was used to winning. He never even questioned it. I parked my car down the road where he wouldn't see it and I was waiting on the roof when he got there. Then I did what had to be done."

"Marcus was your friend," I said quietly.

"That was a long time ago. Before Winter, anyway. That year killed our friendship. We never should have done the deal over the dog."

"You needed Rattigan's money. If you hadn't agreed to the lease, Winter wouldn't have been number one."

"I guess you might say I danced with the devil. I sure as hell ended up getting burned." John sounded bitter, so busy picturing himself as the victim that he'd almost forgotten that Rattigan was the one who'd ended up dead.

"Sometimes it's a shame how things turn out," he said. "You make a decision that seems necessary, even logical, at the time. Then later it comes back to haunt you and there's not a damn thing you can do about it."

His voice was so calm, his tone was so reasonable, that when John lifted his arm suddenly, he caught me by surprise. His hand was fisted, and I thought he meant to strike me. Instead, his fingers opened and a silver choke chain slithered down.

I jumped back but the grooming table blocked my path. Before I could get around it, John had grabbed the free end of the collar with his other hand and pressed it against my throat. His hands crossed swiftly behind my head, the chain wrapping with them.

I should have screamed while I still had the chance, but it all happened so fast. By the time the thought occurred to me, it was already too late. Reflexively I reached for the collar, my fingers scrambling for purchase that wasn't there. The chain tightened and I felt my windpipe constrict.

Breath vanished. Panicked, I struck out with hands and feet, flailing, kicking, trying anything. John side-stepped my blows and applied more pressure. If it wasn't for the bulky turtleneck and jacket I'd worn to ward off the cold, I'd already have been dead.

We moved together in an awkward dance. Briefly I saw his face. John's eyes were black, his pupils dilated. They registered nothing. I tried to scream and barely managed a croak. Stars were beginning to explode in my head. Darkness hovered just beyond them. In another minute it would be over.

John tightened his grip and slipped around behind me. I struck out blindly and my fingers rapped hard against wood. I'd struck the top of Summer's crate. The pain felt good, it let me know I was still alive. For a single moment of clarity, it helped me to think.

I couldn't be stronger than Monaghan, but I could be smarter. I reached out again and felt the crate. This time I raced my fingers down its front. I passed the opening at the top of the door and slipped down further until I came to the latch that held it shut.

Summer was still pressed up against the door. I could feel his hair pushing out through the open grill. Crate doors are usually double locked, but John and I had been talking when he'd put the Fox Terrier inside and he hadn't bothered.

All I had to do was turn the latch. The door would fall open and Summer would be free.

John saw what I was doing and tried to pull me back. The close quarters had trapped me earlier. Now they worked to my advantage. He couldn't get the leverage he needed. My fingers grasped the latch like a lifeline.

"Don't!" he cried.

I knew he was picturing Summer leaping out. After a day of confinement, the terrier would revel in the unexpected freedom. He'd run, and we both knew it.

Maybe it would be a game for him at first. Then he'd look around and realize everything he saw was unfamiliar. People, trying to help, would scream and chase him. He'd see them as the enemy. Pretty soon he'd be running for his life.

There were cars on the show ground and a thruway just beyond, a constricted web of heavily trafficked roads that led to New York's airports. If Summer made it that far, he'd never stand a chance.

I saw Summer's fate just as clearly as John did, and I hated what I was about to do. But John had said it all earlier. I didn't have a choice.

The latch turned in my fingers and I pulled the toggle free. Now my hand was the only thing holding the door closed. The weight of Summer's body pushed against it.

"No!" John roared, lunging for the door.

As suddenly as it had begun, the constriction around my throat was gone. Gasping for air, I fell to the ground and rolled beneath the grooming table. John rushed past me. He caught Summer just as the dog launched himself out into the air.

The Fox Terrier struggled briefly but I knew he wouldn't give me much time. On hands and knees, I crawled out from under the other side of the table. My throat felt raw. The air I craved burned even as I sucked it in.

I tried to stand, but my legs wouldn't hold me. Wobbling, I leaned against the table and pushed myself up. Blood pounded in my ears. If it weren't for that, I'd have heard the screaming sooner.

"Oh my God, oh my God, oh my God!" Kate chanted the words like a mantra. Being a teenager, she prayed at the top of her lungs.

She stared at me in horror and I couldn't manage the words it would take to reassure her. Instead I reached up gingerly to assess the damage. My jacket collar was ripped to pieces, the turtleneck beneath it, shredded. Thank goodness they'd been there. Even so, I could feel the bruises already beginning to form on my throat.

Kate continued to shriek and I was dimly aware that other people were running in our direction. It was about time, I thought. Best in Show was finally over.

． ． ．

It took me a good fifteen minutes to regain some sem-
blance of speech and composure. By that time
Summer had been safely double locked in his crate
and we were surrounded by the members of the show
committee, an AKC rep, my family, and an assortment
of other judges and exhibitors. The local police had
been called and were on their way.

The show chairman, a gruff, blustering man named
Hank DiNardo, demanded an explanation. Immediately John took over, spinning a tale that had no basis
in either fact or reality. Aunt Peg, who had a firm grip
on Davey's hand and an even firmer grip on the truth,
looked ready to interrupt.

I took a deep breath and beat her to the punch.
"She's lying," John said firmly, cutting off my explanation. "It's all lies."

Several people in the crowd nodded. Thanks to
Winter and the rest of the Wirerock Fox Terriers, John
was a well known and well respected figure in the dog
show community. Everyone in the circle around us
knew who he was.

Aunt Peg would have her supporters, but I was
nobody. It didn't take a genius to see who they were
going to believe. Then Kate stepped in.

"Ms. Travis is my teacher," she said stoutly. "And
she doesn't lie."

"Stay out of this, Kate," John snapped.

"I can't. I guess I'm already in the middle of it." She
reached around beside the stacked crates where John

had left some equipment. There were a couple of towels piled on top.

Kate flipped back several layers of terry cloth and pulled out a tiny tape recorder. It was still running. I closed my eyes and offered a silent prayer.

"It's voice activated," said Kate, looking at me apologetically. "I picked it up at The Sharper Image. I know you told me not to get involved but when I saw it, I couldn't resist. I tried to tell you about it earlier. Don't be too mad."

Mad? I was ready to kiss her. My very own teenage Nancy Drew to the rescue.

"Let's hear what you've got," I said.

Kate hit the rewind button. Nobody said a thing as the spool rewound. Halfway back, she stopped and let it play. I couldn't have timed things better.

"Marcus was going to turn me into the AKC." John's voice was tinny, but clear. "Tell them about Winter's breedings and let them take it from there. He would have ruined me—"

"Shut that off!" John's face was purple. He lunged at Kate and tried to snatch the little machine from her grasp. "You taped me without my consent. That's illegal!"

"Tell it to your lawyer," said Hank DiNardo, stepping between John and Kate. "You make one more attempt to hurt someone on my show ground and I'll see to it that charges are pressed."

The wail of an approaching siren announced that the police were near. The show committee, obviously accustomed to working as a team, surrounded John until they could decide what to do next.

Most of the crowd seemed eager to see what was going to happen. I just wanted to get out of there. Now that John's confession was on tape, my presence was no longer crucial. It was easy to fade back to the edge of the circle. Aunt Peg and Davey came around to meet me and I took my son's other hand.

I watched Kate entrust the little recorder to Hank DiNardo and was about to intervene when Aunt Peg stopped me. "Don't worry," she said under her breath. "He's a judge."

"Dog show?"

"Federal court. He'll know what to do with it."

As we walked away, Kate hurried to catch up. "I came with John. I guess I'm going to need a ride home."

"You're with me," I told her. "What about Summer?"

We all looked back. Two officers had arrived. John was arguing vociferously. Others around him were chiming in with other opinions. With any luck, the police would have so many statements to take I'd be long gone before anyone thought to look for me.

"Someone on the show committee will watch out for the dog," said Aunt Peg. "You can depend on it."

"That was fun," said Davey.

Three pairs of eyes turned to look in his direction. "It was?"

"Aunt Peg and I watched Best in Show. She bet me

the Gordon Setter was going to win. I bet on the Afghan and won a dollar. Can we do this again next week?"

Out of the mouths of babes, I thought.

"Not if I can help it," I said.

Twenty-five

In the car on the way home, I asked Kate why she'd brought a tape recorder to the dog show in the first place.

She'd been staring out the window, but now Kate turned to look at me. I'd been concerned she might be upset. Not this girl. She was beaming. "I thought I might hear something interesting. John had said he was going to meet with Summer's new sponsor and I knew he'd never let me stand there and listen. That's the problem with being my age. Whenever adults have something important to say, they send you out of the room."

"The same thing happens when you're my age," said Davey, who had much of Faith's body draped across his lap. Tired from the long day, he'd laid his head on top of hers and was almost asleep.

I smiled at him in the rearview mirror, then went back to the teenager beside me. "I thought I told you not to do any more snooping around."

"Not exactly," Kate said brightly.

"I'm sure I implied it."

"That's not what I inferred."

It's a sad thing when an eighth grader can outtalk you.

The next day I got the rest of the story from Aunt Peg, who'd been in touch with Hank DiNardo. John Monaghan had been arrested for the murder of Marcus Rattigan, and the Stamford police were holding Kate's tape as evidence. I'd probably have to go downtown sometime soon and see Detective Petrie, but in the meantime I was more anxious to talk to Frank and let him know he was off the hook. It was Sunday afternoon before he returned the three messages I'd left on his answering machine.

"Hey, Mel! Isn't it great?" he cried. "The police found the actual murderer. It turned out to be some dog guy."

"The *police* found him?" My voice was heavy with sarcasm, but Frank didn't seem to notice.

"Yeah, a thirteen-year-old girl got him to confess and managed to tape the whole thing. As far as Detective Petrie is concerned, I'm in the clear. Starting tomorrow, I'm going back to work on the coffee bar. It looks like we'll be open by Christmas, after all."

"You're welcome," I said loudly.

"Now, Mel, don't feel bad. I know you put some effort into this and I'm sure with a little more time you could have come up with the answer, too."

"I *did* come—"

"Sure, you came close. You're good, Mel. That's why I asked for your help. Listen, Gloria and I have finally come up with the right name for the coffee bar.

I want your opinion. Ready?"

"Yes," I said weakly. There didn't seem to be much point in continuing to try and explain.

"The Bean Counter."

So help me, I started to laugh. And once I started, I couldn't seem to stop. I could faintly hear Frank's voice squawking in the background. "You like it, don't you? Laughing is good, right?"

"Yes, Frank," I agreed, when I'd finally caught my breath. "Laughing is good."

I made a few phone calls that evening and got to school early Monday morning. I wasn't scheduled to see Spencer Holbrook until afternoon but I caught up with him outside his locker before first period.

"How was your weekend?" I asked.

"Great." Spencer piled his supplies on the floor and slammed the locker door shut. "Big J and I hauled the sailboat out of the water. We spent the whole weekend scrubbing the hull and putting her to bed for the winter."

"It sounds like you wouldn't have had much time to spend on your homework."

"No, we were pretty busy."

"Miss Kinney told me you had a history paper due this morning. Two pages on the Continental Congress."

"Don't worry about that." He patted his folder confidently. "It's right here."

"Do you mind if I take a look at it?"

For the first time Spencer hesitated. "I guess not."

He dug out the paper and handed it over.

"Let's step into my classroom, okay?"

As we walked down the hallway, I skimmed the first page. The report had been prepared on a computer and was neatly typed, with Spencer's name and class filled in on top. "This is good. Clear, concise, all your facts lined up. It looks like you must have done at least a couple of drafts."

"Yeah," the sixth grader mumbled. "Sure."

We entered my room together. I switched on the light and walked over to stand beside my desk. Spencer put his books down on the nearest table and waited to see what would happen next.

"I just have one question," I said. "What's the first sentence?"

"Huh?"

"Come on, Spencer, this should be easy. The paper was only assigned Friday. You must have worked on it over the weekend. And you just told me you did several drafts. What's the first sentence?"

"I don't remember. I did that part Friday. That was awhile ago."

"Okay." I crossed my arms over my chest. "Then what's the last sentence?"

"Uhh." Spencer thought for a minute. He hadn't a clue and we both knew it. "It says, 'That's why the Continental Congress was so important to the history of America.'"

I glanced down at the paper. "Not even close."

He closed his eyes briefly.

"Do we have to discuss the rest of the facts that are in this paper, or do you want to confess now?"

"All right. I guess my memory's not too good."

"Your memory is fine, it's your work ethic that bothers me." I leaned back and sat down on the edge of my desk. "Who's been doing your homework for you, Spencer?"

"Nobody. Honest."

I just sat there and gave him the teacher's stare. You know the one.

Spencer's gaze shifted wildly around the room. He was wondering whether he could get away with bluffing. I decided to make the decision easier for him.

"I spoke with most of your teachers last night. I learned that none of them had ever received a piece of homework from you that was handwritten. Your word processing skills are earning you very high marks for neatness, by the way. And your English teacher credits your writing with a remarkable degree of maturity.

"You're a smart kid, Spencer. I know it, and you know it. That's why I couldn't figure out why you were having so much trouble on your tests, especially when your homework clearly demonstrated that you knew the material.

"Then on Saturday I got into a discussion about a man who had a very good dog that he hadn't bred, or trained, or shown. Even so, he was delighted to put his name on the dog and take all the credit. And when I stopped and thought about that, something just clicked. So here we are. Is there something you'd like to tell me?"

"Parsons," said Spencer. He was looking at his feet.

"Pardon me?"

"Parsons. He's Big J's butler. He majored in history and he *likes* doing homework—"

"I'll stop you now before you try and convince me this is his fault. How long has this been going on?"

"About a year," he said sheepishly. "Maybe two."

"And none of your other teachers ever caught on?" I was incredulous.

"I guess they're just not as smart as you."

"You're not going to flatter your way out of this. Don't even try."

"Are you going to report me to Mr. Hanover?"

"That's up to you. We're only two months into the school year. I doubt that any irreparable damage has been done yet. However, I'll certainly be keeping tabs on the situation. If I were to get the feeling that this was a continuing problem—"

"You won't!" Spencer's relief was evident. "I promise you won't."

"Great." I reached over and dropped the history paper into the wastebasket.

"But . . ." His face fell. "That was due today."

"Get an extension," I suggested. "Tell Miss Kinney your dog ate it."

"I don't have a dog." Spencer picked up his books. Now that he'd weathered the worst of the storm, his cocky grin was back in place. "Maybe I'll tell her *your* dog ate it."

He ran to the door and let himself out.

Kate and Lucia came by later that morning. Though Lucia had done well at her horse show that weekend, Kate was the one who had a clipping from that morning's newspaper with her name in it.

Lucia looked suitably miffed. "I could catch a murderer, too, if I felt like it."

Kate and I exchanged a glance. To our credit, neither one of us laughed. "I need to talk to you later," I said.

Kate's eyes lit up. "Is it another investigation? Do you need some more help?"

Heaven forbid.

"No," I said firmly. "This is about something else entirely."

After our session had ended, Kate hung back for a minute while Lucia went on to their next class.

"I talked to a friend of mine last night," I said. "Her name is Alberta Kennedy. She's a young professional handler, just getting started. I know how much you enjoyed the work you were doing with John and I figured you'd probably miss it. Bertie can't afford to pay you anything, but you'd learn a lot working as her assistant and you'd be able to keep going to dog shows—"

"Oh, Ms. Travis, that's perfect!" Kate threw her arms around my shoulder and hugged me tightly.

"You'll have to get your mother's permission, okay?"

"She'll say yes," Kate cried happily. "I know she will. Thank you!"

"You're welcome." I could see how this might work out well for everybody. And with luck, Bertie would keep Kate so busy she wouldn't have time to think about looking for any more mysteries to solve.

Thursday night was Halloween. Sam arrived just before seven. Davey and I were cleaning up the dinner dishes and listening for the doorbell. Our neighborhood was filled with young children, and the trick-or-treaters would soon be out.

Sam didn't ring the bell, however; he simply opened the door and let himself in. The first notice we had of his arrival was when Tar came bounding into the kitchen. A long black cape had been fastened around his neck, and it fluttered and flapped in his wake.

Faith, who'd been chewing on a fresh marrow bone, jumped up and began to bark. I didn't know whether she was more flustered by the cape or embarrassed that an intruder had managed to make his way inside without her permission. Tar barked right back, then scooted under the kitchen table in case Faith decided to take offense.

"Cool!" Davey jumped up out of his chair. His school had held a costume parade earlier in the day, and he'd been dressed as Batman ever since. "What's he supposed to be?"

"Bat Dog," Sam answered, sounding chagrined. "Can't you tell?"

"He looks great," I said.

Tar had come flying out from beneath the table and was now circling the room at warp speed. Faith looked askance at this demonstration of puppy exuberance, picked up her bone, and carried it into her crate where she could enjoy it in peace.

"Is he going to come trick-or-treating with us?" Davey asked.

"Of course. But this is his first Halloween, so you'll have to show him the ropes."

"Okay," my son said happily. "I can do that."

Sam was staring at me with a goofy grin on his face. After a moment I realized why. I was wearing a black leotard, tights, and ballet slippers, along with a long black tail and small pointy ears.

"Catwoman," I said sheepishly. This was a side of me Sam hadn't seen before. "At Howard Academy the teachers dress up. It's one of those silly private school traditions. I thought there was a certain irony to this particular choice. . . ."

"You're babbling," Sam mentioned. He was still grinning.

"And you're staring." Now I was smiling, too.

"I guess I like what I see."

"Hey!" cried Davey. "I think I hear someone coming!" The doorbell chimed and he went running out to the front hall.

Sam and I followed. Since he seemed fascinated by the swinging of my tail, I made sure it covered a lot of ground. As we complimented costumes and handed out candy, I rubbed it up against his legs a few times for good measure.

"Moves like that could get you in trouble," Sam said when the goblins had disappeared down the steps and Davey had gone to look for the candy bag he'd made that day at school.

"That's what I'm counting on."

"And to think, I've always been a dog man." He slid a hand down my back and over the curve of my hip. "What's keeping that thing on there anyway?"

"Serendipity and safety pins." I wrapped my arms around him. "I'm hoping my luck holds."

"So am I." Sam's tone turned sober. "Peg told me what happened last weekend."

I stood very still. "And?"

"I'm wondering why you didn't tell me yourself."

"I didn't want you to be angry," I said carefully.

"Do I look angry?"

I studied his expression for a moment. "No. But you don't look happy."

"Good. I'd hate for you to think I approve."

I eased back out of the circle of his arms. "I don't need your approval."

"Yes, you do." Sam sounded very sure of himself. "You need it just as much as I need yours, and there's not a thing either one of us can do about it. I love you, Melanie, and I fell in love with you because of all the things you are, even the ones that make me crazy sometimes."

He reached out and took my hand. "I'm sorry, when

I rehearsed this at home, I was much more eloquent. Do you want me to go down on one knee and start over?"

"No, keep going." It was hard to get the words out; I think I was holding my breath. "Don't change a thing."

"Marry me," said Sam.

"Yes."

"Just like that?"

"Just like that."

"It won't be easy."

"Since when have I liked easy?"

Sam groaned softly. I decided not to take it personally.

Davey came racing back into the hall. He'd found his bag and a piece of red ribbon to tie in Faith's top-knot. "I'm all ready. Is it time to go yet?"

"Just about," I said. "Don't forget your Batmobile."

"We're going to be good together," Sam said, smiling as Davey dashed away again.

"Good?" I punched his arm playfully. "Don't sell yourself short. We're going to be great."

Center Point Publishing
600 Brooks Road ● PO Box 1
Thorndike ME 04986-0001 USA

(207) 568-3717

US & Canada:
1 800 929-9108